HER SILENT

OBSESSION

ARLA BAKER BOOK 6

M.L. ROSE

HER SILENT OBSESSION

Copyright © 2020 by M.L. Rose

*****

TABLE OF CONTENTS

CHAPTER 1

The figure watched the woman pushing the pram. His name was Rhys Mason, and he was safely hidden behind a tree, crouching so far low his face was only a few centimetres above the frozen grass of Clapham Common.

Snow was piled up heavy on the sides of the path that snaked into the woods. Rhys had watched the woman for several weeks now. Mother and baby liked to go for a walk in the morning, if the sun was up. It was cold but sunny, melting snow trickling into the gutters by the road, the branches of bare trees lined with a white dusting of snow, as if carefully arranged by invisible hands in the wintry silence of the night. The sky was leaden grey, but the portent of Christmas was in the air, a brief punctuation of light in the closing darkness of December.

Rhys watched the woman stop and stare intently inside the pram. The hood of the pram was up. The woman reached inside, as if she was touching her baby. *Her baby*, Rhys thought with a sudden jolt in the blood.

The mother straightened and appeared to say a few words to the baby safely ensconced in the warmth of the pram. The flicker of a smile crossed her pretty face. For TV serial watchers and Instagram followers, an instantly recognisable face.

Mother and baby came off the path and onto the sidewalk. A car stopped at the traffic lights, and the woman waved her thanks to the driver before crossing the road. The lights changed and the car moved on. On this road of expensive detached houses overlooking the dense woods of the Common, cars were not frequent. Which, Rhys thought, was perfect.

The woman came up to the shoulder-high gates of a house and pressed a buzzer. The iron grill gates swung open.

Mother and baby went inside the house and the door shut. Rhys waited for another five minutes. Then he rose and shook off the flakes of snow stuck to his body. The house had a wide footprint. Four large bay windows watched the iron pillars that enclosed the front garden and sides. Rhys knew there was a side gate, which was an entrance for the housekeeper. He pulled the fur-lined white hood of his parka jacket tighter around the face. Dark glasses allowed no visibility of the eyes. The side gate was open, because the housekeeper had driven off an hour ago to do some shopping. Again, this was a routine Rhys had meticulously observed over the last several weeks.

Rhys slipped to the side of the house and came to the housekeeper's entrance. The door was unlocked. He slipped inside and crouched on the floor. The narrow hallway of the housekeeper's apartment was dark. Listening for sounds but hearing none, Rhys moved forward stealthily. The bedroom was empty, as were the tiny kitchen and bathroom. Finally, Rhys came to the back door, which opened out into the common garden. Rhys stared out at the huge garden, wondering why one family needed *this* much space. He didn't step out into the snow-covered expanse. Instead, Rhys arched his neck upwards and located the first-floor windows. One of the windows was ajar; judging from its size, it was a bathroom. There was a back porch with a flat roof just below the window. Easy access. Rhys smiled.

CHAPTER 2

Rebecca Stone was tired. As joyous as the arrival of the new baby had been, the delivery had been traumatic to say the least. She had lost more than a litre of blood and had to stay in hospital for a week.

She had needed a blood transfusion, and despite still being on iron tablets, she got tired easily and woke up every morning feeling dizzy.

Rebecca turned on the baby monitor in the kitchen, as was her habit. She put the kettle on to make herself a cup of tea. When she walked in the Common it was with slow, measured steps because that was all her body allowed. But it did make her feel better to get some fresh air, despite the freezing cold. Initially, she had been apprehensive about taking baby Reggie out in this weather. But her mother, Christine, was right: Reggie actually liked it. He fell asleep even before she got to the woods, and the moments of peace she got were precious.

Rebecca stood with a cup of coffee in her hand, staring out at the garden, blanketed with a carpet of snow. Small pawmarks crossed the pristine white ground a few metres from the porch. She smiled at the thought of the solitary fox in the backyard, scavenging for tidbits.

The dizziness began as a humming behind her eyes and slowly escalated louder, almost blurring her vision. She sat down quickly, leaning back against the sofa. The light-headedness subsided. Dr Mansfield had said it would be like this for at least two weeks. Well, ten days later, she didn't feel any better.

Rebecca went out into the wide hallway, crossed it, and came to one of the four large rooms that faced Clapham Common. Thick red velvet curtains had been gathered and tied at the corners by the housekeeper. Rebecca stood at an angle, looking out the window.

Her mind wasn't playing tricks. Yes, she was tired and irritable, but she hadn't missed the man who had stared at her when she went out walking with the pram.

He was clean-shaven, in his mid-thirties, and wore a heavy jacket with a hood. The hood was always over his head but she managed to get a good look at his face. As soon as their eyes met, he had looked away. There was a bus stop about one hundred metres from her house. Given how pervasive London's bus routes were, even an exclusive address like hers wasn't immune to the groaning machines.

Rebecca was sure she'd seen the man get on a bus one day. Which meant he didn't drive. She found it odd that a solitary man would be walking around here on his own. Not many people came out to Clapham Common in the winter. It was a desolate, frozen wasteland. Sometimes, she saw joggers cutting their way through the park. But mostly, it was only her and Reggie in the pram. That was why she chose the routes she did—so she had some peace and isolation.

Jeremy, her husband, was trying his best but he didn't really understand. Neither did her mother, however hard she tried. Christine had never had a difficult pregnancy, so Rebecca couldn't really blame her. Thank God Reggie was well. He had emerged perfectly formed and healthy. He was going to be fine, and that thought kept her going.

Rebecca looked carefully out the window, crossing to the other side and making sure she watched both sides of the road. Her heart leapt into her mouth. A vice-like grip squeezed her throat and nausea lurched in her stomach.

There he was.

That same man, wearing the white hooded jacket. He was standing at an angle to the house, but Rebecca could see him. He turned slightly to stare at the window and she pressed deeper into the shadows.

He couldn't see her, but that piercing gaze was too direct, violating. Rebecca's heart hammered against her ribs, her pulse surging to a crescendo as her back hit the wall. She couldn't see the man anymore. Her fists were claws, close to pulling down the curtains. She heard the pelmets creak and let go, fearful of tearing the curtains down. She gripped her forehead and found it covered in sweat. Her breaths came short, rapid.

Then suddenly, he moved. He almost ran down the road till he was out of sight.

A faint but distinctly uneasy sensation forced its way into the back of her mind like the scream of a train whistle inside a tunnel. She blinked rapidly, then ran out of the room, up the giant staircase that rose straight to the first floor. She was gasping when she opened the door of the nursery room, where Reggie's cot stood against the wall, away from the window.

Rebecca came to a standstill. Her vision was frozen, arrested by the sight of the open window. It was raised high enough for a man to duck in and out of. The net curtain fluttered in the breeze. Her head snapped towards the cot. She ran to it. The cot was empty.

Baby Reggie was gone.

Rebecca's mouth opened but no sound came from her throat. Grunting like an animal, she lurched to the window and forced her head out into the frigid air. The garden, and the woods at the back, met her eyes. She spun back into the room, eyes bulging, whole body shaking like she had been electrocuted by a live wire. She ran to the cot again, forcing herself to see the emptiness inside. Her hands became fists and when her mouth opened this time, she screamed.

CHAPTER 3

Detective Chief Inspector Arla Baker stopped at the bottom of the flight of cement stairs that rose up to the double gates of Clapham Common Police Station. She put a hand on the gleaming steel rail and took a few seconds to compose herself. As her pregnancy had progressed, so had the shortness of breath on minimal exertion. She had only walked from the car park to the front gate and already her lungs were heaving.

Unconsciously, her hand rose to touch her abdomen. With an effort she put her hand down by her side. It had become a reflex to pass her hand over her belly whenever she was tired or stressed. It was almost as if she wanted to check with baby if he or she was okay, and hopefully not feeling any of her tiredness.

"Give me your hand," came Detective Inspector Harry Mehta's voice from above her. Harry's tall, gangly form was further accentuated by his position on the stairs.

His eyebrows were wrinkled like his forehead muscles, meeting in the middle. His chocolate brown eyes swelled with concern. But most noticeably of all, the preternaturally smooth-cheeked, self-confessed Eliot Ness of Clapham Police Station had stubble on his cheeks. He had been up the last two nights helping Arla get from the bathroom back to bed because she had a vomiting bug. Arla tried to make light of how much he fussed over her, but it left her with a glowing warmth inside. Even if it made the handsome devil look scruffier than usual.

She frowned at him and swatted his hand away. "I'm pregnant, Harry, not disabled. At this rate, you'll be getting me a stair lift soon."

The corners of Harry's full lips bent downwards. Even at that angle his mouth looked sexy. Despite all the aches and troubles of pregnancy so far, she had to admit their sex life had attained a new level of heat in the last seven to eight months. Heat that coloured her cheeks now as she gazed at him.

Quickly, she averted her eyes and started climbing the stairs, one at a time.

They walked together as the double doors slid open, Harry slowing his pace for her. He said, "On the bright side, if you're going down the hill you could just roll down like a ball."

"Better not stand in my way, then," she retorted, "or I'll knock you over."

A big, slow grin filled Harry's face. It was so infectious she could feel the tug at the corners of her own lips. He leaned over her, no longer smelling of his expensive aftershave, but the mingled smell of bedsheets and clothes, a strange homely odour that she was starting to enjoy.

"Hey, it was me who knocked you up, remember? So, you can't really—"

Her jaws snapped together as her dark eyes blazed at him. "Shut up, Harry," she hissed. She glanced to her left where the front counter was being manned by Robinson, the duty sergeant. He was paying them no attention, his head lowered over a book on the table.

Ignoring the warmth fanning her face, Arla left Harry and strolled to the desk. Robinson looked up as she approached. He was a broad-shouldered Afro-Caribbean man, his curly black hair glinting under the bright halogen lights overhead. Curiosity sparked in his features.

"You here already, guv? Heard you weren't well and not coming in till later."

Arla waved a hand in the air. "Nah, I'm fine. How was the night?"

Robinson shrugged. "Usual. A few drunks, a few drug dealers. No dead bodies—not yet, anyway."

Arla grinned and rapped her knuckles on the wooden counter. "Let's hope it stays that way as well."

"Take it easy, guv."

"I'm good, as you can see. But thanks."

She walked towards the bulletproof glass doors that led to the inside of the station. Harry pressed his fob key on the digital keypad and followed her.

"You know what bugs me?" she asked Harry as they walked down the corridor. Uniformed police officers and plainclothes detectives came in and out of offices. They nodded at Arla and she greeted them back.

Harry asked, "What?" He glanced down at her, a wary look on his face.

"Men assume we become delicate when pregnant. Nothing could be further from the truth. I need to be as strong as ten men in order to produce another body from my own." Her chin lifted and her nostrils flared as she stared at Harry, waiting for his response. Harry merely shrugged.

"If you say so."

Patently, that was not the right answer. Arla crinkled her nose and her eyebrows lowered.

"Even you can do better than that, Harry," she said as they walked into the open-plan detectives' office. Several heads lifted as the couple entered. Officers of various grades were starting to drift in. Lisa Moran, Arla's trusted detective sergeant, rose from her desk and approached them. Lisa was a freckle-faced blonde with her hair always tied back in a ponytail. Her cherub cheeks were rosier than normal as she flashed Arla a bright smile. Her eyes snaked to Arla's bump.

"How are you feeling?" Lisa asked. She had a five-year-old boy herself.

Arla rolled her eyes. "I'm fine, okay? Don't worry, I'm not ready to drop just yet. Still another seven weeks to go."

"Six," Harry corrected.

"Whatever." Arla waved at Rob Pickering, her other erstwhile detective sergeant, and Roslyn May, a new sergeant who had joined them from the Gloucestershire Constabulary. Then she strode towards her office, Harry and Lisa trailing behind her.

Arla adjusted the framed photo on her desk, setting it next to the laptop. The photo showed Arla when she was eleven and her sister Nicole, aged sixteen. Nicole had a possessive arm around

Arla's shoulder, both of them lit up by a forgotten summer sun, an eternal glow encased within the frame of the photo. An image, and memory, that remained constant in Arla's life.

Arla fired up the laptop and went through the emails. Harry excused himself and went to his desk, just outside her room.

Ever since she had become DCI, Arla received emails from the six police stations under her command. Today was no different. In addition, she was the duty senior investigating officer for the week. The duty SIO took responsibility for new serious crimes, including homicides.

She spent the next half an hour responding to the emails and arranging meetings. With rising rank came increasing bureaucracy and she hated it now more than ever. Box-ticking and paper-pushing had never been her style, but she had to do it. The phone on the table rang and she snatched it up without checking the number.

"Yes?" she asked in a sharp voice.

The ominous rumble of her boss, Commander Wayne Johnson, came down the line. "It's me."

Instantly, Arla was attentive. Johnson wouldn't call her if it wasn't something important.

"Just wanted to check you were in," Johnson said, then paused. "How are you feeling?"

"Well enough to be at my desk, sir. But thank you for asking."

Johnson made a guttural noise in his throat, which generally conveyed agreement. "See you in a jiffy."

CHAPTER 4

In five minutes there was a knock on Arla's door, then Johnson poked his head in. He was a bear of a man, standing taller than everyone else in the building. His slate grey eyes were sharp and quick and his shaven cheeks had started to sag now that he was in his late fifties. He wasn't wearing his uniform, which meant no planned visits to HQ up in central London, or media interviews. He glanced at Arla, said hello, then sat down opposite her in a chair that creaked noisily.

There was another knock on the door and Harry entered.

Johnson said, "I called Detective Inspector Mehta."

Harry leaned his never-ending shoulders against the door jamb, crossing his arms across his wide chest and one ankle over the other. Johnson half-turned in his seat and glared at him.

"Sit down, Harry."

Harry's forehead muscles contracted but he knew better than to argue with the big boss. Commander Johnson, as he liked to be called nowadays, was a straight-talking, no-nonsense man, unless it came to buttering up his superiors.

Harry sat down promptly, raising his eyebrows at Arla.

Johnson asked, "Are you on Instagram?"

"I am, actually," Arla said, narrowing her eyes at him. "Why is that important?"

Johnson took out his phone, scrolled to a page, then slid it across the table to Arla. Harry got up from his seat and leaned over the table. Arla angled the camera so that he could see.

The Instagram account appeared to be that of a celebrity called Rebecca Stone. Arla couldn't remember where she had seen Rebecca before, but for some reason the bronze-skinned, long-legged, chestnut-haired beauty looked familiar.

She frowned, scrolling down the list of images showing Rebecca applying her makeup, educating her fans about how to pose for the perfect selfie, even having dermal filler injected into her upper lip. More recent photos saw her posing with a new-born baby in the comfort of her home. Then it hit her. She lowered the phone and jerked her head straight, to find Johnson looking at her expectantly.

"*Chelsea Town Life?*" Arla said, referring to a popular night-time TV drama. She was no expert on it, having caught only a couple of episodes. But the stars of the show had received numerous awards and their faces were plastered across glossy magazines.

"Yup, that's right. Her name is Britney Kemp in the show. Real name is Rebecca Stone."

Arla already had a sinking feeling in her stomach. "Did something happen to her?"

Johnson's cheeks seemed to sag lower, and his grey eyes dulled. "Yes, I'm afraid so. Rebecca Stone's baby disappeared this morning."

There was silence for a few seconds. The sinking feeling was clutching at Arla's heart, pulling it down. "Her baby?" she whispered.

Harry turned to face Johnson. "Nothing's been reported. We asked the duty sergeant."

Johnson settled back further in his chair, which wasn't easy, given his ample bulk. The chair creaked alarmingly. Johnson rubbed his cheek and glanced from Harry to Arla.

Arla's stomach was tightening into a knot, not a pleasant sensation given her current condition. She could guess what was on Johnson's mind, and she came out with it.

"Did the family call you?"

The corners of Johnson's lips turned downwards as his bushy eyebrows met in the middle. "She's married to Jeremy Stone. He's a film producer and also the nephew of Grant Stone."

Harry startled, clicking his tongue against the roof of his mouth. "Pop star Grant Stone?"

Arla's jaw was hanging open and she snapped it shut. "Wow. Really?"

"Jeremy Stone is Grant's only nephew." Johnson shifted in his seat, then flexed his neck once. His Adam's apple rose and fell as he swallowed. "Grant Stone knows Mr Cummings, who's the Member of Parliament in our area. It's Mr Cummings who called me this morning."

Arla nodded, not surprised by the information. The famous and wealthy always had political connections. Wealthy backers were useful to politicians but famous ones came in even more handy when the time was right. Like election time.

"Let me guess," Arla said. "Mr Cummings requested you to keep it hush-hush, not to file a police criminal notice."

Johnson passed a hand over his face. "Along those lines."

He raised his eyebrows at Arla and went silent. Arla narrowed her eyes as a sense of unease crinkled at the corners of her mind. She knew Johnson well. He was sitting very still, shoulders slumped, observing her closely. After all these years of working with him she could read his body language perfectly. Johnson was hiding something.

She didn't waste any time. "What else, sir? We might as well know now."

Johnson pressed his lips together, then blew out his cheeks.

"Mr Cummings is also the new crime commissioner at the Council."

Arla crinkled her nose, as if she was trying to get a whiff of something fishy. She knew that the Council was essentially the local government. But the majority of funding for the police came directly from the state.

"Since when does the Council have a crime commissioner?" Harry asked, glancing at her. They had worked so long together she often thought Harry could read her mind.

"Since the special levy was introduced."

The knot of muscles on Harry's forehead cleared. "Ah, you mean that 30 per cent of our funding that comes from local councils. Mr Cummings is in charge of that?"

Johnson nodded." But that's obviously beside the point," he said hurriedly, noting the scepticism on Arla's face. "The important thing is we have a missing baby."

"So, the fact that Mr Cummings called you up himself is beside the point, is it?" Arla asked, raising her eyebrows. She watched impassively as Johnson's jaws hardened and his nostrils flared.

Arla had a glum satisfaction that her hunch had been correct. Johnson's dog-eared tactic of kissing politically important butt cheeks was becoming depressingly familiar. She waited, braced for the worst.

"Of course it is."

Harry asked, "And I guess you want answers before the media get wind of this, right?"

"Yes," Johnson snapped. "We're dealing with class-A celebrities here. Can you imagine what'll happen if social media gets hold of this?"

Arla had thought of this already. Never mind Rebecca Stone— her husband's uncle, Grant Stone, was one of the biggest rock stars in the UK. He'd also made it big in America, after splitting from the boy band that had made him famous. He was the Rod Stewart of the streaming generation, his songs downloaded more than Madonna's. His name and face were instantly recognisable.

She tapped Johnson's phone, which still lay on her desk, and thought aloud.

"Rebecca's stopped making posts for the last week. Which makes sense as she has a new baby."

She pursed her lips together. She would be in the same position in six to seven weeks' time. A wave of incredulity hovered over her like a rain cloud. It was sheer coincidence this case had just landed in her lap. A sense of dread snaked up her spine, making her shiver. She certainly didn't want her new-born to be abducted. Her heart twisted as she thought of Rebecca Stone and what the poor woman must be going through. She closed her eyes briefly, focusing.

"What time was the missing baby noticed?"

"At eight forty-five this morning."

Harry lifted his hand and made a show of looking at his watch. Arla shook her head. That Rolex Submariner was his pride and joy. Typical man.

"It's ten o'clock now. That was quick."

"Apparently, the husband, Jeremy, heard his wife's screams. He wanted to call the police, but she was afraid of the publicity. So he called his famous uncle to see if he had any contacts."

"Do we know anything else?"

"Rebecca had come back from a walk in Clapham Common, with the baby. She put the baby upstairs, but when she went up to check, he wasn't there."

"How long was she away from the baby?"

Johnson shrugged. "I don't know. That's why we need a statement."

"So, famous rock star calls his friend Mr Cummings, who calls you?" Arla said, leaning back in her chair.

"Yes," Johnson said shortly.

"And because you want to keep Mr Cummings happy, I guess we need to get cracking immediately." The words slipped out of Arla's mouth before she could stop them.

Johnson's spade-like hands became fists and the knuckles turned white. He raised his voice.

"Arla!"

They stared at each other for a few seconds, neither backing down. Then Johnson blinked and lowered his head.

"Just get on with it. I need some answers by tomorrow." He stood slowly, joints popping. His eyes softened as he looked down at her.

It was Arla's turn to look away, because she knew he would ask about her health. Despite all the fire and brimstone that surrounded their professional relationship, Johnson was also the one who had known her the longest. He knew about Nicole, and her parents. His concern for her welfare was genuine.

"I don't want to put you under stress," Johnson said, his voice now a couple of octaves lower. "Are you sure you can handle this?"

"If I couldn't, then I wouldn't be here, sir," Arla said. She stood to emphasise the point, but also to relieve the pain she got in her back from sitting for long periods. There was a rolling in her gut, and a smile crossed her face as she felt her baby kick inside. She rested a hand on her bump.

She found Harry staring at her intently, and when their eyes met, his face dissolved into a knowing smile. Harry couldn't get enough of putting his ear to her tummy or trying to feel some of the baby's movements. He was eager to become a dad.

Johnson observed them quietly for a while. "I had just started my first DI job when my eldest daughter, Kiara, was born," he said. "It's a tough time, but also the most memorable."

He smiled encouragingly. Arla couldn't remember the last time she had seen Johnson smile. The tense lines around his mouth dissolved and, for a few moments, he looked like a completely different person.

"Thank you, sir," Arla said. She meant it. Harry muttered the same.

Johnson shrugged. "To be honest, I expected nothing less of you. But I know how you get when you're on a case. Just make sure you look after both of you." He indicated her bump.

He smiled again and for some stupid reason, Arla felt terribly emotional. Sudden saline drops bulged at the back of her eyes and she swallowed hard, blinking furiously. She turned her back to Johnson, looking out the window.

Harry straightened. "I'll send a report to your desk first thing tomorrow, sir."

Johnson nodded. Arla cleared her throat. "I need permission to see the victim's family, take a statement, and have a look around the crime scene. We have to get SOCO down there as well."

Johnson shook his head. "For now, this stays between the three of us."

"But sir, that's impossible. If we want to take fingerprints, hair or skin samples—"

"I know what you mean, Arla, but please don't involve SOCO till you clear it with me. Keep it between us. Got it?"

Arla knew she wouldn't win this argument. "As you wish, sir."

Johnson held out his phone and Harry scribbled down the address and phone number they needed. When Johnson left, Arla shook her head at Harry.

"Can't believe I have to search for a missing baby before mine's even born."

CHAPTER 5

Arla waited at the rear entrance of the police station, covered by the portico. A light drizzle had started. Harry strode out briskly in the rain, heading for the unmarked black BMW in the carpool. He walked with his shoulders hunched forward, hands thrust into his pockets. Arla knew he was itching for a smoke but over the last week he'd been good. He'd stuck to only three cigarettes a day, which was a huge improvement. Harry could finish a pack of twenty every day, easily.

It was strange to think how Harry was changing. On top of the two-day stubble on his cheeks, his shirt was creased. Arla smiled to herself. She wasn't sure if she was changing too. She was excited, elated, apprehensive—all at the same time. Obviously, her body was changing dramatically. But her mind was still functioning the same way.

She had been hot on the case of a human trafficking ring that worked from Syria to London. The entire operation had taken six months. Although she wasn't able to go out in the field much, she had worked hard at the office, coordinating the various forces involved.

She wasn't sure if she was changing as a person. But Harry had remarked that she was quieter, less frantic. She did feel more at peace—a calmness that was comforting, like waking up from a deep, nourishing sleep.

She smiled and walked out into the drizzle as Harry pulled up in the BMW. He hopped out and went around to adjust the passenger seat. Arla sat down, taking her time. Apart from the back pain, getting in and out of the car was what she found most arduous.

The tyres crunched gravel as the rain whispered against the windowpanes. The filamentous, concrete forest of council estates surrounded them as Harry weaved the car through the winding back roads of Clapham. Snow was stacked to one side on the pavement, turning to grey and black mush on the road. Pencil-coloured clouds scuttled between the square windows on high-rise buildings, reaching down long, morose fingers of rain that whispered against the grimy walls, sliding down like rusty teardrops from black barbed-wire fences that surrounded school playgrounds. London, the city of nebulous clouds and evaporating dreams, where millions gathered their little lives, hopes, and loves, and laid them out like so many diamond studs in an inky night sky.

*****

It didn't take them long to get through the constant knot of South London traffic and head for Baskerville Road, the exclusive address where some of South London's most eye-catching Victorian mansions were situated. From desperate poverty to opulent wealth in the twinkling of an eye.

Arla watched the imposing detached building from the car. There were two large bay windows on each side of the massive dark-brown wooden door. She detected movement at the far left window. Someone was watching.

"Who's at home?" she asked Harry.

"Rebecca Stone and her husband. They have a housekeeper as well, and I requested for her to be present. No one else, as far as I know."

"How long have they lived here for?"

"For the last two years. Before that they lived in her husband's central London apartment."

"What about her family?"

"Her mother visits frequently. She has a sister as well, who lives in London. Married with kids. Not sure how close she is to her sister."

"Look into the mother's background, and the sister as well. I want to interview them both as soon as possible."

Harry nodded in silence. Then he scratched the stubble on his chin. "What are you thinking?"

Arla had spent some time on the phone before she left, speaking to a senior officer in charge of child sex abuse offenders.

"No CSA offender has been seen in this area recently. Which means we have a new person." She shrugged. "Of course, not all offenders report to their key workers on time."

Arla opened the door and went through the usual struggle of hauling herself out. Harry stood watching, his mouth pinched and tight, eyebrows lowered.

"I'm okay, Harry, don't worry," she said, slamming the door shut.

"You don't look okay," Harry murmured. "Should just let me help you."

They walked around the car, Arla stepping carefully on the road. Cars weren't that frequent here, and the snow had hardened to black ice. She grasped Harry's elbow when it was offered and together, they made their slow way onto the pavement.

Harry pressed the doorbell and a small, wizened lady opened the massive mahogany doors with some effort. Arla showed her warrant card and the elderly lady stared at it for longer than necessary.

When she spoke, her tone was brisk, her dark blue eyes sharp.

"Detective Chief Inspector Baker, are you expected?"

Harry spoke as he had made the call. "The call was made to Grant Stone, who conveyed the message to Jeremy, Mrs Stone's husband. Mrs Stone wasn't picking up the phone up, hence I spoke to Grant. I believe we are expected."

"I see. Do come in."

CHAPTER 6

The hallway they stepped into was wide enough to park two trucks side by side. The floor was made of dark parquet-style wood. A huge, stunning Persian rug in red, white, and gold occupied the centre. A crystal chandelier hung from the ceiling, directly above a glossy, varnished round table that held a giant cactus plant.

Modern art hung on walls which bore a kind of silvery, granulated wallpaper that made Arla want to touch their rough texture. It was a home right out of the glossy celebrity magazines, but the design added a touch of originality. Directly in front of them a massive central staircase went straight up to a landing, then divided into left and right as it rose to the first floor.

The carpeted stairway could easily fit a group of ladies trailing the long hems of their ball gowns. On the ground floor, behind the staircase lay double doors on each side. The doors on the right were partially open and Arla could see an open-plan kitchen. The lights were on, allowing a glimpse of the concertina doors at the back of the kitchen that led to a snow-covered garden.

Arla asked, "Are you the housekeeper?"

The elderly lady nodded in silence, her eyes watchful.

"What's your name?"

The woman paused before answering. "Miss Mildred."

"Are you aware of what happened this morning, Miss Mildred?"

She watched them, her eyes flicking from Arla to Harry.

Harry spoke in a soft, reassuring voice. "No one is suspecting you of anything, Miss Mildred. You know we are here for a reason. We just want to know the full details of what happened."

The elderly woman appeared to relax. Harry did have that effect on women, Arla mused. He called himself a natural charmer. She called him a puppy dog.

"I did hear the missus scream. I was in the kitchen, making breakfast. She kept on screaming, so I went up the stairs. She was in the nursery room." The woman stopped, looking to the ground, her tone faltering. Arla noticed her accent was polished, middle class. No trace of cockney twang.

"Carry on," Harry said.

They were still standing by the door in the hallway. The light was dim and they were speaking in hushed voices. No one had seen the figure slowly come down the stairs.

"Edna!" A female voice rang out. Miss Mildred startled, and Arla whipped her neck to the left. A woman was standing there, dressed in a red bathrobe. She stared at them for a few seconds, then came down the last few stairs. She walked towards them with measured steps.

She was in bathroom slippers, and she didn't need heels. Arla was five feet ten herself and the woman stared directly over her head, towards Harry. Her shoulder-length chestnut hair was straggly, and makeup was absent from her face. She clutched the belt of her bathrobe, and Arla noticed her fingernails were well manicured but not polished.

She looked pale and withdrawn, dark shadows underneath her eyes, eyelids puffy. None of that detracted attention from the large, shapely eyes, the buttonlike nose, and the high, naturally sculpted cheekbones. No trace of lines on her marble-smooth forehead. Botoxed to high heaven, maybe, but even in this current state, her inner radiance was unmistakable. Her face stirred Arla's memory. The golden letters RS were sewn on the left breast of the bathrobe.

The woman's eyes swept down to the bulge in Arla's belly. Her lower lip trembled and some of the tightness in her jaw slacked. So did her shoulders, and when her eyes met Arla's, her cheeks were touched with crimson.

Arla asked, "Are you Rebecca Stone?"

The woman cleared her throat. "Yes. Please come this way. Edna, coffee," she added dismissively.

Edna—Miss Mildred—nodded and hurried towards the kitchen. Rebecca led them to a room on the left, one of the rooms facing the Common. Rebecca circled around the rectangular table in the middle of the large room, and Arla immediately wondered if Rebecca was the shadow she had seen from the car.

Harry shut the door behind them. Rebecca turned swiftly when she heard the latch click. Her earlier composure crumbled like old plaster falling off a wall.

She had the haunted, wide-eyed gaze of a woman driven to the brink of desperation. She gasped heavily and grabbed Arla's shoulders with hands that were surprisingly strong. Arla stumbled backwards, taken aback by this sudden change. She reminded herself that this woman was an actress, after all.

"Where's my baby?" Rebecca asked, her voice breaking. She repeated her question, her sea green eyes boring into Arla's. Then tears filled her eyes, rolled down her cheeks. Her head lowered, resting on Arla's chest, and her body shook with sobs. Harry gently separated them, and guided Rebecca into a chair.

Arla pulled out a packet of tissues and handed one to Rebecca. Her head was still lowered, but she accepted the tissue, then dabbed at her eyes. Arla felt a cold hollow where her heart had been, a chill slowly settling into the pit of her stomach. She couldn't imagine the terrifying anguish this poor woman was going through. She was no longer a well-known actress and socialite living in a glamorous house. She was a woman whose baby had been snatched. Those few words conjured up a nightmarish hell so dark and absolute it offered no semblance of hope. Arla leaned over and gripped Rebecca's hand on the table.

"I'm so sorry. We'll do all we can to help you, I promise." She paused and, after an awkward moment, decided to remove her hand. It wasn't like she knew this woman, and her police instincts told her this was a crime scene and everyone was a suspect until proven innocent.

"Tell us what happened," she said.

Rebecca wiped her cheeks and sniffed. Her voice was tremulous.

"I didn't sleep well last night. Reggie kept waking up." Her throat closed and tears rolled down at the mention of her son's name.

Arla gave her two seconds, glancing up at Harry. He stood there like a statue, his face sad and gaunt.

She knew he felt the same way as she did. But more importantly, from the nod he gave her, she knew he was on the same page with Rebecca's response.

If she had carried on with the fortitude she displayed in the hallway, Arla's sixth sense would be ringing loudly by now. Instead, Rebecca had broken down and asked for help, which any woman in her situation would do.

"When Reggie doesn't sleep well at night, I take him for a walk. In the pram, obviously. That's what we did this morning."

"Where did you go?"

"To the Common. We followed the path to the bandstand, then came back."

The bandstand was a familiar place for Arla, for a dark and gruesome reason. A black shadow reared up from the crevices of her mind, but she stifled it with an effort.

"Did anyone see you?"

"No. I don't . . . I don't think so, anyway."

Arla didn't miss the hesitation. "Are you sure?"

Rebecca swallowed and stared down at her hands. "I mean, I was focused on Reggie and walking carefully, so I wasn't looking out for anyone." She paused and Arla waited.

"Do you always follow the same route?"

Rebecca nodded.

"What time did you go out?"

"Seven-thirty this morning."

Arla wrote the time down in the black diary she had opened up on the table. "And what time did you get back home?"

"I would say eight-thirty. Or thereabouts. I only remember looking at the clock when I put Reggie in the nursery and came downstairs to the kitchen."

Arla was watching Rebecca, and noticed the edges of her mouth tighten up, compressing her nose and lips.

"Anything else?"

Rebecca didn't answer; she was still staring into the middle distance. "Rebecca?" Arla asked.

The woman turned her eyes to Arla. The green depths were flat, shallow. "Sorry, I was just thinking."

Arla nodded in sympathy. "I know this is hard for you. But the more detail you can give us now, the easier it will be for us to help you."

"After I made my coffee, I was . . . I was standing here." She pointed to the curtains.

"Doing what?

"Looking out the window."

Arla looked at Harry and she saw the spark igniting in his chestnut brown eyes. Harry leaned over slightly. "You were in this room? In front of this window?" He turned to stare at the long expanse of the bay window.

"Yes. And I . . . I thought I saw someone. Standing to one side, on the left. He was opposite our house, near the Common. Then he walked off very quickly."

Arla narrowed her eyes. "Do you think he was watching your house? Was he standing directly opposite?"

Rebecca shook her head. "No. Like I said, he was standing to one side. That was to not make it obvious. Because I've seen him before."

Harry asked, "Is that why you were looking out the window?"

Rebecca nodded. The knot of muscles on Arla's forehead cleared and she sat back in the chair. She gripped her black pen tightly, and paused over the notebook. "Can you describe this person?"

Rebecca blinked. "He was tall, but not excessively. About six feet. He wore a white winter coat with a fur-lined hood."

"Where else have you seen him before?"

"At the bus stop. He was waiting there, and I was walking past with the pram."

Arla was scribbling away in her notebook. "When was this?" Harry asked.

"A few days ago. In the morning." Rebecca gripped her forehead with long, white fingers. "I can't remember the exact day, sorry. It'll come to me later."

"Don't worry," Arla said, trying to hide the bubble of excitement blooming inside her. It was rare indeed to get a positive lead so early in the case.

"Did this man ever try to approach you?" Harry asked.

Rebecca shook her head. "No. He always covered his face when I looked in his direction."

"Did he remind you of anyone?" Arla pressed. "Someone you knew before you met your husband, for instance. Or someone from work."

Rebecca bit down on her full, pink lower lip. Her hands twisted on her lap as she stared at them. "No. Can't say he did."

"Okay. What happened after that?"

"I went upstairs to check on Reggie. The window was open, and it faces the garden. His cot was empty." Her lower lip trembled again and her eyes closed.

"You're doing very well, Rebecca. This must be very difficult for you. But please carry on."

Rebecca didn't open her eyes. "I looked out the window. I saw nothing but snow in the woods. Nothing." Her eyes opened and she stared ahead with dead, dull eyes. Her face was blank and she breathed heavily.

"Who did you call for help?" Harry asked in a little voice. The woman didn't glance at Harry. She didn't move at all.

"Edna came upstairs. My husband came out of his room. I'm not sure what happened after that. Think my husband called his uncle, who called the police."

Arla asked, "You didn't call the police yourself?"

Rebecca's swollen eyelids fluttered and her attention snapped back to Arla. "I wanted to. But I also didn't want the whole world to know. You know what the media are like."

"I understand." Arla closed her notebook. "Can you please take us upstairs?"

CHAPTER 7

The first floor had a balcony that circled the entire perimeter. Halfway up the staircase there was a landing, then the staircase divided into right and left. Rebecca went up the left staircase and farther down the wide hallway. She came to a door that had the words 'Reginald Stone' written on it in blue wooden letters, stuck on to the wood. She opened it, then stood in silence for a while, like she was afraid to go inside.

When she stepped in, Arla and Harry followed. The first thing Arla noticed was that the window had been closed. It was a shutter window, done in the Victorian sash window style. The shutters were open and folded on either side and there was a small net curtain attached to the lower sash. The room was large; the walls were painted blue, with white clouds painted on the ceiling. It was a large room, and the crib stood to one side, against the wall opposite the window. Built-in wardrobes occupied the space behind the cot.

"Who closed the window?" Arla asked. Rebecca shook her head.

"I'm not sure. Maybe my husband."

Harry asked, "Where is your husband?"

"He's gone for his morning run. He goes every morning at this time, when he's at home."

Arla and Harry looked at each other. What sort of a husband went running at a time like this? Arla turned her attention back to Rebecca, who had caught the glance between the two detectives.

"Jeremy always goes for a run at this time. He asked me if I was okay, and I said yes." Her tone was defensive. Arla stared at her for a while, then decided to change the topic for now.

"Was your son always in this room?"

"Sometimes he slept with us in the bedroom as well. We have a cot there, too."

"I don't wish to pry, Mrs Stone. But, as you know, this is a crime scene now. We do need to have a look at all the rooms."

Rebecca stared at Arla for a few seconds, her face impassive. Then she shrugged. "Sure. Anything that helps you."

Harry was standing by the window. Without touching the windowsill he bent lower and gazed out at the garden. Arla joined him. Neither the window frame nor the sill showed any chipped paint, scratches, or any other signs of tampering. The shutters and the frame were painted white. Arla's practised eyes ran all over the frame, looking closely for smudges of fingerprints. She found nothing. She turned back to the grief-stricken mother.

"You always kept this window shut, when Reggie was in the room?"

Rebecca nodded. "Yes."

"And like all windows, they can't be opened from outside?"

A frown spread on Rebecca's face. "I don't know. But I'm pretty sure they don't open from outside."

Arla ran her tongue over her lower teeth. "Did you lock the window?"

Rebecca shook her head, her eyes widening. Arla held out her hand, softening her voice. "No, please don't worry. I wouldn't expect you to lock the window when you were in the house."

Continuing, she asked, "Are you sure the window was completely shut when you left the room?"

Rebecca pursed her lips together, deep in thought. "Yes, I am sure. This room is always warm, as you can tell. I don't want it to get stuffy so I do keep the door open."

Arla nodded. "That makes sense."

Rebecca leaned against the wall, closing her eyes. Her face was suddenly bone white, eyelids fluttering. Harry crossed the space between them in two steps, grabbing her arm. "Do you need to sit down?"

Harry pulled up a chair and Rebecca sat down heavily. She rested her forehead on her palm, her spine sagging.

"Would you like some water?" Harry asked. Rebecca shook her head.

"No. I'm anaemic from the blood loss during the delivery. That's why I feel dizzy sometimes."

They gave her a few seconds. Harry asked, "Were any of the other windows on this floor open?" Rebecca raised her head, leaning against the wall. She didn't answer.

Harry said, "It's a big house, I get that. I'm only interested in the windows that open to the back. Take the bathroom, for instance. Could that window have been open this morning?"

Rebecca glanced at him. "Maybe. My husband opens it after he's had a shower."

"How far is the bathroom?" Harry asked.

"Just to the right, next door."

Rebecca rose and as she stepped towards the door, Edna appeared. She bore a tray with three cups of coffee. "Coffee with milk, no sugar," she said. "I'm sorry, I should have asked how you like it, but I didn't want to disturb."

Arla and Harry politely declined, thanking both Edna and their hostess. They stepped out onto the balcony that overlooked the giant staircase. Rebecca led them to the bathroom and opened the door. The walls of the bathroom were made of pure stone, creating a stunning effect that made it seem as if they were stepping into a cave.

The floor was crafted of polished chintz tiles, their black surface reflecting the spotlights flashing from the ceiling. The double shower was to the right, wide enough to fit a single bed in. There was also a Jacuzzi, a toilet, and a double sink with two sets of taps.

The mirror above the sinks took up an entire wall and Arla could see her whole length reflected in it. A compliment hovered on the tip of her tongue, but professional etiquette dictated that she keep it to herself. The window that faced the back was above the toilet and Harry strode over to it. The window was indeed open and a draft of frigid air was coming through it. Instantly, Arla's senses were on alert.

"Has this bathroom been used this morning?"

"Our bedrooms are en-suite, so we don't use this bathroom very often. But yes, my husband did use it this morning. I saw him coming out."

"Does he always leave the window open this wide?"

Rebecca shrugged. Harry gestured to her and Arla shuffled closer. Harry took out a pen and pointed it at the open windowsill. A boot print was clearly visible. Arla tried to fight down the nuclear-powered butterflies flapping their wings in her stomach. Not only did they have a suspect, now they also had a method of entry. Which only left a route of exit. The abductor would be carrying a baby, so the exit route was just as important as the entry.

She cautioned her mind, pulling on her neurons like a kite-flyer in high wind. She had a habit of getting excited with new evidence, but something was wrong here. Something she couldn't put a finger on, and it scratched away insistently at the back of her head.

"Take photos. I want Scene of Crime down here as soon as possible." She turned to Rebecca. "The bathroom and Reggie's room are not to be entered anymore. There will be evidence here we need to collect."

Rebecca nodded, observing them. "Who is 'we'?"

Arla stared at her for a few seconds, reminded of Johnson's orders. No SOC. No Forensics, or anyone else. Harry cleared his throat, and she glanced at him.

"Mrs Stone, I know you have suffered an unimaginable trauma," Harry said, his voice warm and low, solicitous. There was even a baritone timbre to it, Arla noted with amusement.

"But without specialist, highly trained forensics officers, we might never catch the person who took your son."

Rebecca frowned, then squeezed her eyes shut. A wave of indecision spasmed across her face as her nostrils flared and her lips downturned. Then she shook her head.

"Please, no," she whispered. "Word will spread. The press know where I live. You can't imagine what they'll do to me."

Arla said, "I can imagine. Believe me, we know how intrusive the media can be. Especially the legions of reporters who live on social media."

She stopped. Explaining the nuances of a complex case like this to Rebecca would take time, and not be useful at all. Arla was riven with conflict, but had no choice. Not involving SOC was like tying her hands behind her back. There was the wider implication of what kind of mess she was stepping into—and what this wealthy, influential family could do if she got things wrong. Or didn't get results. Rich people had a need to blame someone when things went wrong. Quite literally, she was helping Johnson out on a personal request.

Was that a correct, legal use of police resources?

Her attention was wrenched away by a soft, imploring voice.

"Please," Rebecca said. "Just do the best you can."

Arla held eyes with Rebecca for a few seconds, then nodded curtly. She walked past her, out of the bathroom.

She strode into Reggie's room and went over to the window. Without touching the window she tried to make out what lay directly beneath. Breath caught in her chest. She could see the parapet of a flat roof. How hadn't she noticed that before?

"Is that flat roof part of the kitchen?" Arla asked Rebecca, who was standing next to her.

"It's the roof of the back porch, and it happens to be just below the bathroom as well."

Arla's eyes widened a fraction. Synapses were firing at a furious speed in her mind, the wheels whirring and clicking. A pattern was forming, but all she could see was a vague outline. It was enough, for now.

Harry appeared in the doorway. Arla beckoned him over and put sterile gloves on. Harry did the same.

"Do you mind if we open the window?" she asked.

Rebecca shook her head. Arla raised her hand and turned the round metal bolt between the sash panes. She stood to one side as Harry stepped in her place. He put a gloved hand on either side of the lower pane and lifted. It rose up smoothly and a gust of cold air blew into the room. Without putting his hands on the window frame, Harry bent his lanky form at the waist and stuck his head outside.

"Less than six feet drop. Definitely doable." Harry was silent for a few seconds, then he turned to face Arla. She caught the glitter in his eyes.

"What is it?" she asked quickly.

"Footprints. Man-sized shoes."

"Let me see." Arla bustled forward, then stopped short. Her belly was in the way, preventing her from leaning over the window.

"Let me take some photos," Harry suggested, touching her shoulder. She stepped back as Harry leaned over the windowsill again.

Arla wondered at the lack of ingenuity of the expensive architect who had designed this house. This was a huge flaw in the design, lending a helping hand to any burglar who wanted to gain entry. Mentally, she shook her head.

CHAPTER 8

Arla turned away from the window. Harry took some photos on the department camera, then showed them to Arla. Scene of Crime would take detailed images, measuring and showing every inch of the room, but that was not an option right now.

Arla stared at the photo of the boot print, her eyes shining. "Excellent," she whispered.

Rebecca was leaning against the opposite wall, a proprietary hand on the empty cot. She was staring into the distance again, her gaze lost in a vacuum. Arla's chest constricted painfully. She walked over to Rebecca and touched her elbow. The woman's flat, unseeing eyes turned towards Arla.

"Maybe you should get some rest. Have a lie-down for a while," Arla suggested.

The grieving mother shook her head vigorously. "I can't lie down. I can't rest." A distant animosity flared in her eyes, then transformed into panic as her pupils dilated.

"Where could Reggie be? The person who took him, will he look after him? Will he. . . . Oh, God!" Her head sank down, chin touching chest. Arla helped her back on the seat.

Harry said quietly, "I think we should go downstairs, or to a different room. We are done here."

Arla agreed and it seemed Rebecca didn't have much to say. Harry helped her up from the chair. He went out onto the balcony, then guided her down the opulent, carpeted staircase.

Arla stood at the railing of the balcony, committing the building's floor plan to memory. The balcony went round in a circle, closed doors leading off it. From any point on the balcony, one could stand and see who was downstairs, in the foyer. She still had her gloves on and wondered if she should walk around trying the handles on doors. For now, she decided against it.

She went down the staircase slowly. A doctor had told her most injuries happened going downhill. Uphill was strenuous but less prone to accidents. Harry was standing at the bottom of the staircase, hands on his hips. She knew he wanted to help her, but was holding back in case she refused. Which was the right decision. She gave him an encouraging smile as she came off the last stair.

"See? Piece of cake."

Harry rumbled something under his breath, then led the way into the kitchen. Rebecca was already there.

The wooden parquet floor gave way to Italian marble. The kitchen counter seemed to be made of the same black-and-white marble, which created a continuous pattern from the floor to the counter. Arla counted four Rangemaster cookers. Enough cooking power to feed an entire army. The dining table looked big enough for a banquet hall, seating at least twenty either side.

Beyond the dining table lay sofas near the concertina bifold doors. The concertina doors took up an entire wall, providing an unrestricted view of the garden.

Rebecca was sat on a sofa, her spine erect, fingers twisting on her lap. Edna came over with three glasses of water and put them on a small table. This time Arla reached for one.

"We need to speak to Edna in private," Arla said. It was a statement, not a request. Rebecca nodded. "When is your husband coming back?"

Rebecca took a long sip from her glass, finishing more than half. She paused to wipe her mouth. "He left just before you arrived." She glanced at the wall clock. "He should be back in an hour's time."

Harry turned down his lips. "He runs for two hours? How often does he do that? Must be really fit."

"It varies. I think he does it twice a week at least, sometimes more."

Arla raised her voice a notch. "Well, the sooner we can start our work, the better it is. We've got some solid leads here—thank you for the help."

"What sort of leads do you mean?" Hope flickered to life in Rebecca's eyes. She squared her shoulders and her spine snapped straight.

Arla raised her palm, regretting her choice of words. "I didn't mean to say anything definite. It's all conjecture and possibilities at the moment."

Rebecca slumped. A look of irritation creased her face. "Then what did you mean? How did someone get into this house and take my baby?" Her voice choked up at the end and beads of moisture pulled at the corner of her eyes.

Arla took in a deep breath, then sighed. Harry took over. "Given that the bathroom window was open, it is possible that the intruder gained entry from there. He left what looks like a boot print on the windowsill and we will analyse this on our databases to see if there is a match."

Despite her predicament, Rebecca's eyebrows rose. "You have a database for boot prints?"

"It's just an aid," Arla said. "Nothing can replace human intuition."

Rebecca's lips pressed together in a tight line, turning them from pink to white. She spoke between clenched teeth. "So, he came in through the bathroom window, took Reggie, and left through the nursery window?"

"It would seem that way. Please be aware these are very preliminary findings. I'm not saying this actually happened. But it's certainly possible." Harry chose his words with deliberate care and, at the end, glanced at Arla.

"Can we please speak to your housekeeper now?"

Rebecca's eyes flitted from Arla to Harry. She opened her mouth to say something, then thought better of it. "Edna." She repeated herself, turning to the side. At the summons, Edna appeared at the doorway of the kitchen. She walked over and stood uncertainly behind her mistress.

"The detectives would like to have a word with you," Rebecca said.

Arla stood. "Is it okay if we go to the lounge room?"

Rebecca agreed and they escorted Edna to the spacious lounge room where they had first spoken to Rebecca.

Edna sat down and Arla took the chair opposite. Harry stood by the window, looking at the road outside and the dense, clumped trees of the Common beyond.

Arla opened up her notebook. "Where were you this morning, Edna?"

The woman cleared her throat. She tucked a few strands of grey and white hair behind her ears. "The missus told me to buy some groceries and baby food. I went shopping."

"What time did you leave for the shops?"

"Seven-fifteen."

"Are supermarkets open at that time?"

"We have a twenty-four-hour store about fifteen minutes' drive away. That's where I normally go. I don't like the traffic later on in the morning, so I go early."

"And what time did you come back?"

"Just after eight-thirty. I can't remember the exact time. But I remember it being before eight forty-five, as I put the washing machine on timer."

Arla wrote down the times in her notebook and circled them with a pen. She connected the two circles with a line. "When you leave the house, you use the entrance of the annex, right? That's your living quarters?"

"Yes, that's right. I left by that entrance and when I came back, I parked the car and came in. . . ."

"And are you sure you locked the door when you left?"

Edna thought for a while. "Yes, I did."

Harry turned from his position at the window. He walked over and stood behind Arla.

"How long have you worked for this family?"

"Almost one year now. I saw an advertisement online and responded to that."

Arla asked about her last two employers and took down their names and addresses. "You don't mind if we approach them for a reference?"

"No problem at all. Please do."

There was something about Edna Mildred that made Arla pause. She couldn't put a finger on it but her senses, honed from many years of deciphering strange human minds, were tingling, a subtle wave rippling across her mind.

Arla folded her hands on her lap and relaxed back in the chair. "What do you think of Jeremy, Rebecca's husband?"

Edna shrugged. "He comes and goes. Stays out a lot. I don't really know a great deal about him, I'm afraid."

"Have you ever seen his uncle, Grant Stone?"

"I know who he is, of course. Everyone does. But I can't say he's ever been to this house."

"Do you have any children?" Arla asked the question smoothly, hoping the subtle but sudden change of topic would throw Edna. Her curiosity was piqued when the lady took it in stride, not missing a beat. The corners of her mouth didn't tighten. Her pupils didn't constrict. The forehead muscles remain slack. Even the neck muscles, which are the hardest to control when someone is lying, remained relaxed. Most unusual, if she was trying to hide something.

"Yes, I do." Edna's slate grey eyes shone with a sudden intensity. "One son, who's now twenty-five years old. He lives in Aberdeen, works in the oil industry."

"I see. Thank you."

"Do you enjoy working here?" Harry asked.

Edna lifted her chin to look at Harry. She shrugged. "It's a lovely house, as you can tell. Of course, my apartment's rather different." She smiled and Arla permitted a brief tug at the corners of her lips. Edna continued.

"The master and missus are always polite. Things changed after the baby arrived, obviously. I have to take more care of the baby and the missus."

Something in her tone alerted Arla." Do you look after the baby much?"

A genuine smile appeared on Edna's calm and dignified face. The crow's feet at the corners of her eyes crinkled and lit up with joy. "It's been a while since I've held a little baby, so it's lovely, yes. He's gorgeous."

Arla smiled as Edna's eyes travelled down to her bump. "You can't be far off yourself," the housekeeper added.

"Seven weeks and counting." Arla grinned. Then she became serious. "Have you noticed any changes in the husband's behaviour since the baby was born? Has he done anything that got your attention?"

Edna frowned as she thought. Then she shook her head. "Nothing unusual, no. Like I said, he spends a lot of time outside the house. On his film shoots and so on."

Harry asked, "Has he not spent more time at home since the baby arrived?"

"No, he hasn't. He still spends a lot of time away. The missus and I just get on with it." Edna's jaw tightened as she frowned. "Yes, I think that's a bit strange. I did expect him to be more at home, being a new father and all."

CHAPTER 9

After Edna Mildred's interview was over, Harry took her back to the kitchen. Presently, he returned with Rebecca. She had changed into blue jeans and a cream-coloured pullover sweater. Her face remained devoid of makeup, a listless, restive torment in her hazel eyes. Arla stood.

"Miss Stone, we would like to look around the garden and also the woods beyond. Is that okay?"

"Do anything you have to, please. I'm sorry to ask, but will anyone else be involved?"

Arla tried hard not to show her irritation. Rebecca was being polite enough, but her dogged insistence on privacy was beginning to wear thin on Arla's patience. She wasn't here as Rebecca's private investigator. She was a senior detective of the London Met, and she had a job to do.

"No one else will join us at this stage. But you must understand that in order for us to do our jobs, we need help from our colleagues.

For instance, if you want us to find out who the man opposite your house was, we need to check CCTV images. In order to do that, I need to ask one of the detectives in my department to pull up the images. It is not possible for myself or DI Mehta to do everything."

Rebecca folded her arms across her chest and her eyes flashed. "I realise that, of course. But if word leaks out—"

Arla held up a hand, silencing her. "It won't be from any of my staff, I can assure you. I have worked with them all my life, on several high-profile cases not dissimilar to yours. They have never breathed a word to the media."

Rebecca didn't alter her stance. Her jaws clenched together and the stiffness of her spine and shoulders clearly showed her unhappiness.

Arla softened her voice. "I shall abide by your wish not to involve scene-of-crime officers at this stage. You're correct in assuming that the more people we involve, the greater are the chances of a leak. I will confine the details of the investigation to no more than three members of my staff, and I will personally take responsibility for them."

Arla chose her words with care. When it came to Lisa Moran, Rob Pickering, and Roslyn May, she was confident of their integrity. Nevertheless, as she stared back at Rebecca, she was struck by how a woman who had just lost her baby was more concerned about privacy than finding the perpetrator. However, Arla also knew any whiff of bad news about a celebrity was like the scent of blood to shark-nosed reporters. They would probably have helicopters flying overhead, given half the chance. That thought also gave her an idea.

"I can promise you total discretion from my closest members of staff. For the time being, no one will come to see you apart from DI Mehta and myself. I would like to ask your permission, as well, to get a drone's view of your house, the woods behind it, and also the route you take into Clapham Common."

Rebecca nodded in silence. "Very well," Arla said. "We would like to have a short discussion in the car and then return. Is that okay?"

Harry and Arla sat in the car for a few minutes, gathering their thoughts. Harry had the engine on, and warm air blasted from the vents. Arla stretched out her hands to the stream of air, warming herself.

Harry said, "Can't see any CCTV here. I was looking on the way in as well. They must be on the main roads."

"Yes," Arla agreed. "Send Lisa a message to pull the images from the nearest CCTV. Hopefully, we can get some photos of the man Rebecca saw." She continued. "Note down the approximate time and date Rebecca saw the man waiting at the bus stop. It's a long shot, but if we can pick up the registration of the correct bus, then we might be able to see where he got off."

Harry groaned and inclined his head back on the seat. "Trust you to come up with something like that. Needle in a haystack."

Arla squinted at him. "It's worth a try. We can't use SOC right now so we have to keep our options open." She glanced at the clock on the dashboard. It was coming up to mid-day. One of the reasons why she was sitting in the car was to see which direction Jeremy Stone turned up from. Neither the housekeeper nor his wife seemed to know if he had left the house in his running gear. Could he be out on business? Arla found his behaviour strange, to say the least. She remembered they hadn't checked if his car was in, but surely his wife or the housekeeper would know if he had opened the garage.

She said, "We need to ask Rebecca for a photo of her husband. And any photos of the new baby as well. Also, get copies of the hospital notes dealing with the delivery and baby's health."

Harry said, "Baby was healthy, but she went through a tough time. Lost a lot of blood and had a transfusion."

"And she gets tired easily as she is still anaemic. I get that. But having the hospital notes would fill any gaps." She looked at Harry and saw his chestnut brown eyes dancing inquisitively. He rolled his shoulders once, then reached out a large hand and placed it softly on her bump. His eyes were focused on his hand and a smile played on his lips.

"He's moving."

"It's a she."

"No. A girl wouldn't be this restless."

Arla hooked an eyebrow at him. "You call me restless."

Harry made a face. "That's different. You're an adult. But I think you—we, I mean—are going to have a boy."

They grinned at each other, then Arla gently removed his hand. "We have work to do," she reminded him softly.

Harry rubbed the stubble on his cheeks, making a rustling sound. She desperately wanted to feel his stubble, and a lot more besides. A knot of desire untangled low in her belly, spreading heat between her legs. Breath caught in her chest, and she swallowed hard, not taking her eyes off Harry. He glanced sideways, eyes narrowing.

"What?"

"Nothing." Arla looked out the window quickly, to the magnificent Stone residence on her right.

Harry opened the driver's-side door and climbed out. Opening the boot, he took out Wellington boots and a torch. He slammed the door down after he had changed his shoes. He opened the driver's-side door slightly and leaned his long frame towards Arla.

"I'll walk around the garden and also in the woods beyond, then have a brief look at the pavement on the opposite side. Sure you don't want to sit inside?"

"Sit inside the crime scene just because I'm pregnant? Not very professional, is it?"

Harry made a grunting sound in his throat, which meant he was annoyed. "I'm sure Rebecca Stone won't see it like that."

"No way." Arla shook her head resolutely. "Just hurry up. I'll be fine."

CHAPTER 10

Harry used the side entrance and stopped at the door of the annex apartment. This was the housekeeper's residence. He rang the bell, but there was no answer. Edna Mildred was likely inside the main house, working. Harry had gloves on and he depressed the door handle. It was locked. There was no sign of a break-and-enter. Two windows faced him and the curtains were drawn. There was no sign of tampering at the windows either.

He walked to the end of the side passage, with the fence on his right. To his left the patio opened up, continuing all the way to the fence on the other side. He observed the snow for a while, virginal apart from the pawprints of a solitary fox. He went down to his knees and cast his eyes over the stone slabs of the patio. The earlier sunshine had faded and a bank of clouds gave the daylight a dull, greyish glow. Harry shone his torch up and down the patio stones. Satisfied there weren't any boot prints or marks on them, he stepped up to the first stone and then walked down.

From the concertina doors that made up the back wall of the kitchen, a flight of stone steps went down into the garden. He realised the patio stones were heated as well, including the steps. Molten snow had run off the patio, sliding into the steps. He nodded to himself. Since he had first looked out at the garden, he'd wondered why the snow did not settle on the patio. True, there was a portico just below the bathroom window, but that only covered a small part of the patio that ran the full length of the house. Now that he stood here, wisps of steam rose all around him, signifying the heating was still on. He was satisfied one puzzle which had been bothering him had been cracked.

He went to the edge of the patio and, standing on his tip-toes, used his considerable height to scan as far down the garden as he could. Still no footprints. He came to the edge of the patio, shining the torch beam into every nook and cranny. He located the garden shed. It was shut by a latchkey from the outside, but not locked. He opened the door and stepped inside the rickety wooden structure. His six-feet-four frame couldn't stand up straight. Stooping low, he looked around for a light switch, then realised there was none.

The shed only held gardening tools, including a lawnmower. On the floor lay a couple of large toolboxes. Harry kneeled and snapped open the locks. He shone the torch inside the toolboxes, taking out the layers of screwdrivers. He didn't find anything remotely interesting. He examined the ends of the screwdrivers for traces of blackened blood or any other human residue. He found nothing. He didn't expect to find anything; after all, any perpetrator would get rid of the evidence. But he had seen stranger things in his time.

And as his boss, now soon to be the mother of his child, loved to say: An absence of evidence is not evidence of absence.

He came out of the shed and walked back to the patio, his boots leaving deep prints in the snow. He traversed the entire length of the patio and came to the end where it sloped off towards a small fence which came up to his waist. A sliver of land ran between this fence and the next property. A bank of conifers shielded that property from the Stone residence.

Harry looked at the snow-covered land and shook his head. Again, all he saw was the footprints of a small animal, either a fox or a cat. No human prints were visible anywhere. He walked over to the fence. It was steady and not hard to climb over. He didn't. He walked up and down its length, hoping he wasn't disturbing evidence that lay buried under the snow. The fence hadn't been tampered with in any way. Snow lay heavy on the nude branches in the woods behind. The skeleton branches reached out to him like spindly, shapeless, bony arms, almost beseeching for warmth and greenery.

Harry's eyes scanned the frigid, white earth stretching to the woods, then took in the trees themselves. He couldn't make out a great deal. He climbed over the fence and walked down. Luckily, the snow hadn't started again. The tip of his nose was going numb and he rubbed it with a gloved hand. He came to the edge of the woods and stood there for a while. The interior was gloomy and dark, with some evergreen undergrowth interspersed with rotten leaves and fallen branches.

He looked back at the footprints he had left behind. Then he waded into the undergrowth. It was tough. Like claws, twigs scratched at his face, pulled at his hair. Harry cursed and used his gloved hands to pull down as much of the dense shrubbery as he could.

After he had gone in roughly ten feet, he stopped. He shone his light around. This was heavy going, and he couldn't imagine a man carrying a baby going through this. A chill spread down his spine, freezing his heart. Harry was no stranger to the viciousness and cruelty of the human mind, but the thought of that new-born baby being left out here in the cold filled him with a desolate despair. He shivered as looked around, flashing his torch.

There was nothing but glistening, black undergrowth and vines that lay twisted on the ground. They entwined around his feet, making movement difficult. Harry lifted his boots, smashing more branches out of the way. When he stopped, the silence was total, not a whisper to be heard anywhere. All of nature's sounds were withdrawn deep into the breast of its dark, cold heart. It was futile to look around any further. Harry trudged back the way he came, glad to leave this frigid, forsaken place.

Arla was waiting in the car, scribbling in her notebook. She looked up as Harry came back. He deposited the wellies in the boot, changed into his shoes, and opened the driver's door.

"How did it go?" Arla asked. "Not much, right?" She hadn't seen any footprints from the upper-floor windows, and doubted Harry would have uncovered a lot more. But she knew Harry's sharp eyes wouldn't have missed much.

"There's no way out the back. Not unless you've got a machete. In which case, the perp would've left a gash wide enough for me to see. Maybe get the drone up here, and also try to tackle the woods from behind."

Arla took her phone out and, turning on the map function, honed down to her location. "Another row of multimillion-pound mansions behind those woods. Their gardens back on to it, just like this house does."

Harry frowned. "No way out, in other words. That makes the woods an unlikely escape route, unless. . . ." His words died out as the horrible, macabre vision rose in his mind again. He shivered. Arla stared at him, then reached out to squeeze his hand.

"No, I don't think he went down there." She shook her head. "He went out some other way. Look, there's a boot print on the bathroom windowsill, so someone entered the house. The nursery window was open and there's a boot print on the flat roof right below it, so we know he went down that way too."

"With the baby."

"Yes," Arla agreed.

"But how did he do it without leaving any footprints in the snow? Even if he cleaned up behind himself, the snow would be disturbed."

Arla rubbed her fingers thoughtfully under her chin. "Did you do a full circle and come round the left side?"

"Yes, I did. The left side is full of snow and, again, I saw an animal's small pawprints. But nothing else."

"Then it is a mystery," Arla conceded. "I don't like mysteries." She frowned and pursed her lips together.

"Okay, Harry. Please ask Rebecca one last time if her husband is back. If not, tell him to come down to the station to give a statement as soon as he returns. But given that these folks are blue-blooded, they'll probably want us to come back here for another statement."

"Okay." Harry opened the driver's door a fraction. "You wanted the details of her mother and sister as well, right?"

"Yes. And don't forget the photos of Jeremy and the new baby."

CHAPTER 11

It was a peculiarity of human nature, Arla mused, that violent crime and homicide cases tapered down in the winter and increased in the summer. As a result, there were a lot of bored faces at the detectives' open-plan office. Inspectors and sergeants stood around chatting to each other. The incident room had not seen any action for almost a month, an unheard-of statistic in the summer months. Lisa and Roslyn May, the new detective sergeant from the Midlands, were sat together, staring at Roslyn's laptop screen. As Arla got closer, she realised they were shopping for shoes.

"Not disturbing anything, am I?"

Both sergeants jumped. Arla had approached them stealthily from behind. Roslyn lay a hand on her chest. "Geez, guv, you scared the life out of me."

"Good to see you're keeping busy," Arla teased.

Roslyn flushed. She was hard-working and conscientious and Arla liked her.

"We were wondering where you were, and if everything was all right and—"

Arla laughed and stopped her. "I'm only joking. Where's Rob?"

Lisa pointed to one corner, where Rob and three other detectives were sat in a circle. As Arla watched, one of them leaned back and laughed out loud. The man who laughed at his own joke was Justin Beauregard. Justin had always been jealous of Arla's stellar rise up the ranks. He believed he should have been detective chief inspector before her, despite Arla's track record. She noticed that Rob was serious and down-faced as Justin and two other detective inspectors carried on laughing. In silence, Rob rose and walked back to his desk. Arla caught his attention and waved him over.

"What do they find so funny?" she asked.

Rob had a portly figure and a balding head. His chubby cheeks wore a hint of crimson as he shuffled on his feet and cleared his throat. "Oh, just this and that."

Arla narrowed her eyes. She could tell when Rob was lying.

"To my office, now." Arla set off. She took a circuitous route, deliberately walking past Justin's table.

The laughter stopped, and when she glanced out of the corner of her eye, she could see Justin smirking at her. She ignored him, but didn't like it. Justin was a seasoned senior detective. All the years he had spent in the murky underbelly of London's grimy streets had made him a tough cop. But he was known to cut corners, and although Arla could never prove it, she suspected he had planted evidence in the past, in order to secure a prosecution. She had heard it from criminals she had successfully persecuted herself.

The corridors of crime in this secretive city rang with whispers of buried guilt, forgotten crimes, and voices that spoke from beyond the grave. Arla knew her job as a policewoman was to listen for these secrets. A copper's job wasn't unlike that of a doctor, who gets to know the disease better than she knows the patient. Otherwise, she cannot treat the disease. Arla suspected strongly that the disease of corruption had touched Justin Beauregard, tainting him.

Rob shut the door behind him as Arla leaned against a filing cabinet in her office. Rob pulled at the collar of his shirt, his fleshy, corpulent neck folds spilling over it. It wasn't warm, but there was a slight sheen of sweat on his forehead.

"Go on then, Rob, what were those idiots blabbering about?"

"Well, I, the. . . ."

"Something about me, right?"

Rob cleared his throat. He looked down at the frayed carpet, then at the walls, and past Arla's head. Anywhere but stare into the dagger-like intensity radiating from Arla's eyes. She flapped her hands. "For heaven's sake, Rob. Stop acting like a school kid. Just tell me what they were saying."

"It's about what happens when you go on maternity leave."

Arla frowned. "Do you mean the post of DCI?" She knew about this already, of course. Johnson and Deakins, the other deputy assistant commissioner, were looking for her replacement. As far as she knew, they hadn't decided as yet. Breath caught in her chest as a sudden thought bloomed in her mind.

"Yes, your post."

"What about it?"

Rob swallowed hard and tugged at his sweaty collar again. "Justin was bragging, guv. He said things will change around here when he becomes the top dog."

Arla walked to her desk, then lowered herself into the armchair. She tried not to show the shock she felt, her lungs suddenly empty of air. Of all the people who could take her post, why Justin? They could easily have chosen Harry. In fact, she had discreetly suggested Harry's name to Johnson as well. Clearly, it hadn't worked.

"Top dog," she whispered to herself, then pressed lightly on her eyelids with the tips of her fingers. "So, he's going to become DCI when I leave for maternity?"

Rob shifted on his feet, discomfort written plain on his face. "You didn't know about this, guv?"

Arla slapped the palm of her hand down on the desk, making Rob jump. "No," she seethed, "I didn't." Johnson had promised she would have some say in choosing her successor. She would be gone for six months at least, maybe longer. Now, she feared Justin would resent her even more when she returned from maternity leave. The power would go to his head. Given what she knew of him already, it was a dangerous cocktail.

She rose and walked past Rob, into the open-plan office. Harry was seated at Lisa's desk and he straightened when he saw her.

"I'm going to see Johnson. Stay here." She knew Harry would be asking Rob about what had happened. Obviously, Harry hadn't been informed either. She took the elevator up to the fourth floor, and then knocked on the door of Johnson's office. A gruff voice ordered her inside.

Johnson looked up from the file he was reading, his eyebrows rising when he saw Arla. He stood, coming around the desk, something he never did for any of the detectives.

"Why didn't you just ring?"

Arla suppressed the rising tide of anger and spoke between clenched teeth. "I had to discuss this with you face-to-face."

She sat down on a chair at his desk while Johnson took his seat. She had a brief view of his initials, WJ, monogrammed into the gilded black leather before he settled his ample form into it. She didn't waste any time.

"Why did you give Justin my job?"

Johnson's mouth fell open as the delicate skin around his eyes relaxed. His pupils dilated, before constricting like his eyebrows. "Who told you?"

Arla clenched, then unclenched her fists. "The fact that he can't keep his mouth shut should make you worry about your choice of my successor. *Sir.*"

Johnson's nostrils flared. His upper lip rose in a snarl as he shifted back into his chair. He muttered something under his breath.

"I don't think Justin can be trusted. He's a good cop, we both know that. He's done his hard yards. But you know the rumours about him," Arla continued.

Johnson looked genuinely surprised. "What rumours?"

Arla threw her head back and stared at the ceiling for a few seconds. Johnson was such a pen-pusher he had no idea of what happened at street level anymore. Strange to think, she thought, this man had been her first instructor when she took the detective grade examinations. Sparkles of crimson fire burned in her eyes as she stared at him.

"You mean you really don't know?"

Johnson frowned and shook his head. Arla said, "The case against the Albanian cocaine gang members. One of them said a policeman planted the weapon in his house. Justin was the only one who had been to that house. And he went on his own, so there were no witnesses."

Johnson spread his hands. "You're taking the word of a gang member?"

"He was a sixteen-year-old boy, sir. He was scared stiff and wanted a way out. I offered him a deal. He told me the truth to get off a lengthy jail sentence." She straightened her spine and lifted her chin. "And that's not the only case." She rattled off two more instances where Justin's shady activities had come under scrutiny. She shook her head. "At first I thought it was hearsay. Like you said, we can't trust a criminal. But even members of his team and some of the uniformed officers have seen him in odd places."

Johnson eyed her with a flat, calm look in his slate grey eyes. "I know you don't like him, Arla. But you must be careful about smearing the name of a colleague. We live in glass houses."

"He can chuck as many stones at me as he wants. I have nothing to fear."

"No?" Johnson's forehead muscles arched upwards. "Punching a suspect, losing your temper, being rude to your seniors. . . . The list goes on, Arla."

She opened her mouth to speak but Johnson put a hand up. "You have no proof against Justin. Criminals will always try to incriminate police officers. You know how this works. As far as I'm concerned, Justin's a bloody good copper and when you're gone, he deserves your job."

Arla grimaced, then shuddered. "Of all the senior detectives, you had to choose him. Why?"

Johnson shrugged. "The South London Command chose him. It wasn't just me."

"I see." She forced herself to hold her tongue. The South London Command was composed of Nick Deakins, one of the deputy assistant commissioners, and four other senior figures. Nick wasn't exactly her biggest fan. Had they done this deliberately to irk her? She dismissed the thought as petty, but a bad taste lingered in her mouth.

"What about Harry?"

"DI Mehta is your partner, and the father of your child." Johnson's voice dropped as he blinked, then lowered his eyes. "You need him close to you and he needs some daddy time. He could well be a candidate for the top job in the future, but this isn't a good time for him."

She stared at Johnson for a while, wondering if there was an angle here she couldn't see. Maybe there was a connection between Deakins and Justin that she didn't know of. She also knew it was futile to ask about it, or to try to change their minds.

Johnson cleared his throat. "I heard you went to see Rebecca Stone. Thank you for that."

Arla picked the corner of a nail, gathering her thoughts. "No problem, sir."

"What did you find?"

Arla filled him in. "Sooner or later, we need to involve uniformed officers to help with the search of the Common and the woods behind their house. We also need Scene of Crime." She lifted both hands in the air. "But she wants me to keep it just to my team."

Johnson pressed his lips together and rolled them inward. He rubbed his large, bearlike paws on the table. "Well, given who she is, privacy is paramount."

"You mean, given that she's a personal friend of Mr Cummings. The man who controls 30 per cent of our funding."

Johnson snapped his teeth together and his jaws hardened. "That's enough, Arla. This is a police case now and you just need to do your job."

"Do my job? How on earth am I supposed to search all that area with four officers? And if we do involve the uniforms, we can't exactly keep it a secret from them. We need to tell them what to look for. And what about forensics? Dr Banerjee?"

Johnson sagged, the tension dissipating from him like air from a deflating balloon. A wariness rippled across his face as his eyelids snapped shut.

"Okay. I'll try and speak to the family. Just do the best you can, for now."

CHAPTER 12

Arla took the elevator down to the ground floor and trudged slowly back to her office. At the back of her mind suspicion battled with a sense of paranoia. By appointing Justin as her successor, was the South London Command trying to get rid of her?

She knew the department might well look very different by the time she returned from her maternity leave. She sat down at her table and let out a frustrated sigh. Well, she would show them. Her current case was a high-profile one. She had solved cases involving well-known political figures and actors, and she knew how to deal with the media's full glare. She shook her head in disbelief. Justin simply didn't have the same amount or quality of experience she possessed. And yet. . . .

Her office door clicked open and Harry poked his head in, then entered. He shut the door, then leaned his long frame against the wall. He scrutinised her face for a few seconds in silence.

"Rob told me. No, I didn't know either."

Arla glanced up at him, then nodded. Harry wasn't a big fan of Justin Beauregard either. His lips curled upward in distaste. "He's wormed his way into the affections of South London Command."

"Exactly what I thought. He's a yes boy, and he won't mind bending the rules for them."

Arla held Harry's eyes for a second. His normally melting chestnut browns were flat and cold. She knew what he was thinking. The hint of corruption within police ranks was nothing new. With the new monitoring and regulation all police departments had to carry out, corruption was all but stamped out. But occasionally, a waft of it floated in, like the stench from a dying carcass. Harry didn't have to say anything. Neither did she. But from the firm set of Harry's lips, she knew what they had to do.

"We can't go public with the case as yet. But the clock is ticking. We need concrete leads by the end of today. Bring Lisa, Rob, and Roslyn in here."

When Harry left, Arla glanced at the stack of paperwork to her left, in her in-tray. She was still the on-call SIO for the week, but thankfully, her pile hadn't grown any larger.

The team strode in and she was glad to see Lisa with four cups of steaming coffee. Lisa knew exactly how Arla liked it and set the mug down next to her laptop with a grin.

"Thanks." Arla winked at her. She loved her mocha, calories be damned. She was definitely going on a diet after the baby arrived.

She took a sip from the scalding cup, then flipped open her black notebook. Harry locked the door. Arla stared at Rob, Roslyn, and Lisa.

"What we discuss now stays in these four walls. There's no police crime notice on this case as yet. You cannot provide an explanation to anyone who asks what you're doing. Is that clear?"

The three detective sergeants looked at each other. From the bemused look on their faces, Arla could see her comments were as clear as mud.

Roslyn said, "Without a PCN, how can we open an investigation?"

"Good question. This is departmental oversight. The order comes from above me. We have to be discreet, till I get the permission to open formal proceedings." She placed her hands on the desk and leaned forward. "Before then, if any word leaks out, it will be from the people present in this room. Hence, I need your word that this remains confidential."

Everyone nodded and Arla made sure she met their eyes, noting their confirmation. She took them through what she had found so far and the people involved. There was pin-drop silence in the room as the detectives listened to her with rapt attention.

When Arla finished, Lisa whistled. "Rebecca Stone? She's got, like, a million Instagram followers!"

"And she posts ten times a week," Roslyn added.

Arla lifted her shoulders slightly. "If you check the posts from the last six weeks, you won't see a great deal Yes, she did post after childbirth, posing with her new baby. But after the first week, the photos stopped."

"You mean since the baby's birth."

"His name is Reginald Stone." Arla glanced at Harry. "Has the family registered the name yet?"

Harry shook his head. "We haven't spoken to the father as yet. But when I checked the birth and death register, there was nothing on file with that name or date of birth."

"Good. That's one less angle for an inquisitive journalist to prod into."

Lisa spoke up. "She must've been posting photos of her baby bump. And then of the new baby for the first week, as you said. Don't her followers want to see more?"

Arla scrolled through her Instagram feed. "It doesn't look like it. She got loads of comments and likes for the baby posts, but when they tailed off, I guess there are thousands of other Instagram celebrities who took over."

"Yeah," Harry said. He was still leaning against the doorframe. "Instagram users probably have the memory of a goldfish. No dearth of new photos in their feeds."

Arla rose and walked the few steps to the window behind her desk. A small, portable whiteboard stood there. She picked up a marker pen and wrote the number one on the board, then circled it.

"CCTV footage of the man in the parka observing Rebecca's house. The same guy took a bus from the station near her house."

"Got that, guv," Rob said, scribbling on his pad. "I know that area. There should be cameras leading into the street and coming out."

"Good. Let's get those camera feeds and have them analysed by the end of today."

Arla wrote a two on the whiteboard.

"Jeremy Stone. I want to know why he had to go for his run when we were about to arrive. It seemed as if he was trying to avoid us. Either Harry or I will take a full statement from him as soon as he gets in touch. But can you please look into his background. Go all the way back to his childhood, school, and university days. Find out about his relationship with his uncle."

"His uncle being Grant Stone, the rock star," Harry added.

Roslyn gasped. "*The* Grant Stone?" Arla nodded in silence as Roslyn gaped at her. The DS whistled. "Oh my god, guv, I'm such a big fan. Got a Spotify playlist just with his songs!"

Lisa and Rob chuckled. Lisa said, "I must say, I'm a fan too. Went to see him in concert once, many years ago."

"In Wembley Arena?" Roslyn asked.

"Yes. September 2005."

Roslyn's mouth formed a near perfect O as her eyebrows hiked north. "Oh my God, I was there!"

Lisa laughed. "No way. Great concert, huh?"

Roslyn held up a hand, then waved it in the air. Excitement bubbled in her voice. "My goodness, that man is sex on legs. Did you see those dance moves? Just wow."

Arla laughed too, then tapped the table with her finger. "Can we get back on the case, please, ladies? I don't think Grant Stone will be happy with us if we don't solve this case soon."

Smiles faded from Roslyn and Lisa's lips as they sat straighter in their chairs and faced Arla. She pursed her lips and furrowed her brows in concentration as she slowly wrote down the number three on the board and circled it.

"Rebecca Stone. Dig up her childhood and her previous social life. I want to know about school friends, her life in college, what jobs she got and with who. Details about her previous relationships before she met Jeremy Stone."

Lisa looked up from scribbling on her notepad. "Guv, you're casting the net wide now. This will take more than three of us to get through."

Rob said, "Or it will take three of us longer."

Arla blinked. Harry said, "They've got a point. We can't run this investigation on skeleton staff and expect a miracle."

Arla laid the palms of both hands on her bump. "I know that, Harry," she said briskly. "But you and I will help as well." She pointed to the stack of papers on her desk. "I'm going to hand over the on-call SIO role to someone of Johnson's choice. It might well be Justin, but so be it. This takes priority now."

"Are you sure about that?" Harry hooked his eyebrows northward. "After what we just heard about Justin?"

"Yes, I know. But it seems they have taken the decision already. Handing this over to Justin might give him an ego boost, but in practical terms, it also helps him to get ready for the task ahead. Plus, it saves me valuable time."

Lisa's eyes slid from Arla to Harry. "What about Justin, guv? You mean DI Beauregard, right?"

Arla caught Rob's attention. His eyes snapped shut once as he shook his head. She smiled lightly, aware that Rob had kept his mouth shut about Justin. She turned to Lisa and told her.

Her team remained silent. Arla read the look in their eyes. It was a combination of excitement and anxiety. They were eager to start searching for Rebecca's missing baby, but they were also concerned for her and their future.

Arla walked to a table, and closer to them. She spoke softly. "I suspect Johnson has given me this case to prove something. I'm not sure why, and let's not worry about that for the time being. Let's get cracking."

She pointed a polished red fingernail towards Rob. "CCTV images, please. We need to show Rebecca and try to get an ID as soon as possible."

Harry stood straight and stretched his long spine, then flexed both shoulders. He seemed taller when he did that and Arla couldn't help but glance at him, distracted.

"Don't forget the CCTV footage from the cameras at the house. We need to speak to Rebecca or her husband about it," Harry said.

She flashed him a smile. The corners of his eyes crinkled and he tucked his lips inwards and she knew the handsome devil had been saving the best for last. Her chin jutted out and she stabbed a finger in his direction. "You're hoping to get a visual of the intruder, aren't you?"

Harry put both hands on his waist and feigned innocence. "I was just wondering why the famous DCI Baker was missing the most obvious lead."

She frowned at him. "I wasn't missing anything, Harry, just testing you."

Someone laughed and Arla looked at the three detective sergeants who were grinning at them. In the early days, when she kept her relationship with Harry a secret, the smiles were missing but the whispers did their rounds. It was so different now. She was expecting Harry's baby, and while they wouldn't be the first department couple, they had certainly attracted the most attention. It wasn't often that the DCI started a relationship with her trusted DI sidekick.

"Well, you all know your jobs," Arla said, fighting a grin herself. "Let's get this ball rolling."

Her desk phone rang. It was the switchboard. "DCI Baker?"

"Speaking."

"There's a Rebecca Stone on the line for you."

"Put her through, please, thanks."

Arla cupped the receiver and mouthed Rebecca's name to her team. "Hello?"

"Hi. Is that Detective Baker?" The female voice was low and despondent.

"Yes," Arla said. "Hello Rebecca."

"My husband just came back. You told me to call you when he did?"

CHAPTER 13

Rhys Mason watched from his vantage point, sheltered by the dense, snow-laden trees of the Common. He had a clear view of the Stone residence from here, and every time a curtain twitched, he used a binocular to watch the window.

Several times already, he'd caught sight of Rebecca peering out, staring up and down the road and then straight at the plot of trees in the Common.

Once, he was sure, her eyes fell on him. Breath caught in his lungs as his fingers shook. Her gaze was intent, focused. Had she caught a movement that he made? He knew even the slightest movement caught attention so he took great care to remain absolutely still.

How could he ever forget those luminous sea green eyes? Eyes that enveloped his soul like the warm waters on a tropical beach.

Once, those exotic eyes held him captive. Heck, they still did as she stared in his direction now. They pierced like arrows through the orderly symmetry of his mind, bullets smashing into his skull. His breath quickened and beads of moisture appeared on his forehead. The binocular trembled in his hand, distorting his view. But he couldn't pull himself away. Mercifully, after a few seconds, she turned away from the window.

Gasping, he lowered the binocular and raked his gaze over the remaining windows and the front door. She didn't appear in any of them. She was inside, walking around alone in the halls of her gilded prison.

Rhys lowered his head. He was wearing a padded white pullover that blended in with the snow and his white parka on top. He sat on the fallen branch of a tree like he normally did, his back to a trunk.

Memories surged up from a black hole inside his heart, besmirching his mind with amniotic, inky poison. Once, he had thought Rebecca would set him free. And he would do the same to her. But it was not to be. He knew he only had himself to blame, but he had tried to redeem himself.

He couldn't control his urges, his fervent desires. Society regarded them as wrong, but what the hell did society know?

The normal people, busy with their nine-to-five jobs, mortgages, and bills, safely packaged and wrapped in their lives to be lowered into a grave one day. They would never understand. For a while, he knew that Rebecca did. She understood why he indulged his desires. But ultimately, she had turned her back on him, just like the rest of them.

His jaws flexed as his eyes snapped open. The hardened, calloused brown bark of a tree trunk caught his eyes. He wanted to smack it with a gloved fist but couldn't risk the movement. He glared at it for a few seconds, breathing heavily. The moment passed. A smile tugged at the corners of his lips.

That look on Rebecca's face as she stared out the window. The wide eyes. The sunken cheeks. Hollow and emaciated, with eyeballs sunk deep into the sockets. She was scared. Well, she had made him suffer, and now it was her turn. His plan was working. He didn't want to do this, but she hadn't left him with a choice. She had flown from him and taken refuge in Jeremy Stone's gold-barred prison. He would prise out those bars one by one and set her free again. She would know his power. What he was capable of.

A black BMW floated into his view, coming to a stop near the house. His eyebrows lowered and met in the centre of his forehead. He had seen the car earlier this morning. And just like this morning, a tall, wide-shouldered man and a pregnant woman got out of the car.

The woman stood still for a while, staring at the Common. She looked up, down, and sideways, and then she leaned forward, as if trying to peer through the shadows. Rhys knew she couldn't see him as he was too far back, sheltered by heavy undergrowth. But it still unnerved him.

The woman was attractive, even though her nose was angular, a bit too big for her face. Her wide mouth, large eyes, and high cheekbones made up for the nose. She tossed her dark, shoulder-length hair back as the tall man, wearing a grey overcoat, stepped alongside her. He leaned over and murmured something in her ear. She didn't seem to pay him any attention and continued to scrutinise the silent, frozen woods. Presently, she turned and, grasping the man's elbow, walked slowly towards the house.

Rhys raised the binoculars to his eyes again. He took down the registration number of the BMW. The man and woman went inside, let in by the housekeeper. Taking off his gloves, Rhys blew on his frozen fingers, flexed them. He took out his phone to enter the registration number onto the DVLA website. His suspicions were correct. The car belonged to the London Metropolitan Police Service. The smile on his face grew wider. Everything was falling into place. The couple who had just entered the house were the detectives. And the female detective was pregnant. A lucky coincidence indeed.

CHAPTER 14

Arla and Harry waited in the same lounge room, to the left of the entrance hallway. Arla looked out the large bay windows to the snow-covered street outside. A couple walked past, both of them admiring the house. Edna Mildred got cups of tea for them this time without Arla or Harry requesting them. The elderly lady smiled as she put the tray down on the long, rectangular table.

"Mr Stone will be down shortly. Please help yourselves."

"This wasn't necessary," Arla said, eyeing the chocolate biscuits with longing.

"It's perfectly all right. You need to keep your strength up."

Arla couldn't agree more. She had consumed two biscuits and half her cup of tea by the time the door opened and Jeremy Stone walked in. He was much shorter than she had expected. He wore square-framed glasses and his head was balding. She put his age in the late thirties to early forties.

There was a two-day stubble on his cheeks, and his figure was trim and athletic. He came forward and Harry shook his hand, then Arla stood to do the same.

A pair of dark blue eyes searched her face from behind thick glasses. Not a handsome man, she thought to herself, not even good-looking. With his tweed trousers and dark brown sweater, he was a stark contrast to the understated glamour his wife possessed. She was almost a foot taller than him as well.

Jeremy and Harry remained standing while Arla took her seat again. Jeremy said, "Thank you for coming this morning at such short notice. I'm sorry I wasn't here when you arrived. After what happened, I felt the need to clear my head."

His explanation struck Arla as odd, but she could get to it later. "I'm sorry about what you're going through, Mr Stone. I know this must be awful for you, but the more you can remember and tell us, the better."

Jeremy's head lowered and he cradled it on his palm. He remained motionless, but from the stiffness of his shoulders, Arla could see he was holding himself in. Harry walked to him and touched him on the shoulder.

"Would you like to sit down, Mr Stone?"

Jeremy didn't reply, but when Harry pulled him a chair he did as asked. He took his glasses off and rubbed both eyes with the heels of his hands.

Arla opened up her black notebook. "Please tell us what happened this morning."

Jeremy took a while to compose himself. He took out a handkerchief and blew his nose. His eyes were red-rimmed. He swallowed hard and stared at the carpet for a while, a vacant, lost look in his stricken eyes. If this was an act, Arla thought, then it was worthy of an Oscar. She reminded herself, not for the first time, that Jeremy Stone was a director and film producer and was no stranger to high-quality acting. Much like his wife.

Harry walked over to the other side of the table and sat down, observing from a different angle.

Jeremy cleared his throat. "I was up around seven this morning. Reggie and Becky slept in her bedroom. Becky said Reggie wasn't feeling well and she would nurse him. Hence, I slept alone."

Arla remained silent and he continued. "The sun was up and it seemed like a nice morning. I didn't see Becky, and the nursery was empty, so I thought they went for a walk. They do that often."

"Do you join them?"

Jeremy inclined his head. "Yes, of course I do. But Becky knew I was busy this morning on a project that just started. It requires travel to Brighton, to scope out a location. I think that's why she didn't ask me."

"Carry on."

"I had to make some calls and catch up on emails. As it happens, after this dreadful incident, I'm having to postpone my schedule. My assistant producer is stepping in. But I was due to travel tonight. Obviously, that will have to wait now."

"Were you at home when Rebecca and Reggie returned?"

"Yes, I was. I didn't actually hear them come in, however."

"You weren't aware they had returned?"

Jeremy shrugged. "No. I was in my study and I guess I didn't hear the doorbell go. Becky has keys, obviously, but the front door lets off a bell as soon as it's opened, even if with a key."

"And you didn't hear Becky leave either?"

"No."

A sensation crinkled at the corner of Arla's mind, radiating to her ears. A soft sound, like rubbing her finger on paper. She pressed her lips together. "Do you not normally hear the doorbell or other sounds around the house when you are in your study?"

He replied after a few seconds of thought. "Not always. My study isn't soundproof, but it is near the back of the house." He spread his hands. "It's a big house, as you can see. I normally do hear the doorbell, because the chime is on a loudspeaker. But if someone has keys, they can let themselves in."

"And you wouldn't know who came in."

"Yes."

"So, Rebecca let herself in and out with the pram and you didn't know."

A hint of irritation appeared on Jeremy's troubled features. "I think we've established that."

"It's very important to establish that," Arla said, completely unruffled. "If we have a sequence of events, we can build a picture from that. So, when were you aware something was wrong?"

Jeremy took a deep sigh and closed his eyes. "When I heard Becky screaming."

"Let's go back a little while. So you were in your study when you heard Rebecca scream. After you woke up, did you go downstairs?"

"Yes, I did. I got the newspapers and asked Miss Mildred to make me a cup of coffee and some breakfast. Then I came back upstairs."

"Do you know what time this was?"

Jeremy stared at Arla for a few seconds, then shrugged. "I didn't check my watch. But I think sometime near eight o'clock."

Arla wrote the time down in a notebook and circled it. She asked Jeremy to continue.

"I came back upstairs and sat down in my study. Miss Mildred brought the coffee and breakfast up to me. I got busy with answering emails and telling my assistant director what to do. As you can imagine, finishing a film production on time and on budget is a stressful job."

"Sure, I get that. Do you remember the time you heard Becky scream?"

He looked down at his twisting fingers and frowned in concentration. "I remember it being eight forty-five, because I got a phone call. I'm sure it was just after that."

"So, say about nine a.m.?"

"I guess so, yes." He stared above Arla's head for a few seconds, then said, "Actually, I remember that time as well because the internet wasn't working and I had to check the Wi-Fi and router."

"Why wasn't it working?"

He shrugged. "Not sure. It's started up again now, just before you arrived. But all morning it's been down."

Arla swivelled her face slowly to find Harry staring at her. She angled her head, looking at Jeremy askance. "What about last night, or earlier? Did you have problems with the Wi-Fi?"

"Nope. Worked perfectly, normally. We have high-speed, fibre-optic broadband. It was weird how it stopped working this morning."

"What about other electrics? The lights, TV, so on."

"They worked fine. I don't watch TV in the mornings, but the lights worked normally. So did the kitchen appliances, as far as I'm aware."

Arla narrowed her eyes, the wave of a new thought unfurling slowly across her mind. "You have CCTV here, right?"

Jeremy frowned. "Good point. The CCTV is connected to the Wi-Fi. It runs remotely, and we can operate the camera feeds from an app on our phones. I didn't think about that."

He took out his phone and checked. "Yes, the app is working now. But we store the feeds, and have to pay monthly for that. I guess you want to see if the cameras were working this morning?"

"Yes, and last night. In fact, the whole week."

"No problem. But I have to send the company an email."

Harry cleared his throat. "If you give us the details, it'll be easier. We can specify what we need."

Jeremy's eyes switched from Harry to Arla as he considered. Then he nodded slowly. "Our privacy is very important to us. Please ensure—"

Arla interrupted. "You're not the first media figure we have dealt with. Please understand that the CCTV feeds are safe with us."

Harry spoke up from across the table. "Okay, let's get back to this morning. You heard your wife scream the first time, or was it more than once?"

Jeremy took some time before answering. "It's kind of hard to remember. It all happened so quickly, if you know what I mean. But I think there was a faint sound that alerted me. Then I heard a scream." He nodded towards Harry. "You're right. It might have been after she'd screamed a few times."

Harry said, "Your study is directly opposite the nursery room."

"Yes, it is."

"Was your study door open or shut?"

"I never shut it fully, actually. It was ajar."

"And then what happened?"

Jeremy sat straighter in the chair. His nostrils flared and his eyes widened as he recollected those terrible moments.

"I ran across. She was in a state, as you can imagine." He rubbed his forehead and shook his head before continuing. "I couldn't make any sense of what she was saying, apart from the word 'baby'. I looked inside the cot and it became obvious what had happened."

Arla put a hand up. "Okay, let's slow down here, Jeremy. What do you mean by obvious?"

He frowned as he stared back at Arla. "Well, the cot was empty and the window was open. The net curtain was flapping in the wind."

"So, what did you do?"

"I ran to the window and looked out. I couldn't see anything. But that window is normally shut."

Arla wrote something down on her notepad. "Yes, that's exactly what your wife said." She drew her lips in and rubbed them over each other as she stared at her notebook. Then she glanced up at Jeremy. "When you came inside the room, was it cold or warm?"

Jeremy's mouth opened and he appeared puzzled, a frown of irritation spasming across his face. "Warm or cold?"

Arla raised her eyebrows. "Yes?" she asked slowly.

He shook his head. "Pretty sure it was warm. That room normally is."

Arla watched him in silence for a while, then turned her head to glance at Harry. A silent message passed between them. Harry asked, "Did you go inside the bathroom, which is right next to the nursery?"

Again, Jeremy looked surprised. "The bathroom? You mean the main one, on that floor?"

"Yes."

"No, we have an en-suite bathroom in our bedroom and I normally use that. I use the main bathroom for my shower, after I come back from my run."

"So, you're sure you didn't visit the main bathroom in the morning, before we arrived?" Arla repeated.

Jeremy scowled. He held out both hands. "I've told you already, haven't I?"

Arla hardened her voice. "Could you please answer the question."

Jeremy glared at her for a few seconds. "Yes," he uttered firmly.

"Please carry on," Harry prodded.

Jeremy shifted his attention to him. "I wanted to call the police. But I wasn't sure, and Becky didn't know what to do either. So, I decided to call my uncle, and then you guys arrived a bit later."

Arla asked, "What happened between speaking to your uncle and us arriving?"

"Miss Mildred and I comforted Becky the best we could. She was almost catatonic, as you can imagine." He squeezed his eyes shut and leaned back.

Arla gave him a few seconds, then asked, "Did you stay upstairs, or come down into the kitchen?"

"Becky wouldn't leave the nursery. But she wanted me to go outside and check. Which I did, of course."

Harry asked, "You went outside, to the back? But I didn't see any human footprints on the snow."

"I went out to the front door and then circled around the path to the left. I walked down to the edge of the woods before turning back."

Harry relaxed. "But you didn't go into the garden?"

Jeremy's face was calm and flat, like the surface of a pond reflecting the sky. Almost too calm, Arla thought. She couldn't ignore the nagging worry biting at the back of her mind. A concrete, obsidian shape, slowly taking form, but still out of reach.

Jeremy glanced from Harry to Arla. "Like you said, I didn't see any footprints in the garden either. And the snow was heavy, especially at the rear, where the garden slopes down. I didn't see the point."

Harry asked, "So you saw nothing and decided to come back?" Jeremy nodded. Harry leaned forward, putting his elbows on the desk, his chair creaking. He held Jeremy's eyes. "Then you decided to go for a run? At a moment like this?"

Jeremy didn't rise to it, Arla noted with interest. He had been preparing for the question, she thought to herself. A ripple of unease slithered down her spine.

Without moving a muscle on his face, and keeping perfectly still, Jeremy said, "There was nothing more for me to do. I must once again thank you for coming. But it was time for my morning run and I needed some fresh air."

"And you ran all the while we were here?"

A small, mirthless smile tugged at the corners of Jeremy's lips, then vanished.

"I didn't avoid you on purpose. Actually, I used my running time to have a look around in more detail. I ran around the back of the woods and also went inside it, as far as I could. Just to see if I could find anything." His brows furrowed and his jaws clenched together as he breathed heavily.

"What were you looking for?" Arla asked softly.

He shot her a look of pure venom. "What do you think I was looking for? A lost puppy? A stray cat?" His lips curled upwards in a snarl.

It was Arla's turn to remain impassive. She had gotten under his skin and decided to push him a little. "May I remind you this is a serious crime inquiry and we can ask you to come down to the station to give this statement. Would you prefer that?"

Jeremy removed his glasses slowly and made a show of wiping them with his handkerchief. Then, just as slowly, he put them back on. His dark blue eyes were foggy, murky to Arla's gaze, but he stared back at her calmly, his previous poise regained.

"No. I apologise. It's been exceptionally stressful, as you can see." He let out a deep sigh and his gaze floated to the ground. "If you must know, I was looking for a discarded baby. Small body, wrapped in Reggie's clothes."

Arla and Harry glanced at each other. She asked, "Is that the real reason why you went out for a run?"

Jeremy nodded without replying. Harry asked, "Reggie was wrapped in a blue cloth at the time of his disappearance. Is that correct?"

"Yes. I made sure I asked my wife before I went out."

Arla studied his face, his ears, the delicate muscles just under his chin, and the stronger corded muscles of the neck.

It was virtually impossible to stop involuntary contractions of the neck muscles when lying. Jeremy's neck muscles remained lax. She wished they were in an interrogation room and this interview was being videotaped.

She could show it to Nick Marlowe, the criminal psychologist. Jeremy had remembered to ask his wife what clothes baby was wearing before he went out. Then he committed that to memory and deliberately ran around, looking for his son. He was doing a father's duty, of course, but it also showed the working of a methodical mind, not one frazzled by stress.

Jeremy caught her looking at him. He asked, "Is there anything else, detectives?"

Arla shifted in her chair. She arched her spine upwards; the pressure on her lower back was growing. "While you were out, it was only Miss Mildred and your wife in the house, right?"

"I wasn't here at the time, but they were the two people I left here, yes."

A clever answer. Arla was impressed. She decided to change direction, and did so abruptly. "Tell us about your uncle. Glenn Stone."

CHAPTER 15

Jeremy regarded Arla impassively before replying. "I'm close to my uncle, obviously. Hence, I called him."

Harry asked, "I understand your father has passed away, but your mother is still alive, isn't she?"

"Yes, she is. She remarried and lives near Doncaster, in northeast England. I'm closer to my uncle, to be honest. Plus, he lives closer, in Esher."

"That's down the A3, right?"

Jeremy nodded. Arla knew the place. Towns like Esher and Weybridge were bastions of the leafy stockbroker belt in Surrey. Where wealthy bankers rubbed shoulders with rock stars and footballers.

"Have you ever lived with your uncle?" Arla asked.

"No, I haven't. When I was younger, I spent the summers either at his house or vacationing with him. He helped with my first jobs in the film industry. I owe him a great deal." He lifted both shoulders and the corners of his lips downturned. "It's not just me. Uncle is well-known for helping out young actors and singers trying to break into the industry."

Jeremy glanced at his watch. "I'm not being rude, but I do have a few phone calls to make. I will be at home, however, and we can carry on later, if you like."

Arla did a mental head-shake. The upper crust behaved so predictably when it came to using the public services. As if she was at Jeremy's beck and call, to sacrifice her time to suit his schedule.

She kept her voice even when she spoke. "I'm afraid I won't have the time later as we will be busy with the investigation. One more question. Where were you last night?"

"I came back from a location survey in Brighton. We have a beach shoot and I needed to see it in the late afternoon light. I wasn't back home till late evening."

Arla took down the times of his leaving and returning home, then snapped shut her notebook. "Thank you, Mr Stone. That will be all for now." All of them rose. As Jeremy turned to leave, Arla said, "Just a second."

Jeremy turned, a contraction appearing on his forehead. Arla said, "The first forty-eight hours in any disappearance is the most critical. We are four hours into this case already. I appreciate that you want privacy, but without involving forensic officers we might not get an answer quickly. May I suggest you allow forensic officers inside your residence? I know this will cause some disturbance, but we will try and keep it to a minimum."

Jeremy pondered his response for a while, his gaze flicking from Arla to Harry. "Are you sure the media will not get wind of this?"

"I can assure you, these are senior officers who have handled many high-profile investigations with the greatest of discretion. They will never speak to the media."

Jeremy bent his head, then reached up his hand and slowly smoothed the hair he had left at the back. Presently he looked up. "Okay. I will inform Becky. Please ensure they don't erect a white tent outside our house. It's such a cliché."

Arla smiled in victory. "Of course, I understand. No tents."

"And please ask them to put on their white suits or whatever inside the house, not outside."

"As you wish. They don't need to park outside your house, either. How about using your garage?"

"That's a good idea," Jeremy said, his facial muscles relaxing. "I can put one of our cars out on the street. Or even both of them, if you prefer."

"That would be great, thank you. Is it possible for us to take another look upstairs before we leave?"

Jeremy hesitated for a few seconds, then nodded. "I need to check where my wife is," he said quietly.

"We do not wish to disturb her. I just want to have a look at the nursery and the bathroom before we leave."

"Becky said that you suspect the intruder came in through the bathroom?"

"That's just a suggestion at this stage, Mr Stone. We don't know for sure and things will become clearer in due course of time."

Harry took down the details of the remote CCTV provider, and they followed Jeremy. The kitchen door was open but Arla couldn't see anyone inside. The house was silent as they climbed the massive staircase. They reached the first landing and Arla stopped. The staircase divided into its left and right section here. She knew the nursery room lay on the right. She turned to Jeremy.

"Would you mind if we checked the Wi-Fi and router in your study? It would be good to take down the serial number and make, to make sure it wasn't tampered with."

Jeremy blinked at them for a few seconds, shifting on his feet. Then he shrugged. "I can't see why not. But I very much doubt anyone's been inside—" He stopped abruptly and touched the back of his scalp. "Oh, I see."

"If an intruder did enter this morning, they could have gone into your study while you were down in the kitchen," Arla said softly.

Jeremy climbed up the shorter left staircase and spoke to them over his shoulder. "It wouldn't give them much time. Don't think I was in the kitchen for any more than ten minutes."

Arla paused for breath on the upper landing. When she walked again, she noted the rooms with shut doors. The corridor curved around and they stopped in front of a room. Jeremy held the door open for them.

The room was large, with windows facing the front garden and street. A large mahogany table held two computer screens, a laptop, and a desktop computer. Papers were strewn over the desk and on a wall hung whiteboard lists scrawled with a blue marker pen. Stacks of film industry magazines lay on the floor.

"Apologies for the mess," Jeremy stated, striding to the desk. He knelt against the wall and Harry followed suit. He wrote down the name and make of the broadband router, then did the same with the laptop and desktop computer. Then he looked around the four corners of the ceiling.

"You don't have CCTV in any of the rooms, do you?"

"No, we don't. It's only in the hallways, and outside."

They thanked him, then followed him into the hall as he led the way back to the nursery room. Arla stopped in front of the bathroom and she followed Harry when he stepped inside. It was cold, she noted with satisfaction, as the window was still open. Jeremy pointed to it and rubbed his shoulders. "When can we shut that window?"

"If we can get the forensic officers to come in today, then we can shut it as soon as they have taken samples of the boot print."

"In that case, the sooner the better."

Harry walked over to the window and took another look.

Arla walked out and noted the nursery door had been shut. With a gloved hand, she depressed the door handle and walked in. The room was blazing hot and the window was closed.

Her brows lowered as annoyance flashed across her face. "Who shut that window?"

Behind them, a female voice said, "I did."

Arla turned, along with the two men. Rebecca Stone was standing there, still in her dressing gown. She leaned forward slightly and her arms were crossed on her chest, like she was holding herself. She hadn't brushed her hair and still wore bathroom slippers.

"I'm sorry, but I couldn't stand leaving it open." She shivered, although it was warm.

Arla softened her tone. "That's all right. We will come back to take a look here again. I thought you were resting."

"I heard you coming. I was trying to rest, but it's not easy."

Arla nodded at her, then gestured towards Harry. He shook hands with Jeremy and they walked down the stairs.

CHAPTER 16

As Harry turned the wheel of the BMW, a drizzle started. That silvery, almost soundless rain that drowsed across the concrete blocks and tarmac of this crowded furnace called London, smothering its secrets, hushing its million voices.

Arla watched the huge mansions slip past, and then bare-boned woods took over both sides of the road, the trees wearing a melting crown of white snow.

"Not what he seems, is he?" Harry remarked.

Arla tore her gaze from the window and watched Harry's unusual stubble for a few seconds. Unusual for a man whose cheeks were normally smooth enough for flies to slip on. She grinned as she thought of the changes fatherhood would bring to Harry. He glanced at her.

"Did you hear what I said?"

"About Jeremy Stone?" She batted her eyelashes. "I could say the same thing about you."

He frowned, staring at the luminous crimson brake lights of the car in front. "Don't know what you're talking about."

"That's what sleep deprivation does to you. And baby hasn't even arrived yet."

They had deliberately kept the gender unknown. During the latest ultrasound scan, Arla had asked the sonographer to not tell them. Harry said he didn't mind either way, but she suspected he wanted a boy. For her, it didn't matter. It really didn't, and she just wanted the day to arrive.

With an effort she turned her mind to the case at hand.

"Yes, Jeremy is interesting," she conceded. "On first impression he looked like a character from *Revenge of the Nerds*. But he's sharp as a flint. And, for obvious reasons, more in control than his wife."

"Is he a suspect?"

"Everyone is, at this stage. He was alone for most of the morning, and the only person who was on the upper floor with the baby when it happened. Rebecca was downstairs."

"But he didn't come in through the bathroom window and leave via the nursery." It was a statement from Harry, not a question.

"No. I doubt he had the time. But he could have let the intruder in by opening the bathroom window."

Harry indicated and turned left, finding a rare break in the traffic. The engine growled as the BMW leapt forward.

"Why would he kidnap his own son? There's no motive."

"True. But did you see the way he acted when Rebecca came up? I didn't like it."

"He was cold and distant, yes. But we haven't seen them interact much. This is a stressful time for them. People can act strange."

The BMW was crawling along Clapham High Street, cars stuck to each other like the bumpers and fenders possessed magnetic fields. Harry turned the flashing blue lights on and beeped on his horn. A couple of the cars swerved away, opening up some space.

"I still don't buy his excuse for the run. Why take the time to get changed into running gear? Why not just put on snow boots and go out?"

Harry got through the phalanx of barricading cars and finally entered the winding inner-city roads that led to Clapham Police

Station. The scanner at the rear gates read the registration number of the BMW and the steel humps dropped down with a thunk. The gates slid open and he drove in.

He parked right outside the covered sliding doors, where a couple of detective sergeants and uniformed officers stood, smoking.

"Hello guv," one of the detective sergeants said to Arla as she went in. Arla nodded, her mind on other matters. Harry caught up with her at the coffee machine. She picked up the mocha that spluttered out of the nozzle and sniffed it dubiously. Smelled close enough, but the taste, she knew from previous experience, was another issue entirely. Harry got a black Americano, because, Arla told him, he needed to watch his weight.

"Look who's talking," he smirked, then his chestnut browns swirled with warm affection. Her eyes slipped down to his fulsome lips. No man, she had long thought, should have lips as nice as Harry's. Sudden desire pooled low in her belly and her lips parted. She looked away from him swiftly, taking a deep breath. Her hormones were running riot again.

They walked past notices stuck on wall boards, bearing photos of wanted criminals, graphs and pie charts of crime rates in south London.

"Call Parmentier and put him through. Then get the others in my room," Arla said as they walked into the open-plan detectives' office. Harry gave her a mock salute and sat down heavily at his desk, reaching for the phone to call Derek Parmentier, the head of SOC.

Arla entered her office and closed the door. The stack of papers to the right of her desktop had grown in size and she groaned audibly. She called Johnson, who answered on the first ring, like he had been waiting for her.

"Arla, is that you?" Johnson's low, deep rumble floated down the line.

"Yes sir, it is. We went back, as you know. I got a statement off Jeremy Stone. But more importantly, he has agreed to Scene of Crime attending the premises."

"He has?" Johnson sounded surprised.

"Yes. Can I now log a PCN, and make this into a formal police inquiry?" Arla knew that when she activated the normal channels, she would have more manpower at her disposal. She could ask a squad of uniforms to comb the area around Rebecca's house.

"No," Johnson said firmly, quashing her hopes. "Not yet, in any case. This is still an informal missing persons inquiry."

Irritation surged in Arla's veins. "A missing baby is not the same as a missing person, sir. We are treating this as a crime, and it's a waste of time and resources if we do not elevate this to serious crime status."

Johnson was silent for a few seconds, breathing heavily down the line. "I spoke to Mr Cummings, the crime commissioner. As you know, he's close friends with Grant Stone. The Stone family want as much discretion as possible."

Arla tried to keep her voice down and failed. "I need a bigger team, sir. We need statements from both sides of the family and past acquaintances. Right now, we are progressing at a snail's pace. This is a Mickey Mouse operation—"

"Arla." Johnson raised his voice a notch. It was a clear warning for her to shut up. She knew she should bite that hot-tempered tongue of hers, but the words slipped out before she could stop them.

"We can't keep doing favours for important people, sir. The crime commissioner is a member of the public, just like anyone else. I have to tick a hundred boxes every day to make sure we get regulatory approval for our cases, but for these people we have to bend over backwards? If the IPCC ever got wind of this—" She cut herself short, realising her error.

The Independent Police Complaints Commission (IPCC) investigated complaints about the police from members of the public as well as whistle-blowers.

Arla squeezed her eyes shut. Her nails drummed on the table and frustration fumed inside, suffocating her throat. She stood and looked out the window at the rain-swept car park. She didn't want to be a part of this. She wanted to do things by the book, using the normal channels. But she also knew that, with her maternity leave approaching, there were people like Justin Beauregard waiting in the wings to take her place.

She had spoken her mind, foolishly. If she did tell the IPCC about this, they would launch a full investigation. No one wanted that. At the same time, she was sick and tired of doing Johnson's dirty work for him.

"Arla, I would advise you to consider what you're saying very carefully," Johnson said in a quiet voice. He paused, and the silence lengthened between them.

She knew diplomacy wasn't her forte. She was headstrong, emotional. But as she had risen up the ranks, becoming the chief detective over five stations, she had learned to control her nature, even if it meant turning a blind eye to matters like this.

Still, she could only be herself. She couldn't be a sycophant of the assistant commissioners, obeying their whims because she wanted to get in the boardroom one day herself. It was a delicate balancing act.

"All I'm saying, sir, is that I need more resources. You know that better than I do." She paused, knowing her words would hit home.

Allocating resources to a case in these times of budget cuts was done with great care. It was probably one of the reasons, she reflected, that Johnson wasn't giving her much leeway.

"No formal inquiry. Do what you can, and send me a report by the end of today. Then I will decide. I should also remind you that Deputy Assistant Commissioner Deakins is taking an interest in this case. Please don't let us down." Johnson hung up.

Arla stared at the receiver for a few seconds, her heart sinking. She put the phone back on its cradle slowly, wincing when she heard the soft click. That was all she needed.

Nick Deakins was no fan of hers, and she had sparred with him on multiple cases over the years. Old memories returned as she stared out the window at the forest of council estates that surrounded the station.

A police van rolled up to the rear gates, then came inside. A squad of uniformed officers emerged from the van and stretched, some of them pulling out cigarettes to smoke.

She stared at them enviously. At the beginning of her career she had been a uniformed officer for two years, before going down the detective training route. She had no worries then, no one to keep happy, no responsibilities. Unconsciously, her hand went to her bump and slid down its smooth, rotund expanse. A smile lit up her face as she felt baby kick, then her jaw hardened.

It sounded strange, but what she did now didn't just affect her anymore. It also concerned the life growing inside her, a baby who would one day blossom into a human being.

What sort of a world would she leave behind for her child?

A world free of evil was too much to ask for. But free of corruption where she worked? That could be achieved. And she could stamp out as much evil as she could.

She loved her job too much to give it up. And yet, she would have to balance motherhood with it. This thought had occupied her mind a lot recently. She looked to the future with hope and trepidation. At least initially, her job would lose out. She didn't mind that. She couldn't wait for motherhood to begin. But she also knew that after one year, she would have to return to work close to full time, in order to pay back her generous maternity leave.

She sat down, took out her diary, and jotted down, in bullet points, what the rest of the day's plan of action was. She stared gloomily at the stack of papers piled on her desk. It was Wednesday and she had four more days before she could hand over the duty SIO cases. She picked up the phone and rang Johnson.

"Sir, it's me. I'm the duty SIO for the rest of the week, but I need to concentrate on this case. Could you please hand over the on-call role for the rest of this week to Justin?"

Johnson was silent for a while as he considered her request. "Very well. I will inform him." He hung up. Arla grinned and punched the air with her fist. It was a small victory, but it made her feel good. If Justin wanted to step into her shoes, let him take the stress off her shoulders right now.

Her phone rang again, and it was Harry. "Got Parmentier on the line. Shall I put him through?"

"Yes please. Thanks, Harry."

Many years ago, Parmentier had gravitated down south from Lincolnshire in North England, and he still retained his northern accent. "Hello, is that the queen of the serious crime unit?"

"It is, and I hope you're kneeling on the floor."

"I would, but I'm at a crime scene and might disturb evidence. To what do I owe the pleasure?"

"I've got a special case for you—and I mean, just you."

"I'm at the scene of a robbery, Arla. Next up is a house that was used as a drug den. I'm spread thin, and there's work coming out of my ears."

"This takes priority, and I have orders from the top. And I repeat, it's for your ears only."

"Hang on, let me go outside." There was a pause as Parmentier spoke to someone and Arla waited. "Okay, I'm back. Don't tell me you found a dead body in Johnson's house?"

Arla laughed at that. Parmentier, like many others in the department, enjoyed a joke at their boss's expense.

"It's not far off. The case itself is quite distressing." She told Parmentier in detail about Rebecca and the missing baby.

"I know you can't do this alone, Derek. But please don't take any more than one member of staff. Someone senior, whom you trust. My team are sworn to secrecy and from now on, so are you."

"So, where do I upload my findings?"

"For now, you don't upload anything. Report back to me."

"Hang on," Parmentier argued. "You said there was a boot print on the bathroom windowsill, right? I need to get our forensic gait analyst involved. Mary Atkins. She will want to know what's going on. What do I tell her?"

Arla blew out a frustrated sigh. "Just take all the prints and collect any samples you find at the site. I'm not telling you how to do your job, but take photos, get an aerial drone feed as well. Let's hold back showing the prints to Mary."

"Only Mary can access the boot-print database."

"I know that, Derek. For now, please report back to me personally. We will have a better idea of what to do when I have your preliminary report first thing tomorrow morning."

Parmentier yelped like a teenager. "First thing tomorrow morning? Is that a joke?"

Arla grinned. "Does the queen ever joke? I'm serious. I wanted to send the human DNA samples to the lab before five this evening. Send it as an urgent and we should get a result tomorrow. Put down my name and rank as authorisation."

"I better get a knighthood for this," Parmentier grumbled. "Why is this not a formal investigation?"

Arla pressed on her eyeballs gently and slid her fingers down the sides, rubbing them. She wondered how many times she would have to deflect an answer to the same question.

M.L. ROSE

"Please, Derek, do this for me. It's important."

"Okay. Send me their address."

"I will, but don't turn up there by yourself. Harry will come with you. He'll drive you there. No SOC vans outside the house, or tents."

Arla hung up and, almost immediately, there was a knock on her door. It opened slightly and somewhere near the top of the doorframe, Harry's face appeared. He looked almost like a giraffe, she thought, the rest of his body hidden behind the door.

"I got the others, as you asked," he said.

"Okay, bring them in."

CHAPTER 17

Harry parked the car in the hospital car park and got out. He opened the door for Arla, who took some time, but got out on her own. Arla was carrying a shoulder bag with her maternity notes and police radio inside. Hand in hand, they walked towards the imposing red brick façade of the hospital. They entered the spacious foyer and turned left, heading for maternity antenatal classes.

Harry asked, "Sure you don't want me to stay?"

She shook her head firmly. "You're stepping in for me, Harry. Take Parmentier to the Stone residence and then direct the others to search the woods. You're going to lead the search, right?" She looked up to glance at him.

Harry met her eyes with a downward curl of his lips. "I'd rather be back here, and take you home." Home, for the time being, was Arla's apartment in Tooting Broadway, South London. Luckily for them, the hospital was only two blocks away from her apartment.

Harry had his own place in Battersea, a few stops down the bus route, but for the time being, he had moved in with her.

"Please don't walk back," Harry said, his lips pressing into a firm line. "Promise you will call a cab, or I'll be back here in one hour's time."

That made her smile. Harry towered above her, his broad shoulders blocking out the tepid sunlight streaming in through the corridor windows. "I'll call an Uber, don't worry."

She kissed Harry goodbye at the entrance of the antenatal classroom and walked in. A midwife called Lauren was standing in the centre of the room, surrounded by a ring of heavily pregnant women. Arla had gotten to know several of them, and she smiled and waved.

She scanned their faces for Kylie Denham, whom she had become closest to over the last couple of months. Kylie had her back to Arla, and when she turned, her face lit up in a huge smile. She gestured towards Arla and patted the empty chair next to her. Arla squeezed her hand when she sat down.

"Thanks for saving a seat for me," she whispered into Kylie's ear.

"Not a problem. Everything okay at work?" Kylie's grey eyes had flecks of gold in them and their pupils constricted as she stared at Arla.

"Yes, everything's fine. Just busy," Arla said smoothly. Only Kylie knew that she was a police officer. But she didn't know what grade Arla held. When asked, Arla had merely replied she was a detective, and yes, an inspector. Kylie hadn't probed any further, for which Arla had been grateful.

"How about you? How's Greg?" she whispered back.

"Oh, he's fine. Just busy with work, same as you, I guess." Greg was Kylie's husband. Kylie mentioned how he had come to drop her and then pick her up on a couple of occasions, but each time, Arla had missed him. This was the couple's first baby, and she and Kylie had bonded over the fact that they were the only women in the ten-strong group who were first-time mothers. Kylie had also confided to Arla how she and Greg had been through a rocky patch, but were now through it, and were looking forward to starting a family.

Lauren shot them a look and both women went quiet. The midwife raised her voice. "Can we have a vote on what is the most pressing problem today for everyone." She counted off on her fingers, "Moving around, need to pee, difficulty in sleeping."

All ten hands rose for the last option. Lauren stepped back and moved the whiteboard to the corner of the room. She took two pillows and a mat, which she laid down on the floor. "Ladies, could you please move your chairs back a little." As the women obliged, Lauren lay down on the mat. She showed them how to lie to the left and keep a cushion below the belly and also a cushion between their legs while they slept. One by one, the women rose and lay down on the mat to practise.

"If I lie down," Kylie said, "I might not get up."

Arla agreed. "Sometimes I have to ask Harry to pull me out of bed."

Kylie bent her head, staring down at her folded hands. The women were taking turns to lie down on the mat, and no one could hear them speak. "The closer it gets, the more anxious I become. Just hope this time it goes okay."

Arla touched Kylie's elbow. She knew Kylie had experienced two miscarriages before and how much this baby meant to her. She had been through in-vitro fertilisation and had spared no expense in getting the best treatment. "Of course it will be," Arla said softly. "You've come this far; now there's no going back."

"I hope so." Kylie sighed. "But even after thirty-three weeks, you can get early rupture of membranes, and the baby could be born premature."

"Even if they are, babies born at thirty weeks can survive these days. You know that, don't you?"

Kylie swallowed hard, nodded, then looked at Arla. Unshed tears brimmed in the woman's eyes. Arla put a hand around her shoulder.

"After the class, shall we get a coffee?"

Kylie blinked, then rubbed the corner of her eyes. "Just a chamomile tea for me. Coffee makes me want to pee nonstop."

Arla felt a smile tugging at the corner of her lips. It was nice to make new friends, and get out of her workplace. She liked Kylie, who was in her late thirties and had a successful graphic design company. Her husband had a career in finance, in the city, and both of them had worked hard to get where they were today.

The class came to an end, and Lauren stood at the centre of the room and raised her voice. "We need to be aware of headaches, ladies. If you get a headache, you must have your blood pressure checked, your urine tested, and be seen by a doctor. We spoke about preeclampsia last time. A headache is often the first symptom. Bottom line, if you feel funny, please have your blood pressure checked."

The door opened and a few men walked in; they had been waiting outside the room for their wives. Arla and Kylie slipped out, heading towards the canteen.

CHAPTER 18

Roslyn May sat down on the open edge of the car boot and pulled on the winter shoes supplied by the London Met. The detective sergeant looked at Lisa Moran, her compatriot, who was doing the same. "Have you ever tried these boots on before?"

Lisa shook her head, her blonde tresses falling over her face as she bent down to tug firmly on the boots. They were like Wellingtons, coming up to knee-level, but fit more snugly due to the fur lining inside. She stomped both feet on the tarmac. "Surprisingly comfortable, actually."

Roslyn did the same, grimacing. But when she stood and took a few steps, her face changed. "Yes, I could get used to this. Much better than those horrible flat shoes they make us wear."

Lisa shrugged. "You don't have to wear them. I bring my own black shoes."

Roslyn said, "So did I. Till I ran after a pickpocket one day and ended up flat on my arse." She chuckled.

A black BMW came to a halt behind them, and Harry and Rob got out of the unmarked CID car. The two women waited while the men got ready. Harry walked over to them and rubbed his hands together, breath misting in front of his face.

"Right. We spread out, but remain within ten feet of each other and within calling distance." He extracted the radio from his coat pocket and so did Roslyn. Rob ambled up behind Harry, his ample midriff protruding, his gait stiff and uncomfortable.

"Blimey," Rob said. "These boots have given me blisters already."

Roslyn had a joke ready on the tip of her tongue, but thought better of it. "Suits us fine, Rob," she said breezily. She exchanged a glance with Lisa and they grinned. Rob scowled at them.

Harry said, "Let's check the Common first. That will be easier. Then we can tackle the woods, but I suggest we do it tomorrow, when the light will be better."

He looked skywards, and others followed his gaze. It had gone past 1600 hours. and light was fading fast from the gunmetal grey sky. Thankfully, the rain had stopped. Molten snow squelched beneath their boots.

Roslyn pointed to one of the sumptuous mansions behind them. She had observed Harry pulling into its garage. "Is that Rebecca Stone's residence?"

Harry nodded. "Yes. I dropped Parmentier and one of his friends inside. They'll get busy indoors while we tackle this."

Roslyn asked, "Excuse my ignorance, guv, but exactly what are we looking for?"

"That's a good question, Roslyn. I think the baby clothes are the most important. So, a blue wraparound or a purple baby grow, as these were the items of clothing Reggie Stone was wearing at the time of his disappearance. Plus, anything to do with the baby stuff— bottles suckers, shoes, anything." Harry clicked his fingers. "He was wearing black-and-white-striped socks and matching trainers. The blue wraparound had his full name and initials sewn in gold letters."

"Okay, boss." Roslyn shivered as she stared at the gloomy, darkening expanse of the Common. The skeleton trees stood close together, as if guarding a secret.

"Let's get going," Harry said. He was the first to descend the gentle grassy bank that sloped down into the trees.

Roslyn took one last look back at Rebecca Stone's house. Four massive bay windows fronted the ground floor. As she looked, one of their curtains twitched. She narrowed her eyes, and watched the shadow shift behind the window. Someone was watching. She looked away and joined the others as they walked steadily into the Common.

Snow and grey mud sloshed beneath her boots as she went deeper inside.. She looked up at the tall, lonely trees that stood like sentinels, bearing close watch on those who entered their forest. She skirted past a fallen tree, and then had to step over a broken tree stump. Twigs snapped like bones beneath her boots. The cracking sound was loud in the total silence, making her shiver.

She looked to her left, but couldn't see or hear Harry. The foreboding bank of trees seemed to hem her in. For no reason, her mind flitted back to the time she'd gotten lost as a child.

She'd been no more than ten years old and her family was having a picnic by the river. She went into the woods with her brother and got separated. Once she realised she was lost, she had screamed his name. He didn't answer, and neither did her mummy.

She remembered the panic, the chest-bursting anxiety as hot tears had rolled down her cheeks. How alone she had felt, how forsaken. To her childish mind, it was like the end of the world. No one would find her again.

Roslyn shook her head, then stamped both feet on the ground. She splattered mud against a tree trunk. This was silly. She was an experienced detective sergeant, two years into the job and almost five years as a uniformed sergeant before that. Why on earth was she dragging up childhood memories for no reason? She glanced around the frozen landscape, and knew the answer. This place was giving her the chills. She gave herself a wry smile and lifted her chin up.

She walked on farther, and whirled around when she heard the snapping of twigs to her left. Breath caught in her chest when she saw a tall, dark shadow flick between two trees. She watched it move for a few seconds. "Guv? Is that you?" she shouted.

The shape stopped and then turned around. It was indeed Harry. He raised a hand and waved to her. "Found anything?" he shouted back.

Roslyn relaxed, a calm warmth floating into the tips of her fingers and toes. "Not yet," she answered. She kept moving, stepping deeper into the trees of the Common. She looked around her on the ground, in a 180-degree circle, before taking the next step. Then she looked up as well, as she had been trained to do. Most people ignored clues above eye level when searching for objects on the ground.

She pulled out her Maglite torch and turned it on. Her eyesight was good but light was fading from the cloud-enveloped sky. She swung the torch beam around in an arc. Nothing in the trees. She pointed the light to the ground and came to a complete standstill. A small cloth, so tiny that she almost missed it. It was black-and-white striped, and mud had ensured it was well camouflaged. Only the powerful beam had picked it up.

It was a sock, and its size meant only a baby could wear it.

Her hands trembled as a space opened up in her chest, pressing the air out of her lungs. It was difficult to breathe but she stepped forward, then knelt. The beam wavered as her hands shook. She stretched out a gloved hand towards the sock, but something else caught her eye.

It was a doll, wrapped inside a see-through plastic wrapper. At least, it looked like a doll. The head was grey and misshapen, more swollen than it should be, eyes staring, wide open.

Fear surged inside Roslyn's chest like a tsunami. Her mouth opened, and a silent scream forced its way from her lungs. She tried to move back, but ended up falling on the muddy ground.

The Maglite fell from her hands. The cruel beam of the torch lit up the dead baby's face, half-covered in bracken snow. Roslyn's hands were like claws, nails digging into the palms as she leaned forward, turning her back to the ghastly sight.

A primitive, guttural cry erupted from her throat. Her knees sank into the wet grave of the forest floor as she screamed and screamed again.

CHAPTER 19

"It's his mother. She never liked me," Kylie Denham confided, leaning forward towards Arla. "I'm two years older than Greg and she's very old-fashioned." Kylie waved a hand in the air. "She thinks a woman should always be younger than her husband. I mean, in this day and age, who cares?"

Arla shrugged. "Some people don't change. But she must be happy now, expecting to become a grandmother soon?"

The flecks of gold in Kylie's eyes glowed as her lips stretched in a smile. "Yes, you're right. I've seen a little softening in her recently. She even invited us for Sunday lunch for the first time last week."

"There you go."

The smile faded from Kylie's face. "But I just hope everything goes well. My last miscarriage was late at twenty-four weeks and it was horrible, truly horrible. I was in hospital for three days, and depressed afterwards."

Arla reached out and squeezed her hand once. "Don't worry. You're past that stage now, way past. You'll be fine."

Arla had put her phone on the table. It was on silent mode as she had been in the antenatal class. She had forgotten to switch it back on. A red light was flashing on the side.

She clicked her tongue on the roof of her mouth and went through the four missed calls. They were all from Harry. "Excuse me," she said to Kylie and rose from her seat. She walked to an end of the canteen that wasn't crowded and called him. "It's me. What's up?"

"We found the missing baby," Harry said in a grim voice. He filled her in, and Arla was glad she was leaning against the wall. She gripped her forehead, a wave of nausea rising in her stomach.

"I'll call Dr Banerjee. I'll see you back at the station," she instructed.

"Sure you don't want me to come and pick you up? I'm still at the crime scene. Parmentier hasn't finished yet."

"You stay there. Just meet me back at the station." She hung up and went back to the table, where Kylie looked up at her with an inquisitive expression.

"Just work." Arla lifted a palm in the air. "It can get busy without warning for me." She grabbed her tote bag and put it on her shoulder. Kylie rose as well.

"At least with my job, I can do most of it from home, unless I have to meet a new client," Kylie replied.

The two women walked side by side to the hospital's main entrance.

Kylie continued. "You must come to our house one day. I live in Battersea, not far from here. Just straight down Wandsworth Bridge Road."

Arla smiled at her. "Of course. Looking forward to it." She waved goodbye and left Kylie at the bus stop outside the hospital. She had no time to waste. She had already called an Uber and by the time she reached the main road the car was pulling up. She was on the phone as the Uber drove off. Dr Banerjee's mellow, warm voice came down the line.

"If it isn't my favourite police detective. How can I help?"

"Flattery won't get you anywhere this time, I'm afraid, doc. I've got a bad one for you."

In a low voice, and without giving much detail, she told him about the case. The veteran pathologist went quiet for several seconds. When he spoke, his voice was a whisper. "My God. You know, this is the type of case every doctor fears. Adults die before their time and it's sad. But this. . . ." His voice trailed off.

Arla was staring out the window, watching the traffic rush past. "I'm sorry, doc. Can I please ask you to drop what you've got and head down to the crime scene? Harry's there already, with a uniformed squad."

Dr Banerjee sighed wearily. "Okay, give me the address. Do we have a positive identification?"

"I haven't seen the body myself, and in my current state walking that far into the forest isn't really feasible. But the blue wraparound with baby's name on it and the purple baby grow seems to seal it. Now we have to wait for fingerprints and DNA analysis."

"Okay. I'm on my way."

"Thanks, doc."

Arla picked up the phone and dialled Johnson. She knew that Harry hadn't told him yet. After she broke the news to Johnson, there was a prolonged silence on the other end. Then her boss cursed.

"What about the surrounding area? Any clues to who might have done this?"

"Not yet, sir. Baby was wrapped up in a plastic bag. Banerjee is on his way, and I don't know what sort of injuries the body has. As to the perpetrator. . . ." Arla's voice trailed off.

She continued after a pause. "We have to open this up as a formal investigation now, sir. This is a murder inquiry, and has to be dealt with by the official channels." She knew Johnson had to agree, and he did.

"We have no choice, do we?" he said in a resigned voice. "Okay, go ahead. I'll call the crime commissioner, as well as South London Command, and let them know."

The Uber was pulling up at Clapham Common Station by the time Arla got Lisa on the line.

"Get Major Incident Room One ready. I want everyone in attendance."

CHAPTER 20

The station had two major incident rooms and room one was bigger. It was next door to the detectives' open-plan office, separated by a partition wall that was soundproof, but could be folded back.

The apex of the room was taken up by a large desk with three workstations, a laptop, and a pulldown white screen on the wall behind it. Desks lined the sides of the room, bearing printers, fax machines, and telephones. Chairs occupied the middle, where detectives sat.

Johnson's instructions to Arla had been to involve as few people as possible. In reality, she knew that if half of the uniformed squads and detectives were involved, the whole station would know. However, to pacify Johnson, she had agreed.

Justin Beauregard sat in the front row, together with his team. He glared at Arla, making no attempt to hide his displeasure that she was the SIO and not him. Arla hoped he was also rankled by having the on-call duties for the week delegated to him. That should keep him busy, she thought with an invisible smile.

Parmentier was here, as was Mary Atkins, the forensic gait analyst. The financial crimes officer, Julia Ledbury, a plump woman in her mid-forties, was also present. Next to her sat John, the cybercrimes specialist, with straggly long hair from the back of his scalp reaching to his neck and a balding head. He had a perpetual sheen of sweat on his forehead, and he fidgeted constantly, like he was nervous of being in the incident room. John was a classic geek, and Arla smiled at him reassuringly. He was brilliant at his job and if someone had left a digital footprint somewhere, chances were John would find it.

She glanced at Roslyn, who was standing next to Lisa and Rob. "Are you okay?" Arla asked. Roslyn still looked pale, with bags under her eyes.

"Yes guv," Roslyn said, and looked at her shoes. Arla felt a pang of sympathy. Infanticide was thankfully rare, but shocking when it happened. She could only remember one instance when she had come across it and she never wanted to relive the experience again. She thought of what Roslyn must be going through and it made her walk over and rub the woman's back.

She spoke in a whisper in Roslyn's ear. "You don't have to be here if you don't want to," Arla said. "Lisa and Rob can fill you in later on."

Roslyn's jaw hardened and she looked up at Arla with a firm resolve in her dark eyes. "I'm fine, guv. Not the first dead body I've seen. These things happen."

Arla maintained eye contact with her for a few seconds, then nodded. There was a knock on the incident room door and it opened. The slightly stooped form of Dr Banerjee entered the room. He wore a grey suit and his full head of hair was salt-and-pepper. His shoes had flecks of mud on them, despite having worn protectors. He adjusted his glasses, smiled at Arla, and shuffled inside.

"Hope I didn't miss anything." The pathologist smiled amicably. They called him Dr Columbo in the London Met. His bumbling appearance and advanced age hid a sharply analytical mind. Arla relied on him heavily, and to solve this case, she knew Banerjee would be indispensable.

She spread her arms. "Just the man I was looking for. Now we can start."

Banerjee's lips pressed together and the light in his eyes dimmed as he shook his head. All seats in the front row were taken. One of the uniformed inspectors rose to make space for him, despite the elderly pathologist's protests.

Arla pointed to the photo of Rebecca Stone that was stuck on the whiteboard. Next to it she also had a photo of baby Reginald, downloaded from Rebecca's Instagram feed. She gave the assembled officers a quick rundown of what had happened so far.

"The intruder had a small window of opportunity. He used it to maximum advantage. It's the time between when Rebecca returned home, and when she saw baby was missing. It's possible the intruder was hiding in the house before Rebecca returned. Neither the husband nor the housekeeper saw him. Or her," Arla added, shrugging. "It's unlikely a woman would carry out the dangerous task of climbing on top of the flat roof and gaining access through the open bathroom window, but you never know."

She continued. "When we searched the garden there was no evidence of footprints. DI Mehta had a look near the woods that light to the rear of the property. Couldn't see a great deal. But we do have two sets of boot prints in the property. One at the windowsill of the bathroom window, and another on the flat roof. It's reasonable to assume that the intruder climbed on the flat roof to gain entry and jumped back down to escape."

Justin held up a hand. "You said they escaped via the back. Then what happened to the footprints?"

"That's what we need to find out. It's possible he covered his tracks very well. Or there is another possibility." Arla stopped and glanced around the room to make sure she had everyone's attention. Then she looked behind her at Harry, who was staring at her intently.

"The intruder escaped through the front door. Jeremy Stone told us the front door has a chime, but he can't always hear it in his study. I find it difficult, however, to believe that the housekeeper didn't hear it either, if this indeed happened."

Harry cleared his throat. "That would tie in with the body being found in the Common, opposite the house. Not in the woods at the rear."

"Yes," Arla agreed. "And maybe that's why there are no human footprints in the garden. What about the CCTV footage outside the house?"

Harry said, "I rang the company who runs the Wi-Fi-based service. To cut a long story short, the router stopped working for three hours in the morning. The CCTV company has no idea why this happened. All the cameras were working normally, but they weren't receiving a signal and hence were not active."

Harry spread his hands. Arla hooked her eyebrows at him. "So did you check out the router?"

Harry pointed to John and said his name out loud. Arla turned towards the cybercrimes specialist, who appeared more nervous than before. A gentle wave of hilarity swept across the room, because everyone knew what John was like. Arla felt sorry for the poor guy. He was an introvert and computers were his life. He was a whiz kid with anything digital, but human contact freaked him out. She smiled at him warmly. "Glad you're here, John."

John took out a dirty white handkerchief and wiped his forehead with it. "Err, me too. So I, uh, checked out the router make and serial number, and called the manufacturer. They say the Wi-Fi signal was jammed for three hours in the morning."

Silence followed John's statement as several faces looked at each other. Arla said, "You mean like someone used a signal jamming device?"

John nodded. "Yes, like we sometimes do, to block signals from a criminal's phone. It's not difficult, as you know. Wi-Fi signal-jamming devices can now be bought online. Most of them are illegal, especially the high-band ones. For example—" John's voice grew stronger as he spoke. "—we use sixteen-band jamming devices, which can interrupt signals on a wide variety of Wi-Fi and GPS, including police radio. Of course, when we do, we tune our own radios to different frequencies."

Arla held up her hand. "John, I don't need a tutorial. Can you find out what device was used to block Jeremy Stone's router and when?"

John blinked. "It's almost impossible, DCI Baker. Like I said, anyone can buy an illegal jammer these days. However, I can get you the time." He pulled out his phone and stared at the screen for a few seconds. "The jam lasted from seven in the morning till twelve o'clock."

Arla had planted her butt on the corner of the table with her arms folded across her chest. She tapped an index finger on her lips thoughtfully. "Baby Reggie was reported missing at ten-thirty a.m. So that's bang on the money."

A voice cleared from her left and Roslyn spoke up. "My son works in IT, and he told me about this. He wanted to make our router signal safe, so a random hacker can't use it to surf the net and drive up our bills. He said it was easy to block our own frequency, using our router. Pretty sure he showed me how to do it as well, but I can't remember."

A lightbulb switched on at the back of Arla's mind. She snapped her fingers and pointed to Roslyn. "Excellent point. I guess we have to thank your son for this. Jeremy Stone spends a lot of time in his office. Is it possible he jammed his own device?"

She smiled at Roslyn, who was starting to get some colour back into her cheeks. "Guv, are you saying he abducted his own son, then killed him?"

Arla stared at her, feeling a sudden chill sending icicles down her veins. It was a terrifying thought, but one she needed to bear in mind. Most murder victims knew their killers. Why should baby Reggie's killer be any different? Arla looked away, fighting the iron grip of unease twisting in her heart. She faced the room and cleared her throat.

"So, it would appear that we don't have any CCTV footage from the house between seven and twelve this morning. Which was when the crime occurred."

Arla looked at Banerjee, noting the frown on his face. She skipped over him and looked at Mary Atkins, seated in the row behind.

"Mary, do you have the boot prints from Parmentier?"

Mary nodded. "Yes, guv, I've got them. I've run them through the database once, but not come up with any matches so far."

"Anything else you can tell us at this stage?"

"The prints were fresh, obviously, done this morning. They were size eleven, which indicates a tall man."

Arla frowned. "Can you tell us anything more?"

"Just that, for now. I need to see a few more prints before I can analyse his gait."

"Carry on with your testing, Mary. Let us know when you have more information." She turned to Dr Banerjee. "Doc, would you like to come up here? It's best if you face all of us when you present your findings."

"Preliminary findings, and very rough ones, at this stage." Banerjee rose slowly to his feet, knees creaking. He shuffled towards Arla, his lips pinched together, cheeks sucked in. He nodded at her without smiling. Then he turned round to face the room and cleared his throat.

CHAPTER 21

Dr Banerjee said, "Victim is a neonate, which means under the age of twelve months. In this case, I would say no more than five weeks."

He stopped, and his head hung on his chest. There was pin-drop silence in the room, the air as heavy as a concrete block. The individuals in attendance were hardened police officers, but Arla could see the shock and dismay written plain on every face. Her own heart was withered and shrunken. She wished she was standing next to Harry, wanting to feel his arms around her. She rested against the table, both hands clutching its edge.

Banerjee continued. "I need to do a proper examination, as it is difficult to carry out forensic pathology on a neonate. I will also have to get in specialised help from other hospitals. My own experience in these matters is limited." He coughed into a closed fist.

"Bruise marks were present at the throat, which signifies strangulation. I cut through the garments, and could not find any evidence of fractures or other injuries. Non-accidental injuries are suspected in all cases of child abuse, as you know. The tell-tale fractures were missing in this case, which means this baby was not physically abused. However, as I said, I need to take a closer look."

Arla asked, "So, death was by strangulation?"

"Probably. But it would have occurred by asphyxiation in any case, as the body was inserted and then tied into that plastic bag." Banerjee pointed to Parmentier. "Scene-of-crime officers were present and they have taken the garments as evidence."

Arla asked Parmentier, "Did you send off the DNA?"

He made a face. "Sorry. Just as I was finishing up at the house, I got the call from Harry. The DNA samples will go out first thing tomorrow morning. But I did get the prints checked." He shook his head. "No matches on IDENT-1."

Arla had suspected as much. She would've been surprised if any fingerprints from the house matched the UK's most extensive criminal database. But that didn't absolve guilt for any of the residents.

"Time of death, doc?" Harry asked.

Banerjee said, "That's tricky. The body's rectal temperature was lower than ambient, but babies have small bodies, so they lose heat very quickly. It's far more difficult to tell time of death for a child, or a small human being."

Arla fought the black weight pressing against her own throat. She knew everyone in the room was feeling the burden, an emotional weight bearing down upon them. No one wanted a case like this. But they were also the last line of defence, the final barrier against the violent contortions of an insane mind.

"You're doing well, doc," she said encouragingly. Banerjee shrugged.

"Given the limitations, I would say time of death could be anywhere between ten to three hours." He held up both hands as murmurs spread through the room.

"I know that's vague, but it's deliberately so. For such small bodies, we often have to do a post-mortem and get the temperature of the deeper, inner organs. There's also a formula which takes into account surrounding temperature, moisture, and the difference between air and ground temperature. Snow is also a compounding factor. What I'm saying is, I need a couple of days to come up with a reasonably correct time of death."

There was silence for a while, then Arla asked, "Anything else?"

Banerjee shook his head. "I'll extract as many DNA and other samples for chemical analysis as I can."

He turned to Arla. "I'd better get back to my office. You want me to treat this with priority, right?"

Arla nodded. "Yes please, doc. And if you could send off the DNA samples by first thing tomorrow morning, I'd be grateful."

Banerjee nodded, then prepared to leave. She watched him shuffle away slowly, his back slightly more stooped than usual. She called out after him.

"One last thing, doc. Can we come around later this evening, say in a couple of hours, with the family to identify the body?"

"No later than eight p.m.," Banerjee said.

"Okay."

The pathologist shut the door behind him, and Arla walked over to the whiteboard. She pointed to the photo of Rebecca Stone and started writing.

"We need to speak to both of her parents, and her sister. A lot of her life is public already, but let's get talking to people who know her from work, and any friends she has."

She drew a circle around Jeremy Stone's photo. "There's more to him than meets the eye. His father's passed away, but get in touch with his mother who lives up north in Doncaster. Dig up his past as well."

Harry asked, "What about the housekeeper, Edna Mildred?"

"She's an automatic suspect, having been in the house already. She has a son who lives in Birmingham, I think she said. Find out the son's whereabouts this morning."

Arla turned to face everyone, folding her arms across her chest. "Last but not the least, I need to speak to Grant Stone." A ripple of whispers spread across the room.

She said, "We need more information on Grant Stone's relationship with the crime commissioner, as well as his alibi."

Justin Beauregard snorted. "His alibi? He's one of the biggest rock stars in the whole world. Do you really think he'd do a Jackie Chan and climb through his nephew's bathroom window to steal their son?"

"The basis of a successful investigation is to leave no stone unturned," Arla said calmly, pinning Justin with a glare. "I'm sure you remember that from the detective's handbook."

A few voices murmured around the room, while Justin locked eyes with Arla, his nostrils flaring as his jaws clamped tight.

Arla looked away towards the uniformed squads in the back rows. "Darren and Steve." She singled out two uniformed inspectors by their first names. "I want a door-to-door of all the houses on that row, and within a five-mile radius. Ask residents about a car they'd not seen before, or anything unusual. Use the description that Rebecca gave us of the man she saw outside her house."

She continued. "We need the family to identify the body. Harry and myself will sort that out." She glanced at her team, and caught Harry's eyes, who nodded, his lips set in a grim line.

Normally, with a case of this magnitude, there would be a frisson of excitement. This time, the buzz was missing. Instead, Arla could read in everyone's eyes a dull, cold hatred of the beast who had committed this crime.

"How far are we with the CCTV images?"

Roslyn spoke up. "I'm going to sit down in the control room with Rob later tonight."

Arla glanced at her watch. It was nearing six p.m. already. "If it's getting late—"

Roslyn shook her head. "No problem, guv."

Rob chimed in with his agreement. "It's been almost twenty-four hours already. Let's get the images done tonight."

"Good." Arla smiled. "Lisa, please help them if they need anything."

She swept her eyes across the room, then turned to her team, before facing the room again. She clapped her hands together once. "Let's catch this sicko."

CHAPTER 22

Rhys Mason had moved farther back into the Common after he had seen the black BMW for the second time.

He knew they were cops, and there was something about the female, pregnant cop that bothered him. It was the way she had stood and stared almost directly at him, like she could see him. Not much got under Rhys's skin. But that woman made him uncomfortable, for a reason he couldn't pinpoint.

His hunch was correct. The tall detective had returned with reinforcements later on and, judging by the screams he heard, they had found baby Reggie.

Rhys was not in the Common anymore. He was in his room, in the one-bedroom flat he rented for cash under a false name. He was surrounded by four screens, each showing a different view of the interior and exterior of the Stone residence.

On one screen he also had a feed from the Common, looking at the front of the house, and another from the rear. He watched as

Rebecca, wearing jeans and a pullover, came out of her room and went downstairs. He tapped on his keyboard and the screen changed to the large ground-floor landing. Rebecca went into the kitchen. There was only one camera in the kitchen and it faced the concertina doors that occupied the back wall, opening out into the garden. But it was a wide-view lens, and he could see Rebecca at the kitchen counter.

Rhys opened the top drawer of his desk and pulled out the remote microphone controller. When he was inside the house, he had placed microphones in some of the rooms. It was a large house and he didn't have much time, so he had to be selective.

He figured that a lot of household talk took place in the kitchen and living room, so he had placed microphones there. But the house was so large, he had no time to plant them in every room of his choice. He would have loved to put one in the bedrooms, but the house had too many of them.

He cranked up the volume on the remote microphone and heard the hiss of a kettle and the fridge door shutting. The microphones were incredibly small, paper-coloured, and could be stuck to the corner of a white wall, almost invisible. Rhys leaned back in his armchair and put both hands over his head, relaxing. He watched as Rebecca, coffee cup in hand, walked across the floor and sat down on the sofa, facing the garden. He could only see the back of her head, and long hair falling over the sofa. How many times had he run his fingers through that hair? How many times, in the throes of passion, had he pulled on that hair and grabbed her by the waist, moulding her body to his?

A vortex of jealousy and anger spiralled inside him, burning in his bloodstream. His lips curled up in a snarl and he gripped the chair arms.

I could've given you everything, Becky. Everything. You saw right through me. Understood me like no one else. Then you turned away and left me alone. And you left me for that, that. . . .

Rage curdled like lava in his arteries. Rhys stood and began pacing. Of all men, she had to go for Jeremy Stone? Nephew of Grant Stone? How could she?

Rhys stood at the back window staring out at the overgrown, weed-filled garden. Anger bubbled inside him, simmering. He heard a voice and turned. Rebecca was saying something to the housekeeper. Rhys moved closer to the screen. He turned up the volume as their voices were muffled. Edna Mildred was standing next to the sofa. Rhys only caught a few fragments of what they said. Damn the place, he cursed. The kitchen was too big. He should have put more microphones in.

". . . Going out . . . doctors . . . do the shopping. . . ."

Rhys smiled to himself. He knew exactly where Rebecca's doctor's surgery was, having followed her on many occasions all through the pregnancy.

While they were a couple, he had inserted a software into her phone that recorded every conversation she had so he could listen to them at any time. Even better, the software recorded the GPS signal, giving her location at the time of the conversation.

She still had the power of mesmerising him just by speaking. Every word she uttered seemed to be for his ears alone. Making plans to meet with a friend. Speaking to her friend about the nausea and vomiting she suffered, the back pain she lived through, during her pregnancy.

If only she could speak to him about it. Several times, he had been on the verge of pressing the green button and calling her up. But he knew he couldn't. Not after what happened. She had called the police on him. But all he wanted was for Rebecca to be his, for life. He didn't want another man looking at her. No one would ever love her the way he had. The way he still could, if she would just give him a chance.

He could do nothing but wait. And as he waited, the soul-rending visions from the past rose up like acrid, dense, poisonous fumes in the back of his mind.

Of all the women he had been with, only Rebecca knew.

Pain and rage jostled inside his heart, breaking it into two, releasing dark, bitter black vitriol. The poison spread through his blood.

He went to his bedroom, which he had converted into a workshop. Opening the wardrobe door, he pulled down a stack of nail polish bottles. He bought these in bulk from Romania, and picked them up from a boat that docked in Cornwall every six months. A lot of contraband drugs entered the UK through Cornwall, by boats that came up from Holland and northern France. Nail polish contained a volatile chemical called TATP, which was also used extensively in improvised explosive devices or IEDs. During his time in Afghanistan, Rhys had been trained in how an IED was constructed.

He emptied the contents of several nail polish bottles into a five-hundred-millilitre glass beaker till it was almost full. He took the beaker into the small kitchen. There was a Bunsen burner on the kitchen counter and he placed the beaker on it and fired the burner up. He gently stirred the beaker containing nail polish, and added a salt and acid chemical to it, in order to isolate the TATP.

When most of the liquid had evaporated, only pure TATP was left. This was the hard bit. Any spillage, and the TATP would corrode the surface it landed on.

Rhys put on gloves and a mask. Then he poured the thick contents of the beaker into a flat, rectangular steel container. It didn't hold much, but it was enough for his purposes.

He knelt, and from the kitchen cabinet under the sink took out a welder's mask and a blowtorch.

Working very carefully, he fired up the blowtorch and sealed the steel edges of the container to seal the chemical inside. He took off his gloves and mask. Holding the container, he walked back into the bedroom.

He opened a suitcase that was stored underneath the bed. Inside lay a variety of burner phones, wires, and blast caps. He took out a brand-new phone. It was charged already. He wrote down the number, then, using some black tape, fixed the steel container to the phone. He attached four blast caps to the container, then wound more black tape around the entire package, securing it.

All he had to do now was ring the phone, and the electricity from the call would fire the blast caps, lighting up the TATP.

He set the improvised device on the floor. He closed the suitcase and pushed it back under the bed. He entered the new phone number on his mobile. Then he smiled to himself.

Rebecca was going to see the doctor, was she? Maybe that God-awful husband of hers would drive her up there. Well, did he have a surprise for them.

CHAPTER 23

Rebecca stood inside, waiting after Jeremy had stepped out. It was cold and Jeremy had his beanie hat and gloves on. He thrust his hands inside his winter jacket and turned around. His voice had a hint of irritation. "Are you coming?"

She stared out at the packed snow in the corners of the front lawn, and the gloominess of the Common across the road. The darkness between the trees already seemed dense, impenetrable. It made her shiver.

The dizziness returned, swirling in her brain. She put a hand on the door handle to steady herself. She didn't want to go outside. Didn't want to face the outside world. More than anything else, she wanted her Reggie back. She hadn't slept last night. The crying of a baby, incessant and plangent, had kept her awake. The cries seem to pierce through the walls, rising up from the pillow as she put her head down, exhausted. She had tossed and turned, one nightmare after the other filling her night.

Jeremy walked across the porch towards her. She had turned the lights off inside, and behind his glasses, she couldn't see his eyes. His face was impassive.

"Dr Richardson wants to see you. We can't keep him waiting."

It was easy for Jeremy to talk and walk around like nothing happened. He would never understand what she was going through. And if she tried to explain, it would come out the wrong way. Her demure eyes floated down to the parquet flooring. "I don't want to go. I've got nothing to say to him."

Jeremy cocked his head to one side, hands still in his pockets. "We talked about this."

"Like we talked about letting those people into our house?" She couldn't help the sudden, sharp rise in her voice. Her jaw muscles hardened into knots and she pointed a quivering finger at her husband. "I told you not to do it."

Jeremy stared at her for a few seconds, then came inside and shut the massive mahogany door. It was suddenly very dark and he switched the hallway lights on. She cringed under the sudden, harsh glow. She waved her hands above her head. "Turn those bloody lights off."

Instead of listening, Jeremy stepped closer. She was a couple of inches taller than him but his teeth were bared and a scowl deepened on his face. "I'm getting really tired of your attitude," he hissed. "I told you not to go out with Reggie so early. Do you ever listen to me?"

Rebecca swallowed hard and took two steps back. Jeremy advanced on her. "I'm doing all this for you. You need to take better care of yourself, Becky."

He jabbed a finger at his chest. His bottom lip quivered and the tip of his nose turned red. "I'm suffering as well. I'm not showing it and trying to make the best of a horrible situation. You can't fall apart like this. Not now."

Rebecca breathed heavily for a few seconds, locking eyes with him. She regretted the day she had agreed to marry him, but it was too late now. She should have known something awful would happen one day. And now it had. She blamed herself as much as she blamed him. Anger spiked in her tone.

"You didn't answer my question. Without asking me, you let those forensic officers inside, to trample all over our house." She pointed to the upper floor and waved her hand. "Taking away my last shred of privacy, at a time like this. How could you?"

Jeremy's jaw went slack as he shook his head slowly. "Your privacy? You're the one who posts to Instagram a hundred times a day. How could the forensic officers affect your privacy, anyway? All they did was collect evidence."

She jabbed a finger at him again. "Exactly. What sort of evidence do you think they collected? They wanted to come inside my bedroom and take samples from the floor and bed as well."

Jeremy lifted his arms, then flopped them to his side. "So what if they did? If it helps to find Reggie sooner, then what's your problem?"

"How will carpet samples from my room help to find Reggie?" She glared at him for a while, wondering how she'd ever agreed to get married to this insensitive, callous weasel of a man. "I hate you," she bit out between gnashing teeth. She moved past him, and with some effort, opened the door. "I'm going on my own."

Her boots crunched snow as she headed for the sleek black Range Rover Evoque parked on the drive. Jeremy hurried after her. "No, I don't think you're fit to drive. I'm taking you." He reached for her arm and she lashed at him, slapping his hand away.

"Leave me alone!" She didn't mean to shout, but it happened. Jeremy's face fell, but his eyes glittered as he slowly withdrew his hand. Without a word she got into the driver's seat. The keys were already in the ignition.

Rebecca turned the car out of the drive. She screeched to a stop at the red light at the end of the road. A black Honda Accord car was right behind her. Behind the Honda, the road was empty. The lights turned yellow and Rebecca gunned the accelerator, tyres screeching. Her husband's last words echoed in her brain.

'What's your problem?' 'What's your problem?'

The words swirled and ebbed in invisible, inchoate currents in the blackest recesses of her mind, slithering across each other like vipers. *My problem?* she wanted to shout. *My problem?*

Her problems had started the day she became Mrs Stone. After getting rid of that overcontrolling, dangerous dickhead Rhys, she had opted for safety and security. Little had she known what Jeremy Stone was really like.

What was it about her that attracted these control-freak men?

Jeremy had seemed harmless at first, but after a while she realised his true nature. True, he wasn't as bad as Rhys. He didn't follow her around. In fact, sometimes it seemed like he didn't care at all. But when he was around, she had to do as he wanted. Jeremy needed a wife just to show the rest of the world. She was a trophy, nestled inside his beautiful glass cabinet, his own special prison. Saline buds threatened at the corner of her eyes, then lost to gravity and rolled down her cheeks. She sniffed and wiped them with her sleeve. The words came back, reverberating, relentless.

'What's your problem?' 'Problem?'

She turned a left corner to come up to her doctor's surgery. As she did so, she noticed the car right behind her. It was the same black Honda. It had stayed behind her all this time. The car took the same turn as her. In the rear-view mirror she noticed the man driving and a whiplash of fear stabbed her in the spine. Her eyes widened.

That parka with the fur-lined hood. Pulled up over the driver's head. Those broad shoulders. It was the same man she had seen opposite the house, and at the bus stop. Panic gripped her throat, twisting her windpipe. The tepid daylight turned into spots of blackness, darkening photons bouncing inside her dizzy mind.

Nausea rose inside her throat as her hands slackened on the steering wheel. The car swerved to the left and she pulled it back at the last second before it hit a parked vehicle. She hit the hazard lights and pulled to a stop. The black Honda indicated and moved past her slowly. The man turned to look at her, smiling as he did so. He pulled the hood off his head, and for the first time, she could see him.

Fear surged inside her once again, a black wave splashing over her mind, submerging her in panic.

She knew that face.

Rhys Mason.

CHAPTER 24

Twenty-two years ago

Birmingham, England

Nine-year-old Rhys breathed heavily. He clutched his mother's hand tight as he stared at the stage from the side. A group of girls were performing, garishly lit by overhead lights. They were singing a popular pop tune that had recently been in the top ten of the UK charts.

Rhys watched the girls, fascinated at how different it all looked when he was standing here, as opposed to sitting in the audience. The girls were between thirteen and fourteen years old, and were taller than him. The lead singer had an impressive voice and she belted out the lyrics lustily, while the remaining three girls danced, did the chorus, and sang an occasional line. When they finished, striking a pose, the audience in Broad Street Theatre erupted with applause and screams.

Rhys's heartbeat notched up a gear, drumming loudly in his ears. He looked up at his mother, tugging on her hand. Rhys was tall for a nine-year-old and almost came up to his mother's shoulder. He had never known his dad, but his mother told him that was where he got his height from.

"Is it my turn now?"

"Yes," his mother whispered, bending down to catch his ear. "Just wait until they announce your name."

The master of ceremonies strode out onto the stage, a tall man dressed impeccably in a shiny blue suit. Even the tips of his black shoes gleamed in the bright lights.

"Can we have a round of applause for the Daisy Girls, please," the MC shouted on his microphone and the audience cheered and hooted. This was the Midwest England Talent Championships and it was Rhys's biggest gig to date. He had started singing in school choirs, and his teachers had quickly seen his potential. He loved pop music and spent the weekends in front of the TV, copying dance moves. Rhys had been singing and dancing for the last two years and both his voice and dancing skills had improved. He wanted to do this for the rest of his life. He wanted to be like those pop stars he saw on TV, mesmerising the whole world with their beautiful voices and dance moves.

"And now, please welcome onto the stage a young man with prodigious talent. Mr Rhys Mason!" The MC shouted out his name and there was polite applause from the audience, nowhere as loud as they had been for the previous act.

"Good luck, my love." Rhys's mother bent on one knee and they hugged each other. His mother's eyes were shimmering bright, and he thought she was close to tears. He bent over and kissed his mother on the forehead. "Don't worry, Mummy, I'll be fine."

He tried to make his voice as confident as possible, and his mother smiled. Rhys glanced over at the Daisy Girls, who stood with their arms folded across their chests, glaring at him. Rhys saw contempt and arrogance in their eyes. He knew they were favourites to win the competition. That was why their act had been saved as one of the last ones. After Rhys there was a boys' group, and that was it.

His mother pushed him gently on the back as she stood. The MC was standing there, right arm stretched out, head turned in his direction.

This was it. The moment he had dreamt of for so many years.

Well, two years was a long, long time for nine-year-old Rhys. He took a deep breath and let it go slowly, counting to five, like his mother had taught him to. Then he held his head high and walked out on the stage. There was a smattering of applause, which intensified when Rhys looked at the audience, raised his hand, smiled, and waved. He couldn't see a thing, as he had expected, with the lights shining down on him. His heart drummed fast, pulse rising in his ears.

He shook hands with the MC, who introduced him again and then walked off the stage. Rhys kept the microphone turned off and cleared his throat discreetly. The lights dimmed. A hush of expectation fell in the theatre. The first strains of the music started.

Rhys flicked on the microphone. His eyes closed as the microphone rose to a well-practised twenty centimetres from his face. He started to sing, his heart and soul rising as the tune floated out in his voice. He barely heard the audience clapping as they realised this nine-year-old had the mellifluous voice of a seasoned adult singer.

Then the beat dropped, the tune broke, Rhys snapped his eyes open, and he did a 360-degree turn. The beat started again, faster in tempo now and Rhys jerked his hips, swivelled his shoulders, and moved his hands and wrists in repeated jerky, birdlike, frantic movements. He sang about the woman he had lost, who had left him with a child he did not want. There was a gasp of surprise from the audience, then they were silent, spellbound by his performance.

Rhys sang and danced in a daze, cocooned in a zone of his own. The stage had become his living room, his audience the TV screen.

In his mind, he was performing for the millions of people watching at home, but most of all, Rhys was doing this for himself. The stage was his home, a reason for living.

He did his last pirouette, jumped up. then stood with his legs splayed apart, one finger raised in the air, bending forwards as the song came to an end. He switched the microphone off so the audience couldn't hear his gasps. A wall of sound met his ears, growing louder by the second. It was like a gigantic wave rolling towards him and he stared at the black mass of the theatre in confusion. Were they all clapping for him? He could hear screams and shouts, and the clapping just would not stop.

Then the MC was by his side, gripping his shoulder, anchoring him. He looked to the right partition, and could just make out his mother's shape. Both her hands were raised to her face, and she was shaking. He knew he shouldn't be looking away from the audience and quickly faced them again.

Blimey, they were still clapping and cheering. The MC said something, his words almost lost in the relentless applause.

Then Rhys ran off the stage and into his mother's outstretched arms. She hugged him fiercely and when he put his cheek to hers, it was wet.

"Mom, are you okay?" he asked.

Cheryl, his mother, tried to say something but it was a mumble. She hugged him again and nine-year-old Rhys whispered in his mother's ear, asking her to calm down.

There was a commotion behind them as the next act went out onto the stage. Then the MC came around and touched Rhys on the shoulder. Rhys was still holding his mother's hand.

The MC smiled, his broad, handsome face shining. "There's a special guest who wants to meet you, Rhys."

Cheryl asked, "Who?"

A man stepped out from the shadows, clad in a black leather jacket and matching black jeans. He wore a white T-shirt underneath and his black hair was gelled back. Both Rhys and Cheryl gasped. So did the Daisy Girls, and the stagehands.

Rhys blinked, unable to believe his eyes. Was that Grant Stone? The global superstar, a man whose dance moves Rhys copied every weekend . . . and he was *here?*

Rhys rubbed his eyes, then pinched himself. This could not be happening. It was impossible.

Grant Stone came forward and bent on one knee, then extended a hand towards Rhys. "That was an amazing performance, Rhys. I can't believe how good you were."

Rhys was aware that even his mother was so shocked, her grip on his hand had become loose. Rhys stretched his fingers out and shook the famous pop star's warm hand. "Umm. . . . Ah. . . . Thank you," he stammered.

Grant Stone smiled. He looked at Rhys's mother and stood. He leaned forward and kissed her on both cheeks. Cheryl looked like she was going to faint. Her eyes were wide and her nostrils flared. Grant Stone said, "Why don't you come backstage with me?" He put a hand on Rhys's shoulder and gave Cheryl a dazzling smile with his perfectly white teeth. "This young man has a great future."

CHAPTER 25

Twenty-one years ago

Godalming, Surrey

Grant Stone's mansion was built on twelve acres of land. The Surrey Downs Hills rose from the rear end of his massive estate, gently sloping, densely wooded green-and-blue hills that looked like crayon-coloured clouds that had descended to the earth.

Rhys loved to sit on the top floor of Grant's penthouse suite and stare out to the hills, where the line between land and horizon became blurred till it merged into one. He came here often, sometimes with his mother, sometimes in the chauffeur-driven Rolls-Royce Phantom that Grant sent to their grimy counsel flat in southwest London.

Rhys had been on tours with Grant, had photo shoots with him, attended press conferences and glittering music talent competitions. He was only ten years old, but Grant trusted him enough to make him the judge of one competition. That fact alone never ceased to amaze Rhys. He was only ten years old and he was already a judge? Unbelievable.

He hopped off the windowsill, which was like a seat with cushions. He stepped out into the wide hallway and went down the stairs. On the first floor, he came up to the oak door of Grant's study. It was ajar and he could hear voices coming from inside. He had come with his mother today, and he stopped short when he heard her voice.

"You don't have to do this, Grant, you really don't."

Grant had a thin, unusually high-pitched voice. He used it to great effect in his music and it carried clearly through the walls. "It's my pleasure, Cheryl. You have suffered with this debt for long enough. You've raised Rhys into such a lovely boy. You deserve a break."

There was silence for a while, then Rhys heard a sniffing sound. He had heard it before, and he knew his mother was crying.

Rhys knew his mother was fond of wine, and he often found her in the mornings, curled up on the sofa in front of the TV, with two or three empty wine bottles on the floor. On those mornings, he took himself to school. But he didn't know about the debt. He didn't know what the word really meant, but he knew it was something bad. When Cheryl spoke to her friend Janet on the phone, she cursed about it, thinking Rhys was too busy doing his dance moves in front of the TV. She said words like 'loan shark', 'money', and 'debt', then swore.

His mother was speaking again. "But forty thousand pounds is a lot of money, Grant. I will never be able to pay you back."

Grant said, "You don't have to." His voice dropped and Rhys could barely hear him. He pressed his ear closer to the door. Grant whispered, "This is my gift to you, Cheryl. Well, to both you and Rhys. Please accept it."

There was a creaking sound and a shuffling noise. Cheryl was sniffing louder now, then he heard her sob. Rhys pushed the door very gently and it open a fraction wider. Cheryl and Grant were sitting at a sideways angle to him, and neither of them were looking towards the door. Apart from the two housekeepers on the ground floor, busy preparing lunch, the house was empty.

Grant said, "Why don't you leave Rhys here with me for the weekend? I need to write some music and he's full of ideas. I could really use his help."

Cheryl dabbed her eyes and looked up. "Oh no, I couldn't possibly do that. He's going to miss me."

Grant smiled and cocked his head to one side. "Are you sure? He has stayed with me for the whole day before. Staying the night won't make a difference, will it?"

Then Grant put up a hand. "He can do as he wants, of course. The thing about creating music is, I don't know when the creative juices will be flowing and we're on a roll. It's a shame to cut things short, just to send him home. He can stay here and I can send him back tomorrow morning."

Cheryl stared at Grant for a while. Grant said, "Yvonne and Julia, the two housekeepers, will be here. They will look after him as well. Both of them really like Rhys, you know that."

Rhys watched as his mother looked down at her lap. He could see that she was having trouble making her mind up. Rhys knocked loudly on the door and pushed it open further. They turned towards him and Grant rose from his red leather armchair, a big smile on his face. "Hey, look who it is," he said in his thin, singsong voice. "Come inside."

Grant put his hands on Rhys's shoulders and stood behind him.

"He is my protégé, Cheryl. This boy will one day be more successful than I am. Please give me a chance to make his talent shine."

Cheryl's mouth fell open as the skin around her eyes cleared. Her eyebrows rose and she struggled to say something. Then she coughed and Rhys watched her Adam's apple bob up and down.

"But I know it's a big step. You don't have to leave him here with me. Feel free to do as you wish."

Grant walked over to the massive desk in one corner of the room. He opened the drawer and pulled out a chequebook. He wrote the cheque, then walked back and handed it to Cheryl. She stared at it, frozen, unable to move.

"Please take it, Cheryl. Like I said, it's a gift." He gave her the thousand-watt smile he reserved for special occasions. "It's rude not to accept a gift, right?" Cheryl looked at her son, and Rhys saw a glazed, shiny look in her eyes, like she was suspended in a dream. His mother's gaze seemed to look right through him and into the distance. Then she blinked and turned to Grant. "Thank you." She took the cheque and put it into her purse. Grant smiled, looked at Rhys, and winked.

That was how it started. Rhys regularly began staying weekends at Grant's mansion. They would go on long walks and Grant taught him how to horseback ride. Rhys, Cheryl, and Grant would go on holidays as well, to Porto Cuervo in Sardinia, where Grant had a 100-foot yacht he borrowed from an Arab oil tycoon. Rhys even spent weekday nights after school at Grant's place, and in the mornings the chauffeur dropped him off at school in Grant's Rolls-Royce Phantom.

Rhys had a massive en-suite bedroom all for himself in Grant's house. It was twice the size of the three-bedroom counsel flat he shared with his mother. Grant came into his bedroom often and they would stay up too late, talking and chatting. Grant spoke to him about his own childhood, how difficult it had been as he was raised by his father. Rhys got the impression Grant didn't like his father at all. Grant also mentioned how much money he was making, the terms of his contract with the record company, and most of it went way over Rhys's head. He knew that Grant was speaking to him as if he were an adult and he tried very hard to understand. But often he couldn't make sense of it.

When Grant asked Rhys to come to his own bedroom, it seemed like a natural thing to do. Grant showed him a magazine with a picture of a naked man on the cover. Rhys stared at it, not sure how to react. He had never seen a naked man before. Grant turned the pages and showed him pictures of naked men and women who were kissing. Grant asked him what he thought of the pictures. Rhys stared at them in confusion, then shrugged. Grant smiled at him and put the magazine away. They were lying in bed already and Grant hugged him. They had done this before, so it didn't surprise Rhys much. But he was surprised when Grant's face bent down to his own and he felt their lips touch. It was a weird, strange sensation. Rhys froze, not knowing what to do.

Grant's voice was a low whisper. "Don't worry. This is what people do when they love one another." Rhys felt Grant's lips against his again, kissing him.

"Open your mouth," Grant said softly. "It's me, okay? This is a special thing between us. You can never tell anyone else, because they won't understand. Go on, open your mouth, just a little."

Rhys obeyed.

CHAPTER 26

Harry rang the doorbell of the front door and waited. In a short while, the lock clicked and the door swung open. Miss Edna Mildred stood on the other side, her wizened face dominated by her large, dark blue eyes. There was no life in her stare, no curiosity, as if she already knew what they had come for.

Arla stepped forward. In her experience, these tragic matters had to be dealt with using extreme sensitivity, but also with swiftness and clarity. Families wanted to know. They craved closure, one way or the other. The worst part about having a missing family member was the lack of knowledge.

"I wish to see Mr and Mrs Stone, please. It is a very important matter."

Edna's eyes locked with Arla's for a few seconds, searching her face. Then she stood to one side, letting them enter.

Edna directed them to the same living room and they took their seats. This time around, there was no offer of tea or biscuits. The elderly housekeeper didn't say a word. She simply left them standing in the living room, turned, and left. It was Jeremy who came in first. His lips were parted and behind the glasses, Arla could see his anxiety-widened eyes. His Adam's apple bobbed up and down. He shook slightly.

"What is it, detective? What have you found?"

Arla and Harry remained still as statues. Arla only moved her lips. "Where is your wife?"

"She wasn't in her room, but Edna has informed her, I believe. She should be on her way down. Now, if you could please tell me what's going on."

It was dark outside and the curtains were drawn. The two chandeliers in the room were glowing at full intensity and there was nowhere to hide, no way to soften the impact of what Arla was about to say. "Please have a seat, Mr Stone. I would rather wait till your wife arrived, before I inform you of our findings."

Jeremy's chest rose and fell with deep breaths. He took his glasses off and Arla could see the stricken look in his eyes. He wouldn't sit down. "Surely you can just tell me."

Arla's mouth was barely open, but she let out a soft, frustrated sigh. Why did this couple have to be so disjointed in everything they did? Thankfully, there was movement at the door and Rebecca Stone appeared.

Arla noted she was wearing the same clothes as yesterday: dark pullover sweater, jeans, and slippers. Her hair was straggly and unwashed. She glanced from her husband back to them. The corners of her eyes narrowed and her nostrils flared. Her hands were fists by her side, knuckles bone white. "What is it?" She directed the question to Arla. "Edna said it was something important."

Arla kept her voice low. "At 1600 hours today, roughly five hundred yards inside Clapham Common, we found the body of an approximately five-week-old male baby. He had a purple baby grow on with Reggie's name on it. I am extremely sorry to bring you this news. We need you to come and identify the body."

Rebecca stepped forward, gasping and blinking rapidly. Her bone white face had blotches of red on it. Her lips moved but no sound emerged. Harry stepped swiftly to her side as her eyes rolled back and her hands flopped. He was just in time as Rebecca fainted, sagging against him. Jeremy helped Harry to put Rebecca on a chair. Arla opened the door and went into the hall, shouting for Edna. The housekeeper appeared from the kitchen.

"Please get a glass of water. Mrs Stone has fainted."

Rebecca's head was slumped on the table, cradled on her arms. Jeremy sat next to her, rubbing her back slowly. Harry took the pulse on her wrist, then made sure she was breathing. He stepped back and nodded towards Arla. She breathed a sigh of relief.

Jeremy looked at Arla and cleared his throat several times before he could speak. "How can you know for sure that it's. . . ?"

"We don't know for sure, but by appearances it looks feasible. That is why we need a positive identification from you. Then we do DNA samples as well."

Arla hated this part of her job. But the death of a baby was worse than the death of a loved one; this was also the extinction of a new beginning, of hope and expectation.

Her head lowered, eyes seeking out the patterns of the deep pile carpet. She was surprised to find emotion clogging her throat. It wasn't like her to get emotional in the middle of a case. She had delivered bad news to scores of families. She shook her head. Even her battle-scarred heart felt this was different.

A hand touched her elbow and she felt Harry's presence. "Why don't you sit down?" he whispered in a low voice meant only for her ears. She nodded and walked around the table to sit diagonally opposite the grieving couple.

Harry stood to one side next to her. Arla took a few moments to compose herself, then she took out her black notebook. Rebecca raised her head and gently blew her nose with tissue from a holder on the table.

Arla asked her, "When you took Reggie out for a walk this morning, he was wrapped in a blue cloth as well, right?"

Rebecca stared at Arla for a while. Her face was colourless, no trace of any hue to her skin whatsoever. If she had looked washed-out before, now she looked deathly pale. She suddenly blurted out, "I want to see him. I want to go now." Rebecca stood, drawing herself up to full height. Arla remained seated.

Harry said softly, "Mrs Stone, we are here to help. Please answer Inspector Baker's question first." Rebecca breathed, her pupils constricting, eyes roving. Then she glanced down at Arla.

"What did you say?"

Arla repeated her question. Rebecca lifted a hand to her forehead. Her eyes closed and a frown spasmed across her features. "You're here to tell me you just found my dead son, and you're asking me what clothes he was wearing?"

"It's the only way that we can identify your son."

Rebecca put her palms on the table and leaned forward. Her eyes glistened.

"Yes, he was, okay? He was wrapped in a blue quilt that had his name and date of birth sewn on it. He wore black-and-white socks and matching black shoes. I've told you all this before. At a time like this, why do I have to repeat myself?"

"Thank you," Arla said. She stood and went out the door. Harry ushered the couple ahead of him. He had pulled the BMW into the remaining space on the drive already. Rebecca and Jeremy got in the back and Harry fired up the engine.

As the car backed out from the drive, Arla's eyes were caught by movement at the bay window on the right. It was Edna Mildred. She was gripping the windowsill and leaning forward. She was staring straight at Arla. Their eyes locked, till Harry got on the road and the car drove off.

CHAPTER 27

Arla watched Rebecca's face closely when she identified her son's body. Her eyes bulged, then she bent over and vomited on the floor. Jeremy and Banerjee's Chinese helper, Lorna, took Rebecca into Banerjee's office. Shortly after, Harry drove them back. Arla sat in the passenger seat. The grim silence inside the car lay like a cloak upon them. Arla knew that, for the couple, this was the worst news imaginable. But for her, it was the beginning. Her mind was already running loops around itself and she was desperate to get back to the station, despite the late hour.

The detectives' office was empty, apart from Roslyn, Lisa, and Rob, who were huddled over Rob's laptop. Harry strode up to them. He carried two boxes of Krispy Kreme doughnuts and when he put them on Roslyn's table, she cheered. Rob stood, stretching.

"Got all the images here, guv. I think we see their person of interest, but to be honest, he could be anyone."

"Good work. Rob, would you mind getting some coffee?" Rob nodded and walked off towards the small kitchen that housed a sink, a coffee machine, and a fridge. Arla sat down between Lisa and Roslyn and pulled the laptop towards herself. "Show me." Harry stood behind her, leaning forward.

Lisa clicked on the keyboard and four boxes appeared on the screen. She pointed to the top left and pressed play. Cars zipped past the busy road and so did several pedestrians. Many had their coat hoods up, or wore hats. The vast majority of the clothing was dark-coloured, and Lisa pointed to the one man wearing an almost white jacket. The hood was up and when she cropped the view and zoomed in, the fur lining of the hood was visible.

Arla felt a tingle of excitement. The man's clothing, at least, matched the description Rebecca had provided. Lisa clicked on the screens again and the view zoomed back. She pointed to the other cameras, which showed the same view from the opposite side. They saw the man full-frontal now, and noticed he was wearing dark glasses.

"Zoom in," Arla said. The close-up view showed a man whose nose and mouth were covered by a ski mask, in addition to the glasses. Together with the hood of the parka, only the forehead was actually visible. But he was a tall, wide-shouldered Caucasian man and that gave Arla a faint flicker of hope.

"Put signs up on that road, and ask witnesses to come forward. Some people would have noticed him. He's the only one wearing a white coat."

Roslyn asked, "Looks like a ski jacket, right?"

Arla said, "Yes, and I'm sure it would provide camouflage in the snow. If he was hiding in the Common, that would make sense." She pointed at the screen and tapped at the man's legs. "His trousers are also cream-coloured. No one wears that in winter."

Lisa's fingers hovered above the keyboard again and the images started moving. The camera still faced the man, who took a right turn into Rebecca's road. He disappeared from view due to the lack of cameras.

"We pick him up at the end, over here." Lisa pointed to the bottom-right edge of the screen where now the camera showed the man coming out of the street and taking a left. He walked to a bus stop and then got into a bus numbered 240.

Lisa zoomed in to the back of the bus. "I've already sent an email to the schedule master of Arriva, the company who runs that bus route. Doubt I'll hear back tonight, but will chase it up tomorrow. If we can get the bus driver's name, it's worth questioning him."

Arla smiled at her. "Good work, both of you. Help yourself to a doughnut."

Rob returned with a tray of six coffee cups. He knew what everyone wanted and put down a steaming cappuccino in front of Arla. She blew on it and took a sip gratefully. It had been a strange and haunting day. She wondered what tomorrow would bring.

Harry walked around and pulled up a chair at the next table, where Rob also sat. He was the only one, Arla noticed, who wasn't eating a doughnut. "Not hungry, Harry?" she asked between mouthfuls. To her mind, a combination of these doughnuts and cappuccino with chocolate sprinkled on top was her idea of heaven. She swallowed and took a long sip of the coffee. She could finish that whole box by herself! She also realised she had skipped both lunch and dinner. No wonder she was famished.

"Did Parmentier come back from the crime scene?" she asked.

Roslyn shook her head. "I was the last to leave. Darren and his team are still there, together with Parmentier. They might have left by now, but two uniformed squad will alternate to keep watch overnight."

Arla nodded. "Killers often return to the site. It's a ritual for them. You never know what the uniforms could find." She thought of the bleak, inhospitable Common. Icy, wet wind whistling through the trees. It made her shiver.

"Did anyone get in touch with Rebecca's family and Grant Stone?"

Roslyn said, "I did, guv. Her mother has called me back and we can see her tomorrow morning, she says. I didn't tell her what we found today, though."

"No, it's best for mother and daughter to be in touch before we do. Any news from the pop star?"

Harry raised a finger. "I left a message with his secretary. He hasn't got back to me as yet."

Arla put her coffee cup on the table and sighed. "Well, it's early days yet. Get a good night's rest, because tomorrow will be super busy."

Arla stood and put both hands on her bump as she felt her baby kick. She was exhausted and wanted nothing more than to crash. She looked around at the team. It was past eight o'clock and they were still here, doing overtime.

"Go home, all of you. Switchboard has my number and if I hear something, I'll let you know."

She waved them goodbye and walked into her office. She couldn't help thinking of the man in the white winter coat, his face hidden so effectively. He might not be the person she was looking for, but there was something distinctly weird about him.

He knew the camera locations on the main road, because he knew when to hide his face. Which meant he had done surveillance beforehand. That pointed to some training. Was he a former policeman? Intelligence officer? Army?

He had gone to great lengths to keep his identity a secret. She sat down at a table with a sigh and pulled the laptop towards her. She fired it up, and began typing up a report for Johnson.

Harry came in and sank into a chair in the corner of the room. He pulled up another chair and put his feet up on it. She caught his eyes and he gave little shake of his head. Then he closed his eyes and leaned his head back against the wall. She knew he was giving her time to finish the report. The office was empty now; even the cleaners had come and gone. Arla wrote as fast as she could. She had no suspects in mind at the moment, but the main person of interest was the guy on CCTV. She sent the report off as an attachment to Johnson. She got her shoulder bag and put the laptop inside it.

"Why are you taking the laptop?" Harry asked, his hand on the light switch. She walked past him as he flicked the switch off and shut the door.

"I've got to do some work after we get home."

Harry stared down at her and frowned. "I think you need to rest when you get home. This can wait till tomorrow."

Her chin jutted out as she scowled. "No, it can't, Harry. Don't tell me what to do."

She turned and walked ahead of him, safe in the knowledge he would be following close behind.

CHAPTER 28

The snow crunched under Rhys's boot and he stopped. He could see the blue and white police crime scene tape fluttering between the trees. He was a couple of hundred yards away, and from where he stood, he knew the police wouldn't see him. He was dressed as a jogger, in black Lycra and thin runner's jacket. He was taking a risk by coming here, but Rhys had survived so far in life by taking risks. He thrived on them, in fact; the thrill of the chase gave him an adrenaline rush like no other.

A uniformed constable, wearing a heavy black coat which had London Met written in big white letters, stood near the path that diverged into the woods. The man's job was to watch out for any inquisitive visitors or the press, but also to look out for a man who would match Rhys's physique.

Rhys suspected the police had accessed the CCTV cameras from the main road and might have an idea of what he looked like. True, he had covered his face very well, and walked with his shoulders drooped, not meeting eyes with anyone, but there would still be witnesses. Thankfully, there were no cameras on Baskerville Road.

Rhys started to run again, a slow jog. He smirked to himself. Of all the houses that Jeremy could've bought, he had to choose one on the road without cameras. The street had its own private security, a van that rolled up and down both in daytime and after dark. But Rhys had learned its schedule very easily. The idiots never varied their patrol times and it was easy to avoid them.

As the path circled closer, Rhys took a good look at the crime scene. He couldn't see much, but there was movement. Forensic officers would be there still, taking photos, collecting samples.

He felt a pang of remorse and his eyelids fluttered. He hadn't wanted to do this. But Rebecca had left him with no choice. Not only did she leave him, she also married Grant Stone's nephew. How could she? She was the only person who knew.

Well, this is the payback, Becky, he thought. And I'm just getting started.

Rhys cast one last, longing look at the crime scene as he ran past it. The uniformed constable didn't pay him any attention. All he had to do was take a few steps and he could have grabbed Rhys. That made him smile. He made a point of staring at the constable, hoping their eyes would meet. They did briefly, but then the man looked away. Adrenaline surged inside Rhys's veins. If only that stupid policeman knew how close he had come to apprehending the culprit.

Rhys kept running and the crime scene was soon obscured behind the dense clump of trees as the path curled around. He was extremely fit and ran ten miles three times a week. Rhys liked looking after himself. Women fell for his classic good looks and he prided himself on wearing the best clothes money could buy. He increased his pace, pumping his legs harder. He felt better for coming here.

The excitement was worth the risk, but his pace faltered as the baby's face rose up in his mind like a bad dream. Breath shook in his chest as his hands clenched. He couldn't control the unspeakable urges that overcame him. He had learned to live with them, but when they washed over him like a tidal wave, he had to succumb.

He had lived through enough horrors to know how heartbroken Becky must be feeling right now. A tinge of sorrow swept through him. He wished he could comfort her. Tell her what happened. She wouldn't understand, but he would make her. His face contorted into a snarl.

He ran straight down the path, opting to skirt the edge of the Common, making a circle. This way, he could see the crime scene again but from the other side. Unfortunately, the view from here was worse. He could still see their blue and white tape flickering in the breeze, but he had to look for it.

That was one of the reasons, he realised, why there hadn't been much media interest. He had checked this morning's papers and found nothing about Rebecca Stone, or her missing baby. And nothing at all about the body found in Clapham Common yesterday.

Rhys smiled. He ran till he came to the car park and got inside his Volkswagen. He powered up his phone and stared at the screen. It was time to let the world know.

CHAPTER 29

The shrill buzz of the alarm woke Arla up. She reached out one hand and slapped the digital clock on the bedside table. Her head fell back on the pillow as she groaned. She had tossed and turned the whole night, unable to get comfortable.

She had only fallen asleep in the early hours of the morning. She could feel Harry's warmth, and he moved closer, pressing his body against her. Their feet entwined and she could feel his growing erection pressing against her side. He lifted himself on one elbow and leaned over her. His mouth found hers and they kissed slowly. She could feel the heat growing between her legs, and she moaned, pulling him closer. His finger squeezed her already sensitive nipples and she gasped. Harry trailed kisses down her neck, pushing down the strap of the slim negligée that she was wearing. She arched her chest upwards when he took one of her nipples into his mouth. She moaned his name.

"I'm right here, "Harry said. He kissed her swollen abdomen, then down her thighs. Gently, he notched her legs open, then positioned himself in between. "And I'm about to get closer," Harry said, as with one fluid movement, he thrust inside her.

*****

By the time they showered and left her apartment, it was almost seven a.m. While Harry parked the car, Arla picked up a cappuccino and a mocha from the cafeteria and headed to her office. A group of overnight uniformed officers walked past them and they greeted each other. She put down the cappuccino on Harry's desk and entered her own office. She didn't have any messages waiting and now that she had handed over the on-call SIO duty to Justin, the stack of papers waiting in her in-tray was noticeably shorter.

She turned on her laptop to find emails from Roslyn. The enterprising detective sergeant had already gotten hold of the call lists from the phone numbers Arla had given her. She replied to Roslyn, thanking her. Then she printed out the call lists from the phones of Jeremy, Rebecca, and Edna Mildred.

She sipped her coffee as she went through the printouts, circling any numbers she saw more than once. She cross-referenced as well, to see if there were any common numbers. Between the three lists, there were none. Jeremy's call list was the most active and she noted the numbers he had called several times over the last week. In comparison, Rebecca barely called anyone.

Arla noted a number she had called on a regular basis, and wondered if it was her mother. Of course, calls were a minor part of Rebecca's social interaction, which took place mainly on Instagram, Facebook, and other social media apps. Getting hold of those records would take time, Arla knew. She flipped open her own phone and went through Rebecca's Instagram feed. In the first week after giving birth, Rebecca had posted several times, showing off her new baby in different parts of her home, and once even in the garden. But after that, over the last three weeks she had made a handful of posts, and none of them had featured the baby. Arla went through all the comments on the Instagram feed that were posted after the baby photos. She stopped when she came across an odd comment. It was from an account called The Final Countdown.

"Whose baby is it anyway?"

After the comment there was an emoji of a broken heart and an arrow going through it. Arla frowned and scrolled through the rest of Rebecca's baby photo feeds. The same user appeared several times.

"Innocence is easy to kill, sins last forever."

"A baby is for life, not just for Christmas."

An emoji of a dog on a leash followed this comment. Black waters of disquiet rustled at the corners of Arla's mind as she went through the comments. They all took aim at the baby and Rebecca, either being cruel or sarcastic, and a couple of times, frankly threatening. Arla stopped her scrolling when she got to the final comment left by the user.

"Should a child pay for the sins of its parents?"

Arla put the phone down, her mind in turmoil. She glanced at her watch; it was close to eight. She picked up the phone and rang the cybercrime unit, hoping she would get lucky. John Williams answered after the fourth ring, to her delight.

"John, this is DCI Baker."

There was a fumble on the phone, a clearing of the throat, and John's nerdy, high-pitched voice came down the line. "Oh hi, hi, hi. I mean, good morning, DCI Baker."

Arla smiled despite herself. Harry always maintained that John had a soft spot for her. He did act flustered and nervous whenever Arla spoke to him, which she found quite endearing. John was a total geek, but also totally harmless.

"I need to find the identity of an Instagram user called The Final Countdown. And before you ask, I can't find anyone with the same moniker on Facebook or Twitter. I suspect he created this account just to follow Rebecca Stone on Instagram. She does have more than one million followers."

John breathed heavily down the phone for a few seconds, and she could hear a keyboard clacking. "Okay, give me a few minutes, please."

Arla gave John the information he needed, then hung up. He called back in five minutes. "I found his IP address."

"Good. Can you get me a location?"

"There's no geo-link on the IP address. Which means he's probably using a VPN. I can still hack into it, but it will take some time. Even when I do find the VPN, it could belong to a router anywhere in the world. Like China, for example. This is how a lot of social media users hide their true identity."

"Try for me, please, John. This person has threatened Rebecca Stone online. We have to see if similar comments were made on her Facebook or Twitter feeds. He didn't use the same name, but stalkers tend to follow their targets on every platform possible."

"No need to search manually. If you can tell me what the comments were like, I have an artificial intelligence program that will search for similar comments on her feeds. You'll get an answer very quickly."

Arla grinned. "It's all about machine learning these days, right?"

"For searches like these, it's very useful. I'll call you back as soon as I have something interesting."

Arla hung up the phone as Harry walked in. Behind him she could see the detectives drifting in, heading for their tables.

"Any news from Parmentier?" she asked.

Harry shrugged. "I haven't checked my emails as yet. Shall I just call him?" Arla nodded and Harry went back to his desk. When he rapped on the door and entered five minutes later, it was with the bespectacled, veteran scene-of-crime officer himself. Arla leaned back in her chair. "You didn't have to get up just for me, Derek."

Parmentier sighed and sat down. "You're a hard task-mistress, DCI Baker. But you know I'm a glutton for punishment."

He opened up a notebook from his satchel bag. Harry sat down opposite him. Arla lifted a hand. "Don't start till the others get here." She picked up her phone and rang Lisa, who answered. When Rob, Lisa, and Roslyn were in the room, Parmentier started.

"The scene was open to the elements, and that's always a problem. Freezing temperatures are good for DNA samples, but water and chemicals on the ground can cut through the chemical bonds that DNA molecules are made of. Hence, a lot of the ground samples we collected might be negative for DNA."

"We can get to that later," Arla said briskly. "Tell me your positive findings."

Parmentier shrugged. "I was trying to say that when extremes of heat or temperature play havoc with a crime scene, it wastes evidence." He held up his hand as Arla opened her mouth to speak. "I'm getting to it. We found boot prints around the site. They were large, an adult man's print."

A torsion of energy gripped Arla's guts. She leaned forward as much as she could with the baby bump. "Any match with the boot prints we got from the windowsill in Rebecca's house?"

"I don't know, because I haven't had time to check with Mary. I will definitely ask her, but please note this: The print on the windowsill, as far as I understand, was a partial print. But, it still seems as large as the prints we found here."

Parmentier continued. "The prints began from where the concrete path ended. We found some prints on the path as well, back where the Common begins."

Roslyn asked, "So the same person walked off the road, into the Common, and to the crime scene?"

"Yes, it would seem so."

Roslyn and Lisa looked at each other, excitement clear on their faces. Arla raised her hand, grabbing their attention. "No assumptions, please," she warned. "The real criminal could well have been and gone, and another person just came because he heard or saw something."

Harry said, "Which is unlikely, as the baby would've been too small to see, and from inside that plastic bag, I doubt there was any sound."

"Regardless," Arla said, "let's just hear the findings with an open mind." She turned to Parmentier. "How many boot prints did you find?"

"I didn't find any other prints at the ground, apart from ours, of course." He pointed towards Roslyn and Lisa. "I found your prints. At least, I think they're yours. Mary had a copy of our department shoe prints."

"We dusted the nearby trees for fingerprints. We found nothing."

Parmentier cleared his throat and moved on. "The plastic bag was made by a company called Refresh. They are wholesale meatpackers. These bags are generally used to shrink-wrap joints of meat that you find in supermarkets."

Arla said, "Get in touch with Refresh and find out who their customers are in southwest London. See who has made recent purchases. Was there a serial number on the bag?"

Parmentier shook his head. "Unfortunately, no. But there was a barcode, and we can certainly make inquiries about that."

Roslyn and Lisa were busy scribbling in their notebooks. Arla tapped her lower lip, staring at the ceiling for a few seconds. Then she snapped her fingers. "What about the blue cloth that baby was wrapped in?"

"We didn't find it. I looked for any cloth fragments that were blue, but found nothing. However, the baby was wearing all the other garments that Rebecca had specified." Parmentier read from his notebook. "Purple baby grow, black shoes, black-and-white socks. He also had a red-and-black bib on the chin."

For a few seconds, the ghastly image of baby Reggie, lying there grey, mottled, and forsaken, crashed into Arla's mind like a comet. Her body shook as she snapped her eyes shut, lowering her head. She was used to seeing dead bodies, often in macabre, gruesome positions. But she was glad she hadn't been the first person to come upon that crime scene. Her eyes flitted over to Roslyn, sitting on a chair to her far right.

"Thanks for the call list, Roslyn," she said softly.

The DS grinned. "No problem, guv. Anything interesting?"

"Yes, I have circled the numbers of interest." She shuffled through the papers on her desk till she found the call list printouts. Roslyn took them from her hand with a murmur of thanks.

Arla asked Parmentier, "Anything else?"

"Like I said, we are still running tests on the soil samples. Specifically, we're looking for human hair, skin cells, hopefully intact, from which we can isolate DNA. Have we got DNA swabs from the family, by the way?"

Arla nodded. Dr Banerjee's assistant, Lorna, had taken swabs from the parents when they attended the morgue. Before they left the house, Harry had done the same for the housekeeper, Edna Mildred.

Parmentier rose. "If there is a match, or if we find anything else, I will let you know."

Arla stared around the room. "Right, so we have our work cut out. While you guys are busy, Harry and I will pay a visit to Rebecca's parents, and then to Grant Stone."

CHAPTER 30

Twenty years ago

Godalming, Surrey

Rhys had just come back from one of Grant's tours in America. They had visited five American cities and the tour had lasted six weeks. Rhys travelled with his mother, and they stayed with Grant in the presidential suite that was booked for him at every hotel.

Rhys was getting used to the constant media attention, the flashbulbs, and attending press conferences with Grant. When he was alone with his mother, the press still followed them around, asking for interviews. Cheryl was more than happy to speak to the reporters, often in exchange for money. However, she never allowed Rhys to speak to the reporters alone. She would always be present, tackling the questions that were directed at Rhys, and always asked for a piece of paper on which the journalists would have to write down the questions before asking them. For most of the TV and radio interviews, Cheryl did most of the talking, and Rhys only made the occasional response.

Rhys also noticed that when his mother was around, Grant did not ask Rhys to sleep with him. He also avoided Rhys's room, unless his mother was present. Rhys slept in his own room, next door to Cheryl. But after being on the road for four weeks, Cheryl had to return home as she was starting a new job. When she left, everything changed.

Grant started coming into Rhys's room at night. He coaxed Rhys to sleep with him. Those strange moments he had shared with Grant in Surrey started again. Rhys did not understand why Grant made him do these things. But he knew it made Grant very happy, so despite his increasing confusion, he went along with it.

After they returned to England, Rhys went back to school, and to living with Cheryl. Grant had helped Cheryl to buy a house, and they now lived in Surbiton, a nice suburb just outside London.

Rail links to central London were excellent, which was good for Cheryl's job. It was also much closer to Grant's mansion. Rhys would often go and spend the weekends at Grant's place, without his mother. Cheryl would pack him a bag for the weekend and the big Rolls-Royce would arrive on Friday evening after school.

Rhys never complained as it was nice roaming around Grant's house. It was more like a palace, with the whole of the ground floor transformed into a museum. Grant had a thing for toy trains. Each room on the ground floor held a massive toy train track and he and Grant would play for ages, hopping from one room to the other. The ground floor also had a full-size cinema screen, complete with popcorn, hot dogs, and a drinks machine. It was Rhys's idea of heaven. It was September, and a few days of sunshine still remained. Grant had made the garden into an amusement park, with huge rides and roller coasters that were the best Rhys had ever seen.

At night, after dinner, Grant would always come into his room. The routine remained the same. He would hold Grant's hand and go to his bedroom. Grant would kiss him all over very gently. Then they showered, where Grant made him touch his private parts. Rhys was aware it made Grant very happy, but he had no idea how, or what, to feel. That night, as they huddled together, Grant held him close.

"No one will understand what you and I share. You can't tell anyone," Grant whispered softly in his ear. "If you do tell anyone, then they will take me away. I will never be able to see you again. Do you understand?"

This part Rhys did understand. He didn't want Grant to be taken away from him. He wanted to see him again, because they had such a good time, apart from the strange things that happened at night. He nodded and whispered back. "Yes, I understand."

"Good boy."

*****

One weekend, Rhys saw another boy at Grant's house. The boy was his height and age and he was on a roller-coaster ride with Grant. They were laughing hysterically and hugging each other. Rhys felt a pang of jealousy. They came off the ride and walked straight towards him. The boy was chubby with round, rosy cheeks and glasses. His bronze-coloured hair was long and he looked like he needed a haircut.

"Rhys, this is my nephew, Jeremy. Say hello to each other."

After they said hello, Grant went off to do some recording in his studio. Rhys and Jeremy hung out, but Jeremy acted like he didn't like him. The boy didn't say much and when Rhys asked if he wanted to play, he just shrugged like it wasn't important.

"Is Grant really your uncle?" Rhys asked. Jealousy surfaced inside him again. Did Jeremy know how lucky he was? It made Rhys think of something else. Did Jeremy ever sleep with Grant? Did they ever do the things that he and Grant did?

Jeremy rolled his eyes. "Yes, stupid. Of course he's my uncle." Then he narrowed his eyes at Rhys. "You're just his new friend." Jeremy sneered at him, then smiled; it seemed more like a snarl.

"Don't worry, he has a friend like you all the time. You'll be gone soon, and there'll be someone new."

Rhys frowned at him. "What do you mean?" They were in one of the toy train rooms, and an engine whistled as the train passed through a series of tunnels. Jeremy stood and walked a few paces to activate a railway bridge, and brought the train to a stop.

"I mean what I said. Uncle likes boys like you. His last friend even looked a lot like you." Jeremy went quiet for a while, then glanced sideways at Rhys. "What does Uncle Grant do with you?"

They stared at each other for a while, and Rhys could feel his heart thumping loudly. "What do you mean?"

Jeremy said, "Like, I play with him, we have dinner together, then I go to sleep in my room. Does he do the same things with you?"

Once again, the two boys were very quiet, staring at each other. A moment settled between them, dense and foreboding. Then, Rhys realised this was his best chance to understand why Grant did those things to him, with his mouth and his hands. Without taking his eyes off Jeremy, Rhys shook his head slowly. The toy train was stuck at the railway bridge level crossing. There was no other sound in the room, not even the ticking of a clock.

"He does something else with me," Rhys whispered.

"Like what?"

Haltingly, Rhys told him. Jeremy listened in silence, his face devoid of expression, blinking. Then he shrugged. "Okay. Whatever. He's never done those things with me. Come on, let's play."

But Rhys didn't want to play anymore. Suddenly, he wanted to see his mother more than anyone else. He went down to the kitchen, where Yvonne, one of the housekeepers, was preparing breakfast.

Yvonne was his mother's age, slim, with long brown hair. She smiled when she saw Rhys and bent down to give him a hug. Her kitchen apron smelt of roast potatoes.

"I want to go home. Can you call my mummy?"

"Really? What's the matter, my love? Are you feeling homesick?"

Rhys nodded.

"Okay, hold on, let me ring your mummy." Yvonne picked up the phone attached to the wall and flipped open a notebook that held all the phone numbers. She tried three times, but Cheryl didn't answer. Rhys went up to his room, then came down an hour later. Yvonne had almost finished making dinner. She tried Cheryl again, with the same result.

She crouched on one knee and gave Rhys a hug. "I'll try again, sweetheart. But it seems your mother has gone out for the night. Why don't you just stay tonight, and tomorrow morning, as soon she answers, the car can take you back."

Rhys had no choice but to obey. Grant finished his recording session soon and the musicians waved goodbye. Jeremy, Rhys, and Grant had their dinner and then spent the rest of the evening watching a film in the basement cinema hall.

Grant sat next to Rhys. He noticed Jeremy sat two rows in front of them. Grant slid his hand inside Rhys's pants, touching him. From his heavy breathing, which turned into gasps, Rhys knew Grant was enjoying himself.

That night, Rhys walked down the large, dark corridor and knocked on Jeremy's door. When Jeremy opened it, Rhys went inside quickly. Jeremy frowned at him. "What are you doing?"

In answer, Grant's voice floated down the hallway. "Rhys, where are you? Rhys?"

Rhys turned to Jeremy and gripped his arm. "Don't tell him I'm here. Please, don't tell him."

Jeremy frowned at Rhys, then shook his head. "No. If Uncle wants you, then you need to see him."

"No." Rhys pressed on the door to shut it, but Jeremy held it open. He leaned out and called to Grant. "Uncle, he's here."

Grant appeared soon and stood framed in the bedroom light. Behind him lay dense darkness. "There you are," Grant said with a smile. "I was looking everywhere for you. Come on, it's time for bed."

Grant held out his hand, and Rhys stared at it. He didn't move. The smile on Grant's face faded just a fraction, then brightened up again. He came forward, crouched on one knee, and ran his hand through Rhys's hair. "Come on, let's put you into bed." This time, he gripped Rhys's hand and tugged gently. Rhys had no choice.

At the door, Rhys turned and looked at Jeremy. The boy had a sneering smile on his face.

CHAPTER 31

Present day

Jeremy parked the black Range Rover Evoque in the driveway of Rebecca's parents' home. Her mother had already opened the door. Rebecca got out, relieved that there hadn't been an argument on the way here. In fact, there had been nothing but a stony silence. Which suited her absolutely fine.

Her heart was broken and she didn't know what to say, think, or feel. The dizziness persisted, like a low hum that seeped down from her mind, all the way to her fingertips, making her whole body feel prickly, uncomfortable. She rubbed one hand against the other elbow continuously. She found it hard to stay still and ignored the inquisitive looks that Jeremy cast in her direction.

Breathing the fresh air in Weybridge should've been a relief, but all she smelled was the fumes of traffic and a rotting odour from the wet ground. She grimaced and covered her nose. Her parents lived in a leafy, middle-class suburb ten miles down the A3. The two-storey detached residence her parents called home was also where Rebecca had grown up. Rebecca's childhood days had been filled with sunshine. It felt chilly and morose now.

She pulled the coat lapels tighter and shivered in the cold. The neighbourhood was nice, but all the detached houses surrounding her seemed desolate and forlorn. Older people lived here, empty-nesters. Rebecca cast her eyes around the decaying homes, with peeling paint and overgrown, weedy gardens. She was glad she had escaped from here. The bustle of London was far better than being in the country.

Christine, her mother, hurried down the driveway and gave her a hug. Rebecca was stiff for a few seconds, then pressed her mother close. She had a fractious relationship with her mother, but Rebecca was still closer to her than anyone. Both of them wept in silence, bodies shaking subtly. Jeremy put an arm on the small of Rebecca's back.

"I think we should go inside," he suggested.

Christine separated from Rebecca, then gripped her daughter's hand tightly. Together they walked inside. Jeremy shut the door behind them. Her father was standing there, dressed in his habitual blue pullover and blue slacks. Roger was in his mid-sixties, with sunken, sagging cheeks and a forehead lined with worry. He outstretched his arms and enveloped Rebecca in a bear hug.

Her mother wept again as Roger murmured his condolences. Rebecca heard her father sniff and then his body shook. She realised her father was crying, which was a strange occurrence. She had never seen him cry, not even when her grandparents died.

As her parents pressed her closer to them, Rebecca felt loose, detached. She was slowly coming apart, disjointed, her mind and body fading into a vacuum that was sucking her in slowly. Her eyes were open, staring at the still, black arms of the old grandfather clock. The thinnest arm of the clock moved, marking seconds, ticking down the units of a time that didn't exist for her.

Roger's eyes were red as he shook her shoulders gently. But anxiety creased his forehead as his eyes narrowed. "Becky. Becky, darling. Please talk to me?"

Rebecca blinked and opened her mouth to say something, but her throat was so dry she coughed instead. Christine said, "Let's go and sit down. I'll get some water."

Jeremy said, "Make that a tea for me, please."

They sat down in the large living room with its long, Georgian-style sash windows that looked out into the hedges of the front garden. Roger sat next to Rebecca and Jeremy discreetly placed himself in an armchair to the side. They sat in silence, because there was nothing to say. Her parents knew everything, including the identification at the morgue. Mere words could not penetrate the fog of acute misery they were suspended in. Roger held her hand in his, and when it shook, she glanced at her father. She was surprised again to see tears rolled down his cheeks. Roger dried them clumsily with his gnarly hand.

Her rational mind told her she should perhaps comfort her father, or even feel the sorrow. It was weird, but she felt incapable of emotion at the moment, as if her whole being had turned to stone. Her heart felt absent, like it had been ripped out from its bony cage. She sat there, still as a statue, staring into space. Her mother came back, bearing a teapot and four cups. Christine poured out the tea and handed a cup to everyone. Only Rebecca refused.

The doorbell went. Christine said, "Karen's here. I asked her to come."

A knot of irritation creased Rebecca's forehead. Her perfect sister was three years older than her and had a successful career in a city law firm. It was the same firm Roger had worked in, but Karen liked to keep that quiet.

She was on a fast track to become partner, which meant she would become a multimillionaire before the age of forty. Karen had always looked upon Rebecca's media career choice as frivolous.

In school, Rebecca had always played second fiddle to Karen, who was better at academics, sports, and looks. Rebecca was definitely a late bloomer, but when she did come of age, she eclipsed

Karen with her beauty. That caused plenty of sibling rivalry, but luckily Karen left to study law at Oxford shortly after.

Karen was married to another corporate lawyer, one as successful as she was, and they had two baby boys. Everything about Karen was perfect, and she liked to make sure her little sister knew all about it.

Rebecca felt that the only thing her sister liked about her was her choice of a husband. Jeremy ticked all the right boxes for Karen, and sometimes Rebecca thought Karen was nicer to her husband than to herself.

Christine went to open the front door and returned with Karen. Rebecca noted her sister was perfectly dressed for the occasion, in a black silk blouse, black cardigan, long black skirt, and black shoes with heels. Even her Chanel handbag, which must have cost thousands, was black. She was on her own and walked forward rapidly as Rebecca rose.

"Oh, darling. Come here," Karen whispered. "I'm so, so sorry. Can't imagine what you're going through."

Yes, Rebecca thought in silence. I bet you can't. You never even came to see Reggie after he was born. Too busy on a big deal, apparently.

Rebecca stared at her sister as Karen turned her back and greeted Jeremy with a hug as well.

Karen sat down next to her sister. Her expensive perfume stung Rebecca's nostrils and made her want to vomit. "What have the police said?" Karen asked.

Rebecca shrugged. "Nothing."

"I can't believe this. I mean, you have cameras outside, right? Yes, I know you do. Did they not pick anything up?"

Karen's default mechanism of coping was to talk excessively. It was beginning to irritate Rebecca, and she knew that if Karen continued she would end up saying something she regretted. Luckily, Jeremy came to the rescue.

"Our Wi-Fi was jammed, and the CCTV cameras are run off the Wi-Fi. Hence, we have no photos of the intruder."

"How bizarre." Karen shook her head. "But I guess it doesn't matter right now." Remorse tinged her tone for the first time as she stared down at her perfectly manicured and polished nails.

Rebecca glanced at her sister. Karen did look sad, but as always with her sister, Rebecca suspected it was all an act. Karen never had the spontaneous warmth her parents possessed. She looked at Karen's dry eyes, then her gleaming black heeled shoes which screamed designer, and she felt nauseated. She rose swiftly and headed out of the room.

She went into the kitchen and filled up a glass at the water machine on the fridge. Christine appeared next to her.

"I think you should stay with us for a few days, darling. It's going to help. We can go for walks. Jeremy can come and visit, but of course, he's welcome to stay as well. A change will do the both of you some good."

"Thank you, Mum, but it's not necessary. I'd rather be at home."

"At least consider it. The housekeeper will look after the place. I can ask Aunt Grace to come down and visit as well." Grace was Christine's sister and, like Christine, had also been a TV actress. Both sisters had groomed Rebecca to follow in their footsteps. Rebecca hadn't seen her Aunt Grace for many years.

Rebecca frowned and spread her hands.

"Mum, you just don't get it, do you? I have nothing to say to Aunt Grace, or to you. You've not been through something like this, so I can't make you understand."

Christine's head dropped on her chest and she tightened her folded arms, as if she was trying to hold herself.

"Oh, Becky, I know. Believe me, I know."

Rebecca felt herself stranded in that bubble again, a void without compassion or sympathy, a world without noise or colour, white as a blank wall. The dizziness was back in her head, humming around her mind like a swarm of bees circling her skull. She just wanted to lie down and sleep. She had to come and see her parents, but now she was beginning to feel it was a mistake. She wanted to return home.

She turned abruptly and headed back into the living room. It was empty. She went upstairs; the first room on the right was her old room. It had been converted into a nursery for Reggie. The new, blue-coloured walls were like a slap in the face to her. She reeled back, snapping her eyes shut.

She heard voices behind her. Her ears pricked up as she recognised Karen's. She was saying something in an urgent voice, but it was too low to be heard. Rebecca crept forward till she came to Karen's old room. The door was ajar and she pressed her ear against it. She heard a man's muffled voice from inside.

"I've tried telling her, but she won't listen."

Karen said, "Give her some space. Now is not the best time."

Rebecca's heart thudded painfully against the ribs, a booming sound that vibrated against the eardrums. Her throat felt parched and dry. Her hands became fists by her side.

Jeremy said, "I don't know what to do."

"Oh, Jeremy," Karen said, her fake voice sounding genuine for once.

She had heard enough. She opened the door and slipped inside. Karen turned to face her. Jeremy was standing in front of the bed and from the sudden shock on his face, she thought the worst.

"What's going on?" Rebecca hissed. The buzzing between her ears was louder now, drilling into the front of her head.

Karen inclined her head and a carefully crafted look of compassion appeared on her face. "Jeremy was just telling me how much you're suffering, Becky. I think you should see a doctor."

"I *am* seeing a doctor." Rebecca bit the words out, desperately trying to stop saying something she would regret later. "I'm coping and I'm fine. I don't need anyone's help, including yours, Karen." She was snarling now, and breathing rapidly, but she didn't care.

She turned on Jeremy. "When you've finished your nice chitchat with my sister, you can drive me back to the house. I'll be waiting downstairs." Jeremy called after her, but Rebecca turned and left, slamming the door shut.

Rebecca went downstairs but she didn't wait for Jeremy. She stormed into the kitchen, where her mother looked up from the sink as she rushed past. Rebecca ignored her. She slipped on her coat. In the back porch, she put on her Wellington boots and then opened the garden door. In the distance, she could see the barn.

When she was young her father had converted the rear of the barn into a play area for her, as they had no animals. It had become Rebecca's refuge during her teenage years. Frost crunched beneath her boots as she walked. Her head was bent low, hands thrust into coat pockets, tightly clenched. She inhaled the smell of damp, frosty earth. The barn door had the latch on, and after some effort, with a gloved hand she managed to release it.

The tall, heavy door was impossible to open fully, but a sliver was enough for her to slip through. The smell of mildewed old haystacks hit her nose, a comforting odour. It brought to mind the endless hours she had spent in the barn, playing on her own. She switched the light on.

The front area was used to stack their timber, for which her dad had a log-splitting machine. Judging by the number of logs stacked in the corners, she thought her dad must have a farmhand to help. She felt guilty for not coming more often. One day, when her parents were gone, this farm would be left to her and Karen.

Rebecca traversed the floor and went through the small archway that led to her play area. She came here as a teenager all the time. Sensibly, she never brought any boys back, because she knew what would happen if her parents found out. She would lose her private sanctum, where she could hide, secluded from the world.

She clicked the door shut. The tall ceiling was crisscrossed with wooden beams. Cobwebs hung from them now, and she felt sad when she remembered how often she'd cleaned the place when she was younger. There was only one window, so high up that she had to use a prong to open it.

That let some light in, but there was electricity as well. There was a bed in one corner, surrounded by shelves with books, CDs, and DVDs. She could sit on the sofa and watch TV, listen to music, and read her books. She patted the sofa, and retreated when a cloud of dust rose from it.

She looked around the place. There was a double bed in the corner opposite to the TV and sofas. There was also a wardrobe behind the bed, and next to it, covered by the horizontal stacks of wood that made up the wall, was a hidden door. Rebecca smiled. The door was used for sheep and goats to come in when this area was used as a holding pen, many centuries ago. She had implored her dad to let her keep the small door, because it was cute, and she liked using it.

She pulled up the wooden panel and it opened easily, revealing the waist-high door. There was a latch on it, and she slid it back. It was rusty now and it hurt her fingers. The door creaked open, letting in the freezing cold. She snapped it shut and stood.

It was cold and inhospitable now, but as she looked at the bed, happy memories of the time when she just lay here, reading all day, came back to her mind. She wished life could be that simple again. She closed her eyes and leaned against the cold logs as the buzzing in her head circulated again, like a gang of motorbikes rotating around her skull. Her vision shook. She hadn't taken the iron tablets this morning. She slid down the wall and ended up on the floor, knees pulled up to her chest, head buried in her hands.

*****

The drive back to Clapham was filled with the same frigid silence as last time. Jeremy tried to break the ice, but Rebecca told him to shut up. As soon as the car came to a stop, she got out, ignoring what Jeremy was telling her. She slammed the door shut and rang the doorbell, wishing she had brought her keys with her.

Jeremy watched her go into the house, shaking his head. He leaned back on the seat and sighed. He was just trying to tell his wife that he would be going to the post office to drop some mail off. He reversed the car and started to drive.

He couldn't believe what Rebecca had just done. Karen was genuinely concerned about her sister, as she should be. And Becky had just flown off the handle, practically accusing them of speaking behind her back. Well, they were, but only because they were concerned about Becky's behaviour. Jeremy wound the window down to get some fresh air.

There was a smell of gas inside the car, one he hadn't come across before. He sniffed a couple of times as he pressed on the accelerator, and noted the smell was stronger. The sudden, loud bang, like a massive firecracker, took him by surprise. It came from the rear of the car. The back windscreen dissolved in a shower of glass fragments and the car fishtailed out, swerving all over the road. Cold wind blew inside, and when Jeremy looked at the rear-view mirror, he gaped in fear and astonishment.

The entire back door had been blown off and was hanging to the left. Smoke rose in acrid black fumes from the rear seats and it took him a few seconds to understand the car was on fire. He screeched to a halt. Cars were stopping all around him. He stumbled out, then fell on the tarmac. Flames licked the side of the car, rising higher. Fear clutched Jeremy's heart as he stared, spellbound.

"Get back, it's going to blow!" a voice shouted. Jeremy stood, but then slipped on the icy road. A pair of hands gripped and then pulled him farther away. He stood at a distance, watching the yellow and orange flames lick higher over the charred remains of his car. In the distance, he could hear the police sirens.

CHAPTER 32

Arla looked out the window as Harry drove the BMW off the turning on the A3. Open green farmlands stretched out on both sides. A pair of horses were nibbling at the remnants of grass on the frosty ground. It was a bucolic scene, despite the harshness of winter. In less than an hour, Arla mused, they had moved from the concrete jungles of south London, into this green and pleasant land.

"Enjoying the scenery?" Harry asked. He had shaved, his coffee brown cheeks again smooth as a pebble on the beach. His black hair was swept back with gel and the sharp, well-pressed suit was back on his shoulders. They were going to see Rebecca's parents, and Harry had clearly dressed for the occasion. She liked it, but would never admit that to him. Harry got a big head in the blink of an eye. Typical man.

"Funny how the scenery changes so quickly," Arla said. Most of her life had been spent in the melting pot of the city and she often forgot how peaceful it could be in the English countryside. The baby bumps of gentle sloping hills and the crisscrossed hedges that separated the farms were simple and plain, small and contained. But small was also beautiful. And it was precisely this contained nature of the English countryside that appealed to her so much. Order, symmetry, and peace.

There was a loud beeping sound from the dashboard. It was Harry's radio. *There goes the peace*, Arla thought to herself with a smirk.

Harry pressed a button on the steering wheel and the radio came to life.

"Duty controller one speaking. Is that Foxtrot Alpha Sierra?" Foxtrot Alpha Sierra was the codename for the unmarked CID BMW car. Harry cleared his throat.

"Yes, it is, controller one." Harry referred to the switchboard operator by her official name. "This is DI Mehta speaking."

"Hello sir. I was informed to call you by Detective Sergeant Roslyn May. Jeremy Stone has been in an RTA." RTA was road traffic accident in common parlance.

Arla leaned forward. "Is he okay?"

"He is alive, ma'am. Would you like to know the location?"

"Yes please."

Arla thanked the duty controller and raised her hand when Harry indicated left at a roundabout. "Turn the car around. We're going back."

Harry made a noise in his throat. "The family are waiting for us."

"They'll have to wait for longer. I want to be at the site of this RTA."

Harry puffed out his cheeks, but did as he was told. He sped up, too, and when they hit the traffic of the A3 he turned on the siren, at Arla's request.

"Is this necessary?" Harry asked. His fists were bunched on the steering wheel and he was leaning forward, dodging in and out between cars.

Arla suppressed a grin. "Don't tell me you're not enjoying it."

"You didn't answer my question."

She leaned back in her seat as the traffic cleared and Harry cruised on an open stretch of road. He cut the siren.

She said, "After I saw that Instagram user harassing Rebecca, I had a feeling someone was out to get this family. Not sure if that person is the intruder as well, but it might well fit."

"She wouldn't be the first celebrity who attracted a stalker."

"I know. But if you consider the events of the last two days, I'm starting to wonder if there's someone who bears a grudge against Jeremy and Rebecca."

It didn't take them long to get to the destination, with Harry using the siren and accelerator judiciously. Arla saw the flashing blue lights and the uniformed officers' squad cars parked on the side of the road before she saw the burnt-out, blackened heap of the vehicle. Rob Pickering hurried up to her as she got out. His bulbous, rosy cheeks were shining with sweat. He wiped his forehead with a handkerchief, lifting his hand up in greeting.

"What happened?" Arla asked as she got out of the car slowly. She folded her arms across her chest, instantly feeling the cold.

"Looks like an explosion in the rear of the car. Luckily the fuselage didn't ignite, but it could easily have done so. A member of the public used a fire extinguisher from his car."

Arla looked at the remains of the vehicle. The front half of the car was fine. The side and rear had twisted in the heat, bodywork buckled. But the rear door and axle had disappeared almost completely, blown out by an explosion.

Harry said, "If this was a fault with the engine, it's normally the front of the car that's affected."

Yes," Rob said and waved towards a tall man in a uniform. "This is Inspector Stevens of the Traffic Police Unit."

Inspectors Stevens shook their hands. He jerked his thumb in the direction of the burnt vehicle. "Something had to be attached to the rear exhaust pipe. There's nothing in that section of the car that would've caused this big explosion. Any gas leaks would have happened near the front."

Arla frowned. "Are you suggesting an explosive device was implanted in the rear of the car?"

In response, Inspector Stevens led them back towards the wreckage. The squad cars had created an island and uniformed policemen stood guard at the sides. Traffic flowed around them.

A car screeched to a halt, and two men jumped out. They were dressed in full black combat gear, with the word 'counterterrorism' emblazoned in big yellow letters on the front and back of their chest rigs. They jogged over to where Arla was standing. Both men wore black caps, and had a mean-looking weapon strapped to them. Their index fingers rested lightly on the trigger.

The lead man said curtly, "Agent Murdoch, Counterterrorism Squad." He showed his ID. "This is Agent Sullivan," he said, introducing his partner.

"What happened here?" Murdoch asked. Harry explained the event and the two officers listened impassively.

Inspector Stevens pointed at the base of the car. There wasn't much to see, and Arla didn't know what she was looking for in the wreckage. Stevens flashed a torch and showed the remains of a pipe which had clearly snapped off.

"This was the rear exhaust pipe. Half of it's still attached to the back chassis." He straightened, but kept the light shining on the remains. "My guess is someone packed a device inside this thing, or strapped it to the sides of the pipe."

"And how did it detonate?" Arla asked.

Murdoch replied. "It would either be a timed device, or detonated by an electrical signal, like a mobile telephone call. Five rings is normally enough electricity to spark an improvised explosive device." His gaze flitted from Arla to Stevens and then Harry. "Are we suspecting a terrorism-related offense here?"

Arla shrugged. "I can't see why. This is the car of a well-known film director. It's hard to think why he would be involved in terrorism. Also, there was no loss of life. This appears to be a police crime issue."

Murdoch nodded. "Going after one person is not the hallmark of a terrorist."

They discussed the case for a while longer, then the counterterrorism officers bid their goodbyes. Arla pointed to the remains of the car. "Is Explosive Ordinance on their way?"

Inspector Stevens nodded. "Yes, I've called them. Their lab is waiting for the samples. Hopefully that'll give us some clues as to the nature of the device."

*****

Clapham Common lay on the left of the road and smaller, separated parklands to the right. Rhys Mason had parked his black Honda Accord a couple of blocks down in a lay-by, then jogged back into the Common. He was now securely hidden in the undergrowth, watching the police cars parked on the road.

He could see the pregnant police officer inspecting the wreckage. More officers appeared, and they had an animated discussion, no doubt wondering about how the explosion occurred. Rhys smiled. Jeremy got lucky this time. There was enough explosive in the device to blow up the whole car, but for some reason, it didn't ignite. Well, this was just the beginning.

There was a long, long way to go, and by the end of it Rebecca would be begging him for forgiveness. Unless they were dead, of course, and what a shame that would be! The only problem was the police, who would now be suspicious of someone stalking the family. Rhys had tipped his hand, and in the process, raised the stakes. He watched the female police officer closely. Although she was pregnant, she was obviously the person in charge. Officers ran up to her and took orders. She had an unmistakable air of authority and Rhys knew she was a person who could become a thorn in his side. He had followed her back to Clapham Station and already unearthed newspaper clippings about some of her previous exploits.

"Detective Inspector Arla Baker," he whispered to himself. "Stand in my way, and I'll take you down."

Rhys felt his phone buzz in his breast pocket. He looked around him quickly, making sure he was alone. In the deep silence of the Common, not even an insect stirred. He answered.

"Are you okay, my love?" a female voice asked, slightly breathless. Rhys recognised the anxiety in her tone and spoke quickly to reassure her.

"I'm totally fine. But it didn't go as planned."

"As long as you're all right, I don't care about the rest. But tell me what happened."

Rhys spoke, and she listened in silence.

"The police will be on your case now. I'm worried," she finally replied.

"The police have been on my case since yesterday. I jogged past that spot, and a stupid copper actually stared at me. If only the idiot knew who I was."

There was a sharp intake of breath on the other end of the line. "No, Rhys. You need to stop this. Taking these risks will get you caught."

"Don't worry," Rhys said soothingly. "The coppers don't know where to start looking. They've got nothing on me."

There was silence for a short while, then she spoke again. Her voice was almost a whisper. "Be careful, Rhys. Please."

Rhys gripped the phone harder, pressing it to his ear. "I will. But also remember what the end goal is. I will not be deflected from my aim."

The woman's voice was sad and low. "Your aim is happiness, Rhys. Isn't that more important than anything else?"

"Yes, it is. But we also have to be free. You understand, don't you?" He held his breath, closed his eyes.

"Of course I do, darling. As long as you look after yourself."

Rhys chuckled, hiding his relief. "I am, don't worry. The countdown has started."

"The final countdown. You used to listen to that song so much."

"Yes," he said, grinning against the receiver. "I did. And I still do."

CHAPTER 33

Arla stood next to the whiteboard in Major Incident Room One and stared at the three rows of expectant faces looking up at her.

"What we have seen today represents an escalation in what I think is a series of attacks on the Stone family."

She took up a marker pen and tapped on the photo of a smiling Rebecca holding her baby and then a close-up of the baby's face. Both photos were stuck next to each other, followed by another photo of the crime scene where Reggie was found.

"I think it is now safe to assume that the abduction and subsequent death of baby Reggie fits a pattern. Rebecca has been harassed extensively on her Instagram feed by an account called The Final Countdown." She half-turned, where Lisa and Roslyn stood to her right. Lisa stepped forward and read from a piece of paper.

"There are a couple of other accounts on Facebook and Twitter which post similar derogatory messages about baby Reggie and Rebecca's motherhood. In fact, on Facebook, one account goes back almost three years. The messages are rude, negative, and amount to cyber-bullying. They comment on Rebecca's weight, how she's a cruel and unforgiving person, and how she got married to Jeremy because she's a gold-digger."

"Blimey," Justin said from the front row. "And do we know the identity of these accounts?"

"Anyone with Internet access and an email account can open a Facebook account. John is chasing them up at the moment," Arla said, indicating the cyber expert sitting in the second row.

"Ah, um, yes," John mumbled, then wiped the sweat off his forehead. "It's all about getting the IP addresses from where these accounts were opened. I have now looked at all the accounts, and they belong to different IPs, and all originate from untraceable VPNs."

Arla shook her head in frustration. "Have we contacted the social media companies? They should have some details on the identities."

"We can try, but unfortunately it's very easy to hide your true identity online. However, I have noticed that all of the accounts that bully Rebecca Stone use a VPN. The location of a VPN can change, but I'm trying to see if there's a pattern. If I find anything, I'll let you know."

Sergeant Smith, one of the new detectives, raised his hand. "Celebrities often have trolls on their social media accounts. Rebecca Stone has more than a million Instagram followers. Some of them are bound to post negative comments. Is it worth the time and money to chase them up?"

"Good point, Smith. But this is not just any troll. These people are posting deeply personal comments, not just about her but about her new baby as well. Many of the comments are frankly threatening."

Harry cleared his throat. "Which brings to mind why Rebecca has never reported them."

Smith said, "Maybe she's just used to them, or perhaps like most of the Instagram celebrities I follow, she hardly ever bothers to check her posts."

"Maybe." Arla puckered her lips and drew them inwards. "But we must ask Rebecca about this. Maybe there's something in her past we don't know about."

Arla turned to her team. Roslyn nodded and stepped forward. "Celebrities often announce their relationships online. Having been through Rebecca's social media accounts with two of our researchers, I can confirm that she had at least one relationship whose photos she removed from her social media accounts."

Arla frowned. "Really? How do you know they were deleted?"

"Four years ago, several of her followers had posted, congratulating her on how she looked with her new date. They even used a name. Rhys. We only know the first name. But it seems Rebecca has deleted all photos of her and Rhys."

Roslyn continued. "Exactly eighteen months later, she gets engaged to Jeremy Stone. Those photos are all present on her accounts."

Lisa spoke up. "The abusive messages on her accounts started around that time too. The researchers found two accounts on her Facebook, and one on Twitter." She gestured towards Arla. "And you found one on her Instagram account."

"So four in total," Arla said. "Can we find out more about this Rhys character? Check all the newspapers and tabloids. There might be some photos or a news clip in the gossip columns. He might not be famous himself, but dating Rebecca would get him attention."

"If only we had his last name, then we could search for him on social media," Rob said. "I'll get the researchers to look for media articles on Rebecca's love life." He turned to the table next to him and picked up the phone receiver.

"Excellent," Arla said, rubbing her hands. She felt a warmth in the pit of her stomach, and her instincts were ringing like a klaxon alarm. She had something here finally, something concrete. Maybe she was assuming some of it, but with experience, she had also learnt not to ignore her sharply honed instincts.

"And we have the explosion this evening. I know it's premature, but any news from Explosives Ordinance?"

Parmentier spoke up. "Not yet. But my team have been collecting samples as well. We did a mass spectrometry of the debris from inside the exhaust pipe. One molecule spikes high on the spectrometer frequency. It's a chemical called TATP. It's frequently used in nail polish, so obviously has no business inside an exhaust pipe. However, TATP is often used by terrorists to make an explosive device."

Silence followed Parmentier's remark. Several faces looked at each other and Arla frowned, looking at Harry. Then she glanced at her team. "The Stone family and Rebecca have no connections with terrorism, do they?"

Harry answered for them. He shook his head firmly. "No, there's no political angle here. This was a homegrown device, designed for personal use. If it was a terrorist, they would have chosen a packed bus or Tube train. Targeting one person is of no use to a terrorist."

"Good point, Harry." Arla turned back towards Parmentier. "Can we get anything more from the TATP samples?"

"Unfortunately no," Parmentier said. "Nail polish is widely available, and even though someone has to buy large amounts and stock them, they could buy them from different stores, over a period of time, so they don't get noticed. Or even by mail-order from foreign countries."

Arla slapped her palm against her thigh and sat down on the chair. She hated blind ends. Her mind raced around in loops and convolutions, synapses triggering and firing in her brain. She touched her temples and closed her eyes briefly.

"The priority now is to find who this Rhys person is. We need an answer in a couple of hours and then start to track him down."

Rob said, "The researchers are on it already, guv. I will let you know."

"Good." Arla turned to Parmentier. "Anything more from the crime scene where we found baby Reggie? You were looking at the plastic packets from the company called Refresh?"

"Nothing."

"What about the boot prints? Did Mary Atkins get back to you?" Arla lifted her neck, looking around the room. Mary should have been here, and she was annoyed at the woman's absence. Apparently, she was busy with another case, as forensic gait analysts were precious people, their expertise shared over all six police stations in the borough.

"The boot prints of Roslyn, Harry, and three uniformed officers have been cleared. The only print that she can't find a match for is the other large, male boot print."

Arla frowned, tapping her cheek. "Did she mention any similarities between the boot print found in the Stone residence window and the one at the crime scene?"

"Yes, they are of a similar size, but she's still running her gait analysis software on both of them."

Arla opened her mouth to say something but the incident room door was flung open and the mountainlike form of Wayne Johnson entered. He glared at everyone in the room, his eyes falling lastly on Arla. He slammed the door shut, the sound loud in the sudden silence. His nostrils were flaring and his lips were bared, white with fury.

"The media have turned up at Jeremy Stone's house. Who leaked the news?"

CHAPTER 34

Rebecca lay on her bed, curled up like a foetus. Tears seeped out from the corners of her eyes, soaking into the bedsheets. A black weight was pressing down on her, smothering her from above, like a malevolent cocoon. She was a prisoner inside it, and couldn't break free. The buzzing inside her head was ever-present, a dim hum at the best of times, but now more like a swarm of hornets, stinging her skull. She had no strength to move her fingers, lift her head. At times, it seemed she was incapable of thought.

From the recesses of her memory, Rhys Mason's smiling, evil face reappeared. He was following her around. She was trying to ignore the truth, but she couldn't anymore.

She had always known he was mentally unstable. True, he loved her with a passion no man had done before. Their sex life had been incredible and Rhys had made her feel like the most desired woman on earth. He showered her with gifts, too. But at the slightest indication she was being friendly with another man, he would fly into a fit of rage. Once, he almost hit one of her co-actors on the set of *Chelsea Town Life*. When they got home that evening, they had a blazing row and he smashed a chair over the table. He pushed her into the sofa, and as he towered above her, fists bunched, eyes wild and crazed, she had known their relationship was over. Because it wasn't the first time.

Over the ten months of their relationship, Rhys veered from being loving and caring to a demonic monster who could beat the shit out of her. He had been in the army and was tall and strong. She knew he had issues from his childhood, and had once intimated to her that he had been abused. But he wouldn't say by whom, or how.

After one of his fits of fury, he had broken down and begged her for forgiveness. She felt his childhood problems had shaped his current personality and each time, she had taken him back. But that evening, she knew there was no going back. Rhys would never change, which was exactly what he vowed to do every time he lost it. Every time he wept and begged her for forgiveness. But she knew better. She did feel sorry for him, but he needed a doctor's help, something she couldn't provide.

He cleared out his stuff from her apartment when he realised she was serious. And then the visits started.

She would come home from work and find him standing outside. He would be there at her workplace in the morning, just to see her and make sure that she was all right. He called her day and night. When she threatened him with reporting him to the police, he stopped. A restraining order meant a criminal record, and Rhys was clever enough to avoid that.

That was when she noticed the abusive trolls appearing on her social media feeds. She could never prove it, but she suspected it was him.

And now, he was back again. He had taken Reggie, she knew it. She had no idea how he got in, but Rhys was nothing but if not resourceful. From his time in the army, he had learned many skills, including, he would boast, how to break into any property and how to make bombs. She shivered. She had no doubt Rhys was behind the explosion in Jeremy's car. It was pure luck that Jeremy was still alive.

Her phone buzzed as it got a new message. She ignored it, but it kept buzzing. She lifted her head and the room tilted, then spun around her. She felt dizzy again and lay back down.

Groaning, she moved to her back and lifted the phone. Her eyes bulged in shock as the breath froze in her chest. A whiplash of fear lashed down her spine, dispelling the fog from her brain. She lifted herself on one elbow, wide eyes fixed on the phone.

The screen showed a countdown, the numbers disappearing, and then an explosion. The loop kept repeating itself, but the message that followed was even more disturbing. It was a video of the song, "The Final Countdown." It had been one of Rhys's favourite songs and he played it often. In happier days, they danced around to it. He said when they got married it would be their first dance as husband and wife. Message after message followed, all of the countdown GIF and the explosion.

Rebecca felt sick. Bile rose up in her mouth as she scrambled out of bed. There was a knock on her door and Jeremy appeared. His glasses were raised on his head and a heavy scowl creased his face.

"Have you seen my uncle's memorabilia? All the stuff that was in the museum." The museum was a room where Jeremy kept things Grant Stone had once used—clothes from a performance, signed books, and records.

Jeremy caught the stunned look on Rebecca's face. "What's the matter?" he asked, coming forward.

Rebecca shoved the phone in her jeans pocket and stood. "Nothing," she said briskly. "I haven't seen your uncle's stuff. What happened to it?"

She walked out into the circular hallway and Jeremy followed. "That's just the point. It's all gone."

Rebecca turned around, an emptiness spreading inside her chest, numbing her body. "Gone?" she whispered.

"Yes, all gone. I hadn't checked on it the last couple of days and this morning I saw the door handle missing. The room was empty."

Rebecca touched her forehead, feeling faint again.

"This is ridiculous," Jeremy said in a tight voice. "This had to be the intruder who came in yesterday. But how could he have taken it all?"

Their eyes met and both knew they were thinking the same thing. Jeremy whispered, "Unless he came again. Last night."

"I need to check if the cameras were working," Jeremy said, running a hand over his balding scalp. "How could he even dare to—"

Rebecca interrupted him. "We don't know yet. He could have taken it all yesterday."

Jeremy frowned at her. "Maybe there was more than one person? That makes sense. Two people could take all my uncle's stuff and Reggie too."

His voice broke as his eyes closed and his head hung down. He leaned against the wall. Rebecca reached out and touched his shoulder. The tears threatened again, and she was so tired of them. She was tired of crying, of wishing she were dead, not her baby boy. Before she could say anything, a voice floated up from downstairs.

"Missus! Missus!"

It was Edna, and her tone was raised, urgent. Rebecca spun around and grabbed the banisters. Edna was coming up the staircase rapidly. She stopped when she caught Rebecca's eyes, and pointed in the direction of the road. "There's vans outside, parked opposite. People with cameras. I think they're reporters."

Anxiety lurched inside Rebecca's stomach. She rushed to one of the upper-floor windows facing the street. She counted five vans, two of them with satellite dishes on top. Three photographers were setting up tripods on the road, with telephoto and zoom lenses focused on the house. Jeremy swore loudly and smacked one fist into another.

"That's all we need! I'm calling the police right now." He stormed off towards his study. Rebecca glanced at Edna, who had come upstairs and was standing on the landing.

Edna met her searching gaze with candour. "It wasn't me, missus. You can check my phone, and my emails. I've always been loyal to you."

Rebecca held her eyes for a few seconds longer, then nodded. In her own mind, she knew who had leaked the news to the media. It was Rhys. He had returned, and was hell-bent on destroying her entire life. Now she knew he wouldn't stop. *She had to stop him.*

Her jaws flexed as a new anger gathered strength inside her. Had Rhys taken Reggie? How dare he? She would show the bastard. . . .

"Get your car ready. I will hide in the back, while you drive. Don't drive too fast; otherwise, they won't be able to see your face. Do you understand?"

"Yes, missus, I do."

"I'll meet you in the garage."

As Edna hurried downstairs, Rebecca got ready. She knew where Rhys lived. Or rather, where he used to live. He boasted of having more than one property in London, left to him as part of his inheritance. She would start with his three-bedroom house in Brixton, where she had stayed on occasion. As she got dressed, her hands shook uncontrollably. Not for fear. She wasn't afraid anymore. But she had to confront him, and asked the devil why he had killed her son. If she died in the process, she didn't care.

Rebecca went downstairs and opened the garage door. Her own Range Rover hadn't moved for the last couple of days. From the dashboard she took her torch. From the trunk she extracted a small shovel kept for snow and also a screwdriver from the wheel well. Edna came in, nodded to her, and raised the boot of the Ford Mondeo. Rebecca got inside. It was large enough to fit her comfortably as she pulled her knees to her face, then nodded at

Edna. The housekeeper slammed the boot shut, then fired up the engine.

As the car pulled out on the road, Rebecca heard the muffled shouts from the reporters. She knew that Edna would follow her instructions. She heard the cameras clicking, and hoped the paparazzi were taking photos of the back seat as well. *Nothing to see here, you vultures.*

As the car gathered speed, she breathed in relief. After driving for a few blocks, Edna pulled into a side road and parked. She opened the boot and helped Rebecca out. She looked around, making sure she wasn't followed.

"Go back home," Rebecca instructed Edna. "Not immediately. Take a detour. I'll be back in an hour or two, not more than that." She breathed out, and focused on Edna. "If I'm not back in three hours, call the police."

The elderly woman swallowed hard, concern creasing the corners of her eyes. "Where are you going? Is it safe?"

"Don't worry about me. I think it's safe, but I won't know till I get there."

Rebecca put the small shovel, torchlight and torchlight into her shoulder handbag. She waved goodbye to Miss Mildred, who stood watching her as Rebecca walked to the bus station across the road.

CHAPTER 35

Rebecca was dressed in a waist-length black coat which had a large hood. She had large dark glasses over her eyes and wore gloves on her hands. She wore sensible flats and clutched the shoulder strap of her handbag tightly as she walked.

Brixton hadn't changed a great deal, she thought as she walked. The Victorian-era terraced buildings were charming enough, but the entire area had a grey and weary look, accentuated by the overflowing rubbish bins, unemployed youth lounging on street corners, and police cars patrolling the streets in watchful circles.

She dodged a dump truck and a group of men standing outside a barbershop. She avoided eye contact, knowing they were checking her out. Her feet moved swiftly, till she came upon the street she wanted. She stopped at the corner and swept her eyes up and down. If memory served her correctly, it was a mid-terrace house. The number was thirty-one and it had a green door.

She walked past a couple of boarded-up windows and a car with its windows smashed in. She kept moving till she came to number thirty-one. To her surprise, the door was ajar and the curtains were open. It was late afternoon, and lights were coming on in the surrounding houses. But number thirty-one remained dark. She walked to the end of the street, then did a loop.

Tendrils of cold breath rose in front of her eyes, shaped like question marks. Her lungs moved rapidly, heart cannon-balling against the ribs. She took her gloved hands out of her pockets and held them rigidly by her side. She could do this.

She had to do this.

Rebecca opened the rusty gate that was leaning to one side. It creaked noisily as she went in. The tiny front yard, no more than ten by fifteen feet, was overgrown with weeds. She remembered coming here. They had shared nights of passion in the bedroom upstairs. It was all dusty, distant memory now, replaced by this derelict, desolate reality. With a shaking hand she nudged the door. It opened wider without a sound. She stood for a while, prepared for someone or something to come barrelling out. Nothing happened. She heard no noise from inside. She swallowed hard, then stepped through the doorway.

The smell of damp and rotting wood hit her nostrils. The carpet was threadbare, and the floorboards creaked beneath her feet.

Wallpaper peeled off the walls, showing thin plaster that had crumbled in places. To her left the staircase rose up, getting lost in darkness.

The radiator on the wall to her right was stone cold. The silence was absolute, as was the freezing cold. Her teeth chattered. Fear drummed inside her heart, but she had come too far to walk away now. It was obvious this place was uninhabited. No one had lived here for years. There was no furniture in the living room, the shelves barren, the carpet stained and torn up in places. The dining room behind was the same, and from the kitchen next to it came the acrid stench of either rotting food or a dead rodent.

Rebecca stepped back, nausea curdling in her guts.

She took out her torch and shone it up the stairs. The hallway upstairs was deserted, as expected.

She raised her voice. "Rhys? Rhys Mason? Are you there?"

Nothing but silence greeted her words. She called out again, but there was no answer. She climbed the stairs slowly, shining her torch around. In the other hand she held the spade.

She was braced for a figure to appear out from one of the rooms. But nothing happened. She got to the landing and flicked on a light switch. It didn't work. There were three rooms in front of her, and a bathroom. All the doors were open and when she shone the torchlight inside, she saw nothing but old carpets and dirty walls. The furniture was gone. She turned the beam to the ceiling, and saw the square opening for the loft space. It was shut, and she had no intention of going up there.

"Let's get this over and done with," she whispered to herself. She crept forward and entered the first, and largest bedroom. If memory served her, this was the room where she and Rhys had. . . . She banished the memory from her mind with a shake of her head.

Like the other rooms, there was no furniture here. She shone the beam around the corners and stopped at the far left. The carpet had been lifted in the corner and wasn't properly nailed down. She went over to it and crouched. She looked over her shoulder once to make sure she was alone. Then she put the torch down and grabbed the corner of the carpet with both gloved hands. It came up easily, revealing a piece of floorboard that had been sawn off.

She lifted the torchlight and flashed it inside.

Her mouth opened in shock as she realised what she was looking at.

Her fingers loosened, and the torch almost fell into the hole. The humming was louder in her brain again, bombarding the inside of her skull like a manic drilling machine. She shrank back, almost falling. She leaned against the wall, waiting till her breathing quietened. Then she looked inside the hole again.

She reached inside and pulled out a blue cloth. She knew this cloth very well. It had 'Reginald Stone' embroidered in golden letters in the bottom-right corner. She put the cloth to one side and looked down the hole again. She found a pair of man-sized trekking boots. With a shaking hand, she pulled the boots out. The jagged edges of the cut floorboard got in the way, and she dropped them once. She had to pull them out one by one. Then she leaned against the wall, gasping. The torch beam flickered on the two items, lying side by side on the carpet.

The blue cloth that had covered Reggie when he disappeared.

A pair of boots with dry, caked mud all over them.

CHAPTER 36

Light was fading from the December sky, a slow suffocation as the grip of dark clouds tightened over the dead, one-eyed gaze of a useless sun. The heavily pregnant woman had ventured out into her garden as she heard a noise. *Must be the foxes again*, she thought.

Martha looked out from the glass panel of the back door, towards the garden fence. Like most Londoners, she lived in the latticed framework of terraced houses that crisscrossed the city.

Behind her back garden fence laid the railway lines. There was also a path that ran alongside the lines. Often foxes came into her back garden, and she had to shoo them away. Her eyebrows creased as she looked around her small, twenty-by-thirty-feet back lawn.

The grass was hoary with frost, which was starting to melt. She couldn't see the fox, but was sure she'd heard something. Martha was thirty-seven weeks pregnant, and as she got heavier, movements were increasingly laborious. She held the base of her baby bump and wished he would arrive quickly. Yes, it was a boy;

the scan had verified that. A tiny expectant smile hovered on her lips as she took the kettle off the boil.

She had her antenatal classes this morning, but just didn't feel up to walking to the bus stop and taking a ride to their community centre. Her friend, Kylie Denham, had asked her last night if she was going, and she had replied yes at the time. But this morning she felt slower and heavier than usual. A few Braxton Hicks contractions had also occurred, which her midwife had said was normal at this stage.

Her husband left for work early in the morning, and bless Tony, he had offered to start late so he could give her a lift to the antenatal class. She had refused, because even the midwife acknowledged that at this late stage, rest was more important. She had to stay active, however, because blood clots in the leg veins could easily occur at this point of the pregnancy if she didn't keep her legs moving.

Martha heard the sound again, and this time it was a knocking sound against the wooden steps that went down into the garden. Pesky fox.

She picked up the broomstick that lay in a corner, meaning to rattle it against the stairs to give the fox a scare. The animal was probably sniffing around below the patio. She opened the back door and stepped out onto the small patio that led to the three stairs that descended into the garden. She banged the broomstick, hoping that would get the fox out from underneath.

She tried to look through the cracks, but it was dark under there. Martha advanced towards the stairs, wondering where the fox was. She heard the sound again and, a split second later, from the corner of her eye, the blurred image of a black shape came into view. It was a man, and he was upon her so quickly she didn't have time to breathe. Before she knew it, he had clamped his hand over her mouth and was pushing her back towards the open door. Fear bulged inside her in a crimson wave and her eyes widened with shock. The man was dressed from head to toe in black running gear. His face was covered in a ski mask and the dark glasses over his eyes gave him a ghostly, demonic appearance.

She screamed but the hand was clamped tightly over her mouth. The man marched her back to the door, then shoved her inside. Martha landed on her back. A shattering spasm of pain ripped across her abdomen, making her cry out in agony. The door slammed shut.

Wave after wave of pain engulfed her, and she could barely see. Bile rose in her stomach and trickle down the side of her mouth. She opened her eyes in fear. The man was still there, and he was crouching next to her. His hands were covered in dark plastic gloves. In his right hand he held a kitchen knife, its gleaming tip shining brightly.

"Now," the figure said, in a surprisingly light, almost sing-song voice, "give me your baby."

*****

Kylie Denham had driven to Martha Smith's house to check on her. Kylie didn't attend the antenatal class either, but had come to see Martha instead. She was worried about her friend, who wasn't responding to phone calls or text messages.

That was unlike her. Martha was normally a chatterbox, only too glad to speak to her. Kylie knew Martha stayed alone at home while her husband went to work. They had gotten to know each other quite well over the last seven months. Apart from Arla Baker, Martha was the best friend Kylie had made through the class. Arla hadn't replied to her text either, but she knew Arla was busy with work.

She called Martha and again there was no response. The landline rang till it went to the answer phone. Kylie got out of the car. She heard the rattle of the railway lines behind the row of houses. To her surprise, the front door was ajar. She pushed it and the door fell open. Across the narrow hallway she could see the kitchen, with the windows and back door looking out to the garden. The house was silent, but soon she heard a sound. It was a grunting, moaning sound, as if someone was in pain. It made Kylie shiver, and the hairs on the back of her neck stood to attention.

277

"Martha?" she called out. She got no response, but the grunting sound came again. It was coming from the kitchen, and Kylie trembled as she felt her heart rate go through the roof.

She stepped closer to the kitchen, noting the moaning sound was getting louder. Then she saw the feet on the ground. Then the pool of blood spreading around Martha, who lay on the floor. Kylie's eyes opened wide in shock as she stumbled backwards.

She couldn't breathe. Her eyes couldn't comprehend what she was seeing. There was enough blood to fill an entire bathtub. The kitchen floor was soaked in blood, and all of it came from Martha's abdomen. It had been hacked open and the abdominal cavity was a mangled mess of blood and tissue. There was a hole where the large uterus had been, and the baby was missing. The placenta lay collapsed, like a ruptured balloon, and an artery still pulsed out blood from within. Martha lay with her eyes closed, her face white as a sheet.

Kylie scrambled backwards, reaching for her phone. Her fingers shook, but she managed to dial 999.

"My friend, my friend. . . . She's been stabbed to death; her baby's been stolen. Please help."

CHAPTER 37

"Bloody hell!" Arla whispered as Harry drove the car down Baskerville Avenue.

Vans lined both sides of the road, several with satellite dishes on top. In front of two vans, journalists were reporting, with a camera and soundman in front of them. Several reporters leaned against their vans, smoking. An electric spark seemed to touch them as soon as they saw the black BMW. They straightened, getting cameras ready.

Harry parked the car on the road, as the drive was already full. Rebecca's Range Rover was outside, as was another Audi SUV that Arla hadn't seen before. She glared out of the window at the reporters who now stood outside the car. Harry opened her door, then reached out a long arm and pushed away the microphones that were thrust in Arla's direction.

"Are you Detective Inspector Arla Baker?"

"Inspector Baker, do you suspect anyone in the family?"

Arla's jaw muscles bunched tight as she tried to hide her shock and disbelief. How on earth did they know her name? She didn't know exactly what the media knew, and the media liaison officer, with whom she'd had a meeting before she left, wasn't any wiser.

Arla had reassured Johnson that it wasn't any of her team, and she doubted that on such a high-profile case it would be any other policeman. Reporters never revealed their sources, but if a copper was a snitch, word got out eventually. Even Justin Beauregard wouldn't dare leak anything on a case like this.

Which meant the person who had informed the media also knew who she was. That left a bitter taste at the back of her tongue. An unease that lay coiled, like a dormant serpent with sharp fangs. She couldn't shake the nagging suspicion that the same person was behind this chain of events. Alerting the media was the best way to pile pressure on the Stone family.

Now the perp was dragging her into it as well, and she couldn't help wondering if their paths had ever crossed.

The reporters clamoured for her attention, snapping photographs and firing questions. Harry shielded her with his broad back and arms outstretched like a giant condor, and she turned and walked towards the house. The front gate was unlocked, as the family had been informed that Arla was on her way. The media had to stop there as well, but they became even more voluminous.

"Detective Baker, when will you make an announcement?"

"Is Rebecca Stone a suspect? What about the husband?"

"Is Grant Stone inside?"

The iron gates shut, but the media vultures kept taking photos through the grills of the gate. Finally, they withdrew as Arla and Harry entered the house. Jeremy Stone opened the door for them, then slammed it shut. He stood there with arms folded on his chest, feet spread wide. His eyes were blazing and open hostility was carved into every line of his face.

"Well?" he fumed. "After all your assurances, one of your staff did leak the news, didn't they? This is all your fault, Inspector Baker. We trusted you and look what's happened."

Anger ignited inside Arla, a red heat that made her clench her teeth.

"None of my staff or any other policeman leaked this news. You would do well to remember that it was one of my detective sergeants who found Reggie's body." She leaned forward and jabbed a finger at Jeremy's chest, raising her voice.

"Right from the beginning, I've been bending over backwards trying to help you. We've given you every privilege in the book, acting like your private security force. Who do you think you are? I don't give a damn who your uncle knows; if you want me to help you, then you have to listen to my advice!"

"Arla," Harry whispered urgently in her ear, restraining her by the shoulder. Arla shook his hand off and ignored him.

"I understand this is stressful for you, Mr Stone. But your assumption that the police are somehow to blame for this is completely off the mark. If you don't want us to help you, I am more than happy to walk out of here, right now."

Jeremy's chest heaved as his eyes flicked from Arla to Harry. A sheen of sweat had appeared on his balding frontal scalp and he wiped it with his sleeve. "I'm sorry. I just don't understand who could have done this."

"Have you considered it could be the same person behind everything?"

Jeremy frowned. "But why would they inform the media? Doesn't that put *them* into the spotlight?"

"Yes, it does. But in my experience, individuals like them crave the limelight. They want the world to know what they're doing. It gives them a sense of empowerment."

Jeremy's mouth fell open. He struggled for words. Harry said, "Why don't we sit down and discuss this. Is your wife at home?"

Jeremy nodded. "I think so, but I don't know exactly where she is."

Arla said, "Sitting down would be a good idea."

Jeremy went to call Edna, while Arla and Harry sat down in the living room. Harry whispered, "You can't lose your rag like that. Not good for you in this state."

Arla hiked her eyebrows. "What state do you mean? I'm still capable of doing my job, Harry."

He raised both hands. "I know that. But you know what I mean. You always get into trouble when you don't control your temper."

Arla frowned. He was right, of course, but with him, she could speak her mind. "He accused me, and my staff, of leaking the news. What did you want me to do, shake his hand?"

Harry lowered his eyebrows, stared at her intently for a while, then shook his head. He rose and went to the large bay window; the curtains were now drawn. Arla watched him for a few seconds as he took a peek outside from one end of the curtains.

"Okay, I know what you mean."

Harry turned and shrugged his wide shoulders. "It's for your benefit."

That made her smile. She was carrying his baby, after all.

The door opened and Jeremy walked back in, followed by Edna. She carried a tray with a teapot and cups. She proceeded to pour tea into the cups, and Arla took the opportunity to question her.

"Miss Mildred, you were the first person to notice that the media vans had arrived. Is that correct?" Arla had already spoken to Jeremy on the phone, and was aware of the details.

Vapour from the hot tea rose up in fragrant tendrils, masking the elderly lady's wizened face. Her sharp blue eyes became fixed on Arla's. She straightened and spoke in a clear voice.

"Yes, I did. They looked like paparazzi."

"When did you first see them appear?"

"I can't be sure of the time, but I know it was after ten o'clock in the morning."

"And you notified your mistress straightaway?"

Edna Mildred's gaze seemed to bore deep inside Arla's skull. Not a muscle moved on her face. "Yes, of course I did."

"And you haven't seen these vans there before?"

"No."

"Has any reporter ever approached you? For example, in the supermarket when you are out on your errands?"

The elderly lady blinked once and her jaw hardened. "Detective Baker, if you are accusing me of being the leak, you are wasting your time. I know that people who service households like this are targeted by reporters for inside information. I can assure you, even if I was approached by a journalist, I would ignore them. This is my livelihood, and believe it or not, I have bills to pay."

Arla didn't break contact with her eyes. She smiled slightly. "Thank you. May I inquire what sort of bills you are responsible for?"

Edna fluttered her eyelids, and a shadow seemed to pass over her face. Arla waited patiently.

"I have an apartment in Birmingham, where I used to live. It's empty at the moment and I have to pay the household bills, or the electricity and water can be cut off."

"So, there's no one living there at the moment?"

"No."

"May I ask why you came to work in London, if you are from Birmingham?"

Edna drew her breath in sharply, and splashes of colour appeared on her neck and cheeks. Arla noted this with interest. She prodded gently. "I would remind you, Miss Mildred, this is a police investigation, and you are required to tell us the truth."

"I have nothing to hide," Edna said briskly. "I have been living in London for several years now, only because it's easier to find employment here. I can give you the addresses of where I have lived. I have worked as a housekeeper in several notable families. If you ask Mr Stone, you will find my references are impressive."

"Very good. Could I please have the address of your property in Birmingham?"

Arla wrote down the address. When she looked back up at Edna, the elderly woman was studying her carefully. Her sharp eyes had dulled, and her shoulders relaxed from the rigid posture earlier. Arla's eyes roamed over her features, noting the hands tightly gripping the chair she was standing next to.

"Thank you, Miss Mildred. That will be all."

They sipped their tea in silence for a few seconds. Then the door opened again and both Jeremy and Rebecca walked in. They took seats opposite Arla, while Harry took his usual position, standing behind her.

"I'm sorry about the mess outside," Arla said. "But I've already explained to your husband, it wasn't our fault. In fact, I strongly suspect the person who abducted your baby is behind everything."

Rebecca's eyebrows creased on her paper-smooth forehead. But she didn't speak. Arla asked, "Miss Stone, I want you to think carefully. Did you know someone whose first name is Rhys?"

The knot of muscles on Rebecca's forehead cleared slowly. Her jaws relaxed as she opened her mouth to speak, then thought better of it.

Jeremy reached out and touched her arm. "What is it?"

Arla observed intently, making sure her expression remained neutral. In the heavy silence, the only sound was Rebecca's rapid, shallow breathing. Then, without a word, she rose and left the room. Jeremy looked at Arla and Harry in bewilderment.

"I'll get her back. By the way, she used to have a boyfriend called Rhys Mason. She told me that once. He was an aspiring actor, but I don't know anything else about him." He raised his hands, then left the room.

It was Rebecca who returned first. She carried a backpack. In silence, she crouched on the floor and took out its contents. A blue felt blanket, and a man's pair of boots. The blanket had flecks of brown and black stains on it, and the boots were caked in mud. Arla stared at the items, a riot of thoughts surging in her brain. Jeremy walked in, and watched in silence.

Rebecca was the first to speak. "Rhys Mason was my boyfriend. He was abusive and controlling; that's why I broke up with him. Yesterday, I went to his old house in Brixton. It was deserted. I found these things hidden underneath the floorboards in his bedroom."

She pointed to the blue cloth. Her voice broke and a solitary tear trickled down her left cheek. She made no attempt to wipe it. "This is Reggie's blanket, the one I wrapped him with the day he vanished. I don't know whose boots these are. But I'm wondering why they were hidden with Reggie's cloth, in Rhys's house."

CHAPTER 38

Arla couldn't take her eyes off the two items on the floor, especially the boots. She remembered the size of the footprints in the Common where baby Reggie was found. Harry bent forward to take a closer look, and when their eyes met, she saw a glint of excitement flashing in his chestnut eyes.

Arla stared at Rebecca. "What made you go back to look for Rhys Mason?"

Rebecca didn't reply for a few seconds. Then she took out her phone, pressed a few buttons, and handed it to Arla. The countdown GIF played on the screen, followed by the song. An electric bolt of clarity jolted through Arla's mind. *The Final Countdown. The name of the Instagram account that bullied Rebecca.*

"I saw him," Rebecca whispered, staring into nothingness. "He followed me."

Arla frowned. "When? And why didn't you tell us?"

"On my way to the doctor's. I couldn't be sure it was him. But then I realised. The man I saw opposite my house was also him."

Harry leaned closer. "Do you have any photos of Rhys?"

Rebecca swivelled her eyes to him. "I deleted all my files with him. But I might have an old photo album. I'm not sure. I need to search."

Arla nodded slowly, handing the phone to Harry, who wanted a closer look.

"The Final Countdown is the Instagram account that has been harassing you."

"So you know." Rebecca voice was as dry as the rustle of winter leaves stirred by a breeze.

"No." Arla shook her head. "We didn't know his identity. You forgot to delete some of the Instagram comments from your followers who congratulated you on your new relationship with Rhys."

Rebecca narrowed her eyes, trying to remember. She glanced at Harry, who was still looking at the GIF. Arla continued. "We believed you deleted all the photos of Rhys from your account. We only had his first name, nothing else. Now we know who he is."

"I can show you the emails he has sent me, and the paper posts as well. His bullying never stopped, even after we broke up. He stopped turning up at my place and following me around when I threatened him with a restraining order. But he targeted me on social media."

Harry said, "We suspect three accounts on social media that could be his. All of them have been harassing you for the last two years."

Rebecca nodded. "When I became engaged to Jeremy, he went through the roof."

Harry handed Rebecca her phone back and she scrolled through her messages.

"These emails are from him. I blocked his address and his phone number, but I saved the messages in case something happened."

Her head sank down on her chest and she covered her face with both hands. Sobs shook her body. Jeremy pulled her into a hug.

Rebecca dabbed at her eyes and nose with a tissue Jeremy gave her. "Not in a million years did I think he would become this vicious. What did I do to him?" She spread her hands and her voice became high-pitched, almost a wail. "It's like he wants revenge."

Arla spoke quietly. "He has dangerous obsessional character traits. From what I know now, we need to discuss this with our forensic behaviour analyst. But from past experience, I can tell you people like him are very focused and determined. They have a goal, and their whole life depends on fulfilling that."

Jeremy asked, "Do you think he really. . . . I mean, could he. . . ?" Words faded from his lips as his eyes fell on the blue cloth and the boots.

Arla nodded. "There has to be a very good reason why these items were present in his house." She turned her attention to Rebecca. "It was remarkably brave of you to go there. Weren't you afraid?"

Rebecca sniffed and dabbed at the corners of her eyes. Hair was plastered across her forehead and fell in unwashed clumps around her face, but she seemed past caring about her appearance. "Someone just killed my baby." A piercing agony contorted her face and fresh tears budded in her eyes. She placed a hand over her chest.

"And when I got that message this morning, it made me think of all the stuff he's written during my pregnancy. I had to know if it was him." She paused for a few seconds, breathing heavily. Her eyes moved from Arla's bump to her face.

"What would you have done if you were me?"

Arla considered her for a while. From the beginning, she had known there was an inner core of strength in Rebecca. What she now could feel was a palpable fire of anger, burning inside her soul, consuming her.

"I would've called the police, Rebecca. I wouldn't have taken a risk like this."

A sad frown flitted across Rebecca's face as she shook her head and leaned against the chair next to her. "How do you know, Detective Baker? After Reggie's death, I barely feel alive myself. I have no fear of death. I could be dead tomorrow—" Her eyes closed and she sighed deeply. "—and I would be grateful for it. Life has no purpose for me anymore."

Emotion strangled Arla's throat as she stared at the stricken woman. She blinked away tears as she watched Jeremy removed his glasses and wipe red-rimmed eyes. Then he shuffled closer and put a hand on his wife's shoulder, squeezing it gently. As Arla stared at the grieving couple, from deep within her soul a firm conviction began taking hold. Rhys Mason had done enough harm. It was time for him to pay.

"So, you went there yesterday?" Arla asked Rebecca. She nodded.

"Have you left the house since then?"

"Yes," Rebecca said. "I went this morning to see the doctor. I had a blood test. My iron levels are still low, and I'm on tablets for that."

Arla wrote all of this down in her black notebook, including the address of Rhys Mason's Brixton house. Then she snapped the book shut and rose. "We need to get all the data pertaining to Rhys from your phone. And these items." She pointed to the floor.

Harry lifted the blue cloth and boots with gloved hands and put them into three separate specimen bags.

"Don't worry, we'll catch him," Arla said.

Rebecca shook her head, staring at the ground. "It won't be easy. He used to boast of having more than one identity and multiple addresses. He used to be a child actor, and had a trust fund. Money isn't an object for him. He has the means to hide away for long periods of time."

Arla opened her mouth to speak, but both her and Harry's phone rang at the same time. Harry was the first to pick up. As he listened, he frowned and his shoulders stiffened. Arla had a horrible premonition as she stared at him. Harry locked eyes with her as he slowly removed the phone from his ear.

"A pregnant woman has been killed. The foetus was cut out from her abdomen. A woman called Kylie Denham called it in. She said she knows you."

CHAPTER 39

Rhys never told anyone.

He couldn't, because as a child he never understood what Grant Stone was doing to him. When he became an adult and started having sexual relationships with women, he still couldn't make sense of it. He was thirteen years old when Grant last laid his hands on him. He had hit puberty. He remembered Grant saying how they would be separated soon. He mentioned this with an air of sadness and clutched Rhys tight to his chest.

By then, through Grant's contacts, Rhys had landed several movie contracts. He excelled as a child actor, singing and dancing in his movie roles. He also appeared in West End shows, and received glowing reviews from critics. His career in show business was beginning. But with Grant his relationship was increasingly strained. Over the three years he had known the rock star, Rhys had felt Grant's attention wane as he had grown older. Rhys was getting tall, and for some reason, that seemed to put Grant off.

Rhys stared out the left window, over the endless chimney stacks that stretched to the horizon like punctuation marks, brief aphorisms in the bitter confusion of his life. It was a cold, sunny day and the scimitar rays of light slashed through the meagre defences his mind erected, laying bare the tyrannical memories. They exposed what he had become: a twisted and tormented soul, capable of violence he couldn't comprehend himself.

The first time a woman had touched him down there, he was embarrassed by his erection. He was almost seventeen, and she was two years older than him, and more experienced. He was embarrassed because that was how he had felt when Grant touched him, or took his erection in his mouth. Rhys moved away from the girl and left the room, leaving her perplexed and hurt.

He learned to avoid women after that, but it left him lonely, as he had no sexual interest in men. For a long time, he lived in this murky twilight that Grant had stranded him in, where he was embarrassed by what should be normal. He knew that now, and as he watched the sunlight wink off windows and vaporise the hazy white, serrated clouds in the blue sky, his soul twisted and burned inside.

He wanted to hate Grant for what he did, but the truth was, he felt ambivalent. He knew Grant had destroyed him and he wished he felt the sort of violent anger Grant deserved. The kind of violence Rhys now inflicted on others.

But no, instead, Rhys had been left with a hatred of children. Not every child deserved to be alive. Not every life was worth living. He had written page after page on forced sterilisation camps for women who came from broken families. Sometimes, the kindest thing was not to bring a life into this world, a life that would end up like his, a scarred, scorched destiny.

His lips lifted in a snarl. He thought of the adulation he'd received as a child actor. He was in every Sunday newspaper. When he realised how shallow and vacuous that life was, he had slowly shunned his TV and stage obligations, till he barely had a job anymore. Despite all the money he earned, Rhys despised the media and show business in general. He strongly believed he wasn't the only abused child in the industry.

Just like him, there were many who bore their burden in silence. Just like him, they didn't know how to make sense of it, or who to speak to.

Maybe he should've sought help earlier, but it was too late now. Too late to turn the tide that had borne him down this river of blood, consumed his senses, made him who he was now.

And Rebecca?

He shook his head. Despite his emotional closeness to her, she strengthened his belief in the inherent coldness of human nature. People were cruel. Only the fittest survived, and they did so by killing others. Rebecca had killed the last crumbs of love that were alive in him. After her, he vowed he would never try to gain the trust, or love, of another human being again.

Instead, he would make sure that certain human beings never lived to see the light of day.

Rhys looked at the three envelopes on the table, addressed to three individuals. These envelopes contained his manifesto. Rhys had written down how to detect a child sexual abuser like Grant. In his opinion, any famous person with access to children was a predator unless proven otherwise. Why? Because, like him, the children didn't have a voice. They could never say anything. Even if they did, no one would believe them.

He felt a knife plunge deep into his chest, and misery darkened his mind, blotting out the sunlight. He, too, had wanted to speak to someone. He'd wanted to tell his mother. But she was so gloriously happy at the complete transformation of their lives, she wouldn't have listened even if Rhys had found the courage to tell her.

Rhys walked to the wardrobe in the corner, next to the bed. He opened the door and knelt, carefully pulling out a black briefcase. He snapped it open and stared at the tubular structures inside it. Both were sawn-off plumbing pipes, available at any plumbing hardware store. They were stuffed inside with the chemical that Rhys had made, and connected by wires and blasting caps to mobile phones strapped to the outside. They were close replicas of the IED he had used on Jeremy's car.

He shut the briefcase quickly when he heard footsteps outside. They walked down the stairs, not disturbing him. He listened for a while. He rented this loft room above a Pakistani butcher shop in Tooting for several months of the year. He always paid with cash and used a fake name. He wore a fake beard, and covered his short hair with a skullcap, pretending to be a Muslim for the Pakistani landlord. He was never asked any questions. Rhys had spent four months as a squaddie, as a British lance corporal was known, in the Helmand province of Afghanistan. He had picked up a few words of Urdu, and used them liberally when he spoke to his landlord.

This room was one of four places Rhys had scattered around southwest London. He also rented an apartment in Hounslow, ten minutes' drive from Heathrow. He'd paid cash for that as well, and as those parts of London were now heavily populated by Polish and other Eastern European immigrants, he had used a Polish name. Rhys was good at picking up identities. He searched the birth and death registry for children who had died at the age of one year. He applied for their birth certificates, pretending to be a relative. He used that birth certificate to get himself a passport. From there, it was easy to create a life story, and hoodwink people into believing him. He used to be an actor, after all.

Rhys smiled to himself. Using one of his identities, it had been easy to register himself with a doctor in Godalming. A doctor whose name Rhys remembered from the last time he had been to Grant Stone's house. Grant had a urine infection, and the doctor had come to do a home visit.

Rhys had sweet-talked one of the receptionists and found out Grant still attended the surgery. He was in his sixties now, and understandably, his visits to the doctor had increased.

He attended occasionally to see the nurse, in the winter. One day, while sitting in the waiting room with a newspaper in front of his face, Rhys saw him. Grant looked surprisingly good for his age. His skin looked fresh and young, probably the result of a facelift. He had a full head of hair and looked at least a decade younger than the sixty-five years he was.

Rhys remembered how Grant never got his face tanned while he was on holidays. Getting tanned from the neck down was fine, but sunlight on the face made a person look older. The memory of that casual conversation made Rhys's hands tremble as he watched Grant now.

His tormentor sat down on the other side of the waiting room and proceeded to read from a magazine. Rhys had his fake beard on and was wearing a baseball cap and glasses. He knew Grant wouldn't recognise him. Grant had to wait far less time than the other mortals in the waiting room. The moment Grant walked in and sat down, trying to look as inconspicuous as possible, the whispers began. He was still instantly recognisable.

When Grant was called in, Rhys rose and left. He was shaken, disturbed at having seen Grant again. Slowly, the conviction had grown.

Grant Stone must pay.

*****

Rhys put the three envelopes inside the black briefcase, snapped it shut, and locked it. He checked his beard and moustache in the mirror, making sure they were fixed on correctly. He put the skullcap on, which he would replace later with a baseball cap. He had a pair of glasses inside his coat pocket. He put the backpack on his shoulder and picked up the briefcase, then locked the room and went out.

CHAPTER 40

Harry switched off the BMW engine and then put a restraining hand on Arla's left arm. "I don't think you should go in there. You heard what Darren said."

Uniformed Inspector Darren Clark was in charge of the crime scene at Martha Smith's house. Arla had just switched the speakerphone off, after Darren had filled them in with the grisly details.

Arla lifted her chin and squinted at him. "Because I'm too delicate?"

Harry rolled his eyes and huffed. His large right hand became a fist, and he rubbed his knuckles on his thigh. "Damn it, Arla. You know what I mean."

Arla reached out a hand and caressed the side of Harry's smooth cheeks, feeling the hard bunch of his jaw muscles. She wanted to pull him towards her and give him a kiss, but they were on duty.

"Can I tell you something?" she said.

It was Harry's turn to squint at her, raising his eyebrows. He cleared his throat. "What?"

Arla slid her hand down his neck, massaging it lightly. Her facial expression softened as she leaned forward, smelling his dense, musky pinewood aftershave. "If you can push another body out from your own, Harry, it gives you a strength no man will ever possess."

Harry stared at her blankly for a few seconds. Then he blinked and shook his head. He lifted both palms and slapped them down on his thighs. "So stubborn." He spoke almost to himself.

"But also true," Arla said, smiling. "Don't worry about me. SOC are there already, so a lot of the goriness must be contained. That will stop you from fainting."

Harry snorted. A slow grin appeared on his face as his eyelids hooded. "A red-blooded man like me doesn't faint, sweetheart. It's actually you who fainted once when you came so hard—"

Heat fanned Arla's face and she smacked Harry on the chest. "Stop that, now!"

Harry grinned and got out of the car, then came round and opened the door. Three squad cars were parked in front of them. Blue and white tape stretched around the house and the road had been cordoned off. Darren was standing on the pavement, thumbs hooked into his chest rig, his radio squawking in his breast pocket.

"Rough in there, guv." Darren was a veteran of the London Met. He had seen his fair share of gruesome scenes. From his sunken, white cheeks and listless eyes, Arla knew Darren was shaken. He had two school-aged children, and had been first on the scene. Arla reached out and touched his shoulder.

"Thanks for securing the scene, Darren. Has Dr Banerjee arrived?"

"Yup, they're all in there."

A white tent had been set up on the road. A uniformed constable wrote down Arla and Harry's names on a sheet of paper attached to a clipboard, and they both signed.

Inside the tent, they put on shoe covers, gloves, and surgical masks. A forensics officer Arla hadn't seen before was putting on his blue Tyvek suit. When she came out of the tent, she saw the blue plastic duck boards that were laid all the way up to the front door, and then in the hallway. She could see a couple of blue-coated figures kneeling on the kitchen floor. She looked at the duck boards in distaste. She was wearing flats, but she still hated walking on them.

"Come on, hold my hand," Harry said, moving ahead of her.

Harry shielded Arla's view of the scene. She took a deep breath and shifted to one side.

The scene was a ghastly one. The entire floor was stained dark crimson with blood. Arla's lungs clenched tight, expelling air through her open mouth. Frigid numbness laid claim to her fingers and toes, and she folded her arms across her chest, forcing herself to look at the macabre scene. She had, of course, seen Martha in the antenatal classes. She had never been friends with her like she was with Kylie, but she had chatted with the woman once or twice. She had never imagined that Martha would endure this ghastly fate one day.

The woman lay on her back, her abdomen cut open in a roughly circular shape. She was naked. Banerjee was leaning over the open abdomen, partially blocking Arla's view.

She looked at the back door. It was open and a forensics officer was dusting it for prints. Another one was kneeling on the stairs just outside the door, picking up samples of evidence with pincers, storing them in specimen bags.

She leaned against the wall as Harry turned to her. "Do you want to sit down?" His voice was a low whisper. She shook her head, but wouldn't meet his eyes.

"I'm fine." She took a step inside, trying to find a spot away from the bloodstains.

"Doesn't look good, doc, does it?"

Banerjee half-turned towards her, lowering the mask that covered his face and raising his glasses. "No, it doesn't."

He wore the blue Tyvek suit and his purple-gloved hands were dark with blood. "Not seen anything like this, Arla." He shrugged. "From me, that's saying something."

Harry pulled up a chair for her, then touched her forearm. "Sit down," he said gently. Arla fluttered her eyelashes at him, then obeyed. It was a relief to sit. She wanted to kneel down and get a closer look, but her current state prevented that.

"What do you think happened?"

Banerjee pointed at the rough marks around the abdominal wound.

"Whoever did this was no surgeon. More of a butcher, in fact. He was obviously in a rush and performed this as quickly as possible." Banerjee put his hand inside the wound and lifted up a piece of clotted tissue. It was attached to the abdominal cavity. "This is the uterine artery. It inserts into the placenta and the foetus gets all its nutrition from it. This was cut off when the placenta was removed."

He pointed to the floor surrounding him. "Bits of placental tissue were scattered here." He lifted a specimen bag and squeezed the contents. Arla saw the papery thin tissue bulge out like the sides of a balloon being puffed.

"The placenta is nothing but a fluid-filled sac. He ruptured this, then took the baby out and escaped."

Arla frowned. "You can't just take a foetus out from its womb and run off, can you?"

"I'm not suggesting that. This woman was almost thirty-eight weeks, so the foetus was at full-term maturity. In other words, a live baby. He obviously had a mechanism to carry the baby in. A bag, maybe, or a heated container."

Banerjee's eyes flickered to the ground. His facial muscles were contorted as he moved his head sideways. "I'm not far off from retiring, Arla. I hoped I could see off my working days without coming across something like this."

His words caused a silence to descend, both Arla and Harry at a loss for words. It was broken by a sound at the back door, and Parmentier entered. He didn't have his customary sardonic grin. His grey eyes were flat and dull, brows lowered. He murmured a greeting, then pointed at the floor. Arla saw the boot prints, marked out by white squares.

"To my eyes, the prints seem to match the crime scene in Clapham Common." He took out his phone and flicked to the relevant photo. He showed it to Arla.

"They do look the same. And the same size. He probably has multiple pairs of the same make," Arla said, her breath quickening.

"There's traces of mud on the floor as well, but that probably came from the garden outside. We can analyse it to see if it is the same as the soil we found from the boot that Rebecca Stone gave you."

"That would be great. Please get it done as soon as possible." She handed the phone back to Parmentier and shifted her attention back to Dr Banerjee. "Time of death?"

"Recent. Rigor mortis hasn't even started in the small muscles like the eyelids and lips. I would say no more than four hours."

Parmentier said, "No fingerprints. Nothing on the body, either. She was wearing makeup, in any case only light foundation, but that can be enough to smudge fingerprints. However, the marks on the throat and face were by a gloved hand."

Arla nodded and stood. She walked outside, helped by Harry. She took a deep breath as she pulled out her phone. Wayne Johnson answered on the first ring. His voice was a low rumble, and he didn't even bother greeting Arla.

"I heard."

"We need to inform the public, sir. He can strike anywhere, anytime."

"I'm calling Media Liaison now to organise a press conference. Are you okay to lead?"

Arla faltered. This was the kind of attention that Johnson normally craved. His name, up in lights, the centre of attention. "I thought you would do it, sir?"

"No, Arla. It's best if you lead on this."

CHAPTER 41

Inside Clapham Common, Rhys had changed position. Uniformed police still guarded the crime scene and it was a shame. He had lost the vantage point directly opposite Rebecca's house. Now he was forced to see it from an angle more than two hundred yards away. He crouched on the damp, muddy ground, feeling his boots sink deeper into the soil. Through the binoculars, he saw Rebecca's Range Rover reverse out of the house.

Photo bulbs flashed from the media vans opposite and several paparazzi ran into the road. They held their cameras out, snapping photos at the dark-tinted car windows, which were fully raised. Some even crowded around the front of the car, literally throwing themselves at the fenders, taking photos of the windscreen, through which Rebecca was visible. Lips bared, Rebecca turned the wheel savagely, shaking her fist at them as she gunned down the road. The paparazzi scattered like insects, lucky not to get hurt.

Rhys left his watch point and ran out on the road. His car was parked in a side alley and he was just in time to see Rebecca's car roar down the main street. He got in and followed. He kept a safe distance as she joined the flow of traffic on the three lanes of the A3, heading out of the city.

She took the turning for Weybridge. Rhys followed till she drove onto the narrow winding road that led to her parents' farm. He reversed and went back to the A3. He joined the traffic artery again, and eventually got to the doctor's surgery in Godalming. He checked his watch as he waited in the car.

According to his timetable, Grant Stone was due this morning to see the nurse. Rhys passed the time by posting some messages on one of his fake accounts, trolling Rebecca. He drank coffee and munched on some biscuits while he waited. His patience was rewarded an hour later.

Grant's gold-coloured Porsche Carrera 911 entered the parking lot and parked opposite Rhys. He watched as Grant came out of the car, then walked inside. Rhys waited for five minutes, then came out. He had dressed for the occasion, wearing blue overalls that proclaimed him to be a mechanic from AA roadside assistance.

Rhys walked slowly across the car park, his eyes darting sideways, checking out the other vehicles. The only windows that looked out onto the car park belonged to the doctors and nurses and the curtains were always drawn, for obvious reasons.

Luckily for Rhys, the waiting room was on the other side of the building. There was CCTV, but he couldn't do anything about it. His disguise would have to suffice. He had his fake beard and moustache on and his baseball cap was pulled low over his face.

Rhys didn't rush. Movement attracted the most attention.

He knelt by the side of the Porsche and opened up the toolbox. Now, he worked with speed and precision. The sports car's twin exhausts were large. Unlike Jeremy's Rover, where he had to strap the IED to the outside of the exhaust pipe, with the Porsche, the IED slid easily inside.

Which, of course, presented a problem of its own. When the car started, it could dislodge the IED.

With Jeremy's car, he had made a mistake. The bomb had not been strapped firmly enough. It didn't ignite the fuselage as he had hoped. This time, he hoped to have better results.

With gloved fingers, Rhys smeared adhesive to the sides of the IED, then made sure the mobile phone inside it was working. He could see the flashing green light that told him all was okay. He slid the IED inside the exhaust pipe with a steel prong, pushing it in as far as he could. He turned the prong around and use the handle to push it in further. Then he used the handle to press it down firmly, making sure it was attached to the steel structure.

He pushed the IED gently after a few seconds and it would not dislodge. He looked around him. No one had come out of the surgery, or driven up as yet. Rhys pushed the IED again, and was satisfied when firmer pressure could not move the object.

*****

Christine Walton opened the door to find her daughter standing there. They embraced without a word, then Christine shut the door.

"Where's Dad?" Rebecca asked, her voice tremulous.

"He's gone to the farmers' market," Christine said. Mother and daughter went into the kitchen. Christine put the kettle on to boil and they stood in silence for a while, then stared at each other. No words were necessary. Rebecca had already told her mother how she had gone to Rhys's old house and what she discovered.

"What do you think will happen?" Rebecca asked.

The dark pupils in Christine's blue eyes constricted. Age strips away the vigour of youth from all of us, but in some it replaces that with a toughness, a sense of reality that only experience can bring.

"Well, he's going to get what he deserves," Christine said, her nostrils flaring as her back teeth clamped down tight. She handed a cup of steaming tea to Rebecca. "You must take care of yourself, darling."

They went upstairs, to Rebecca's old room, which had been converted into a nursery for Reggie. It was still inexpressibly sad to be here, Rebecca thought. The walls had been painted blue.

Roger was so overjoyed at having a grandson he had even hired an artist to paint Superman and Batman figures on the wall. Rebecca stared around the room, at the fluffy cushions on the bed and the cot next to it. She didn't want to change anything. The word 'mausoleum' was a bitter, cold, dreary word. This was where, she realised, Reggie's spirit would live on. True, Reggie had his own nursery back at her house. But the house belonged to Jeremy. The only place she had to call her own was her parents'.

Christine was observing her daughter with steady, calm eyes. "And are you okay, dear?"

"Yes, Mum. I like this room."

Something broke inside Christine's heart, a ripping that was so intense and profound it almost drove her to her knees. She had never experienced sadness like this before. It had changed her as a person, maybe more than her daughter realised. The sadness was so deep, she could only express it with a ghostly smile as tears prickled the corners of her eyes.

"I know you do, dear. So, don't worry. It will stay like this as long as you want."

They picked up a few things from the room, then went downstairs and walked over to the barn. Christine had got the farmhand to clear up Rebecca's old hideout. The carpets were hoovered, all the surfaces scrubbed and polished, and even the old bookshelves had been dusted. Rebecca went over to the bed and sat down. "This place looks great, Mum. Thank you."

Christine put down the things she was carrying and Rebecca helped her mother. They rearranged the furniture, putting the table over the small door at the back, barricading it. When they were done, Rebecca wiped a sheen of sweat from her forehead. "I think I'm going to rest here for a while, Mum. Shall I see you back in the house?"

Christine hugged her daughter and gave her a kiss. "As you wish, dear."

CHAPTER 42

Grant Stone walked slowly out of the surgery. Several people turned and pointed at him as he walked past them, whispering. It was unwanted attention and it irritated him a great deal. A doctor's appointment wasn't the place to take smiling selfies with strangers. He enjoyed doing it at social occasions, but not now.

The catheter was inserted and the contents of his bladder were emptied. The nurse had kept the catheter and given him a new bag, and he carried the paraphernalia in a backpack. It was bloody painful, he mused, when that damned tube went up his penis. Grant had a condition called gonococcal urethritis, a disease which causes a stricture, or narrowing, of the urinary passage. Grant's case was not severe, but it still caused intermittent urinary retention or blockage of urine. He knew first-hand how painful that condition could be, and it was also a medical emergency. He had been taken by ambulance twice to the nearest hospital, and the second time he had insisted on being taken by helicopter to shorten the time.

He opened the boot of his car and flung the backpack inside in disgust. It struck him as very unfortunate that despite the fame, adulation, and money he had earned throughout his life, one sexual encounter in the backstreets of Tangier, Morocco, had left him with this condition. Admittedly, he visited Tangier and also Sri Lanka frequently, as it was easier to get boys there. No one knew he was a rock star in Tangier and he could live there for weeks in total anonymity.

Grant got into the car and sighed. Well, life was what it was. He had lived it to the fullest, and he had no regrets. He could only be himself, and in that way, he was no different to any other human being.

He had needs and desires that seemed natural to him, although he knew the rest of the world wouldn't see it that way. Hence, he had learned to keep his sexual life private. Tongues wagged about him being a sixty-five-year-old playboy. He had never married, and he wasn't gay. The media thought him to be gay and he had never agreed with nor refuted that opinion. Because in his own mind, he didn't feel the need to accept a standard that society set on him. Why could he not be who he was?

It never struck Grant that the way he thought and felt was wrong. Indeed, he was narcissistic to the point where he cultivated his deviant tendencies with great care.

The world would never know who he really was. The few children he had abused in England had taught him a valuable lesson. It was hard to keep them quiet. That was why he travelled abroad frequently. In third-world countries, adults seldom had a voice, never mind children.

Grant pressed on the accelerator as he hit a country road, and was satisfied with a mighty growl from the four-point-six-litre engine. He zoomed down the road but had to slow down as a junction arrived. He stopped to let a tractor pass. He heard his phone beeping and glanced at it. A text message flashed on the screen.

"Hi. This is Rhys Mason. Remember me?"

Confusion mounted inside him as he stared at the screen. Then a light bulb clicked, flooding his mind with clarity, then drowning it with dread. Rhys Mason. How the hell. . . ?

Grant indicated left and turned in to a smaller lane, where he could pull up on the grass verge. He grabbed the phone and stared at it. Maybe he could just ignore it and it would go away. Was this a prank? If it was, then how did someone know. . . ? In fact, what did they know?

Could it be Rhys, after all these years? If it was, Grant wasn't that worried. Rhys had an enviable career, thanks to him. And if he bore a grudge and wanted to go public, Grant had his army of lawyers to come down on Rhys like an avalanche. No. Rhys wasn't going to be a problem, if this really was him.

The phone started to ring. Grant didn't recognise the number and stared at it, feeling a cold knot encircle his gut. He also heard a different sound. A buzzing, a vibration, like something rattling inside a pipe. It came from deep within the car, faint but present.

Grant frowned and lowered the phone. He turned his head backwards, listening intently, wondering if he had something in the boot. Did the nurse put her phone in his backpack by mistake? That would be highly unusual. Grant opened the door of his car.

He put a foot on the grass when a loud explosion ripped through the Porsche. The fuselage ignited and a red fireball lifted the car with savage force, hurling it several feet forward. The force of the blast cleaved the car in two, crumpling the steelwork with heat, showering glass fragments in the air. The shock waves rippled through Grant's body as well, fracturing his spine, pushing his shoulder joints out from the sockets. He ignited like the wicker man in a bonfire, flames consuming his body. He screamed in agony, but the sound was lost in the blast of the explosion.

The last thought in Grant Stone's mind, as he died, was of the boy he once knew as Rhys Mason.

CHAPTER 43

Rebecca looked around the well-lit room in the barn, a sense of comfort settling inside her.

She could be alone here, far away from the real world. The distance insulated her from the harsh blows life had dealt her. Her defences had crumbled, but one by one she would build a brick wall, enclosing her grief and solitude. Here, she would be like a plant that grows bereft of light, possessing a life of its own, its roots piercing into the velvety darkness of her soul.

Her phone rang, interrupting her thoughts. It was Christine. "Jeremy's here, darling. He wants to speak to you."

Rebecca's jaw hardened. "On his own, is he? Karen's not with him?"

Christine sighed down the line. "Becky, please. You know there's nothing going on between Jeremy and Karen."

Rebecca hung up. She had stayed the night here, and Jeremy had come to check on her. Well, she had nothing to say to him. But it would be rude not to see him. Despondently, she made her way across the field, wishing she could stay back in the barn.

Jeremy was seated in the living room, and after Rebecca entered, Christine discreetly shut the door behind her. Jeremy stood and spread his arms.

"Why didn't you answer my calls? I was worried stiff."

Rebecca shrugged, not saying anything. She stood behind an armchair, opposite Jeremy. He frowned. "Why are you giving me the silent treatment?"

Rebecca's sea green eyes were naturally luminous, but they sharpened.

"You gave me the silent treatment during the pregnancy. And after Reggie was born, you acted like you didn't want him."

Jeremy hung his head back and stared at the ceiling for a few seconds. Then he put both hands on his waist. "Come on, Becky. I never did that! I don't even know what you mean by not wanting Reggie. He was my pride and joy! And after he came, you know how busy I was with getting this new production off the ground. I was travelling all the time."

"Of course, that was so much more important. You've got your priorities all sorted out, haven't you?"

"I was there for you. Who took you to the doctor's? Who bought you medicine when the heartburn was so bad you couldn't sleep?"

Rebecca held up two fingers. "Like a broken record, Jeremy. You keep talking about those two times. What about the rest?" She huffed in frustration. "Why can't you just admit that things changed between us after I got pregnant? It's not been the same since." Her voice dropped to a whisper and she looked down at the carpet. A bubble of silence enveloped them both. When Jeremy spoke, his voice was scratchy, barely audible.

"I know what you, we, have been through." He shook his head. "But don't let that break us, Becky."

"What's left to break?" Rebecca said, not meeting his eyes. "I'm sorry, but I just feel like there wasn't much to begin with, anyway. I thought Reggie would make a difference, but I was wrong." Her eyes widened, then became glassy as she stared at him. "It made things worse," she whispered.

"What are you talking about, Becky?" Jeremy's voice was plaintive, entreating.

She didn't answer. Jeremy sat back down on the sofa, then leaned forward and cradled his head in his hands. "You're overthinking this. Maybe you need some time to . . . just rest."

Rebecca squeezed her eyes shut. The buzzing headache was back, a swarm of insects pinging against her skull. She put her hand to her forehead and pressed. Sometimes that helped, but not now.

Jeremy said, "Staying here with your parents might not be a bad idea after all. I think you need a break. Karen said the same thing."

The buzzing sharpened to a scalpel point in Rebecca's brain, slicing through the misty fog that engulfed her. Rage erupted inside her, a heatwave that flooded her body. Her spine snapped straight. "You love discussing me with my sister, don't you?" Her voice was shrill and high-pitched and Jeremy looked up, startled.

Rebecca pointed a trembling finger at him. "What else has she told you about me? That she was Miss Perfect and I had to live in her shadow? That stupid, arrogant, selfish cow!" Rebecca stepped forward, her eyes blazing, teeth grinding. "How dare you conspire against me behind my back!" She didn't care that she was screaming.

Jeremy stood, a scowl appearing on his face. "That's total bullshit, Becky, and you know it. Karen's just concerned about you, as any sister would be."

She shook her head, a smile appearing on her face, mirthless. "You don't know the first thing about Karen. The only things that matter to her are money and career."

Jeremy said, "I'm not here to discuss your relationship with Karen. I'm here to talk about us."

Rebecca stared at her husband for a few seconds, breathing heavily. Her anger faded suddenly, leaving her weak, washed out. She stumbled backwards and sat down on the sofa.

"Just go. Leave me alone." She closed her eyes, pressing the sides of her forehead as she leaned her head back on the sofa. She heard the door open and then her mother's voice. "Is everything okay?" Christine asked. She had obviously heard her shout, Rebecca realised.

"Yes," Jeremy said, his tone low and resigned. "Becky wants to stay here for a while, and I think it's a good idea. I'll be in touch." He brushed past Christine and left.

Rebecca opened her eyes when she heard the front door click shut. She rose, not meeting her mum's eyes.

"I'm going to the barn, Mum. Leave me alone for a while, please."

Rebecca walked through the frost-hardened field, over the stone slabs that had been put down as a pathway. She entered the barn and stood still for a while, listening to the silence. Her nose crinkled at an unfamiliar smell. She sniffed. It reminded her of filling her car up with petrol. Was it a diesel can that her dad had left lying around when he filled up the tractor?

She froze when she heard a sound behind her. She turned around quickly, but she wasn't quick enough. A hand closed over her mouth, and the stench of diesel and smoke was stronger. Another hand restrained her arms as she was pulled tightly against a hard body.

"Alone at last, Becky," Rhys Mason whispered. "It's been a long time."

CHAPTER 44

Arla looked over the rows of expectant faces in Major Incident Room One.

The room was packed with forensics staff, financial and cybercrime officers, and extra uniformed units who had been pulled up from the surrounding stations.

The whiteboard next to Arla had Rhys Mason's photo on it. There were also two photos below it, of Rhys when he was a child actor.

"Okay, people, so this is our man. He is upping his game, and we need to catch him before he strikes again." Arla glanced down at the notes in her hand. "He was born in Southampton; his mother was a cleaner and his dad left when he was a baby. His mother moved to London and they lived in a council flat in Battersea. From the age of nine, he started winning local talent shows. It's well-known that Grant Stone took Rhys Mason under his wing. Rhys was a talented singer and actor and Grant helped to sharpen his skills.

Through his mentor, Rhys landed several film and TV contracts. We have contacted Grant Stone, right?"

Arla glanced at Roslyn, who nodded. The detective sergeant said, "Grant Stone spends a lot of time abroad. However, he still does concerts and occasional interviews. I have contacted his press secretary and am waiting to hear back from her."

"Thank you, Roslyn," Arla said. "After Rhys left school, he gave up on his lucrative showbiz career. No one seems to know why." She frowned as she glanced at her team. "We know that Grant Stone, despite his fame, is quite media-shy. Maybe Rhys learned that from his mentor?" Arla faced the room and shrugged.

"Anyway, after quitting showbiz, Rhys joined the army, which seems quite a sudden move from his previous life, but there you go. He was in the army for two years and even completed a tour of duty in Afghanistan. But he was kicked out from the army for his views on soldiers bearing children."

Arla paused. She met the eyes of the people staring at her. "This is the first time we've heard of Rhys's thoughts on children. Quite simply, he didn't believe soldiers should have children as they serve long tours abroad, and in general, he seems to think a lot of children should not be born."

Arla picked up a battered and torn notebook. "Uniforms raided Rhys Mason's house in Brixton. We found this notebook and it expounds his philosophy." She shook her head in disbelief.

"He encourages the government to start forced sterilisation camps. He wants the population of the UK to go down by a million a year, and he says this can be achieved by less babies being born. He says it's a sign from God that fertility rates for Western women are dropping."

Behind her, Lisa muttered, "What a freak." It was loud enough to be picked up by the first few rows, who nodded in agreement.

Justin Beauregard asked, "What happened to his mother?"

"That's a good question. After Rhys left for the army, we don't hear of Cheryl Mason anymore. Maybe she changed her name, or is living under a different identity. But we have looked up and down and there's nothing in our databases."

Another hand went up; it was one of the new detective sergeants, James Conrad. "So, the evidence that Rebecca Stone collected from Rhys Mason's house proves that Rhys killed her baby?"

Arla held up a finger. "The boots are definitely his, as Mary has confirmed now. And the blue cloth definitely belongs to Reggie. Matching DNA is found from the cot in the nursery room. We are still waiting for the analysis of the mud sample from the boot to see if it matches the Common."

Arla looked pointedly at Parmentier. The veteran scene-of-crime officer cleared his throat. "I checked that. The mud on the boot has the same chemical composition as mud from the crime scene."

Arla smiled. "Then, beyond the shadow of a doubt, it puts Rhys Mason there. So, he had the opportunity. His toxic ideology provides the motive. And we all know the means he used." Arla shuddered as she thought of the plastic bag baby Reggie was found in. But now she had a textbook murder case: motive, means, and opportunity.

Another inspector asked, "What about DNA samples from Rhys Mason?"

Parmentier said, "We don't have any, unfortunately. The house in Brixton doesn't have reliable human skin samples. It's been derelict for too long."

Harry said, "He's an actor, and Rebecca mentioned how he likes his disguises. We are looking for a person who has several identities."

"E-fit images are circulating later today," Harry continued. "I've asked for his face with a beard, glasses, and also bald. We are putting posters up all around Brixton, Lambeth, and southwest London."

Sandy Burton, the senior financial crimes officer, raised a hand. "Under Rhys Mason's name, six hundred thousand pounds was stored in a NatWest bank account. Last week he took out all of the money, in four instalments, and all in cash."

Arla said, "He's looking to go off-grid for a long time. Probably even escape this country. We need to catch him before he gets away."

She asked Sandy, "What other properties does he own?"

"Last year he sold two properties. The money from the sales went into his NatWest account, but again, he took the money out."

Arla said, "How much did he make from selling those two properties?"

"Roughly two hundred thousand," Sandy said, glancing at the notes in her hand.

"He can't be carrying all that cash around with him. He's either invested it in something, or kept it hidden." She continued. "If he has more than one property, as Rebecca has indicated, it's possible he's buying them in cash. That way, he doesn't leave a trail, although land registry should have some details of his buying and selling."

Sandy said, "Not necessarily, guv. Land registry can only put down the name and details given to them. If he uses a fake name and identity, that's all we have to go with. And having been through land registry records, I can tell you there's no evidence of him having bought another property. So, if he is buying them, it must be with cash and a different name, as you say."

"What about the CCTV footage?" James asked. "Outside Martha Smith's house, I mean."

Rob stepped forward. "Roslyn and I spent the morning in the media lab. No one came in to Martha Smith's property this morning. There are railway lines behind her house, and it's possible the intruder came into her garden through the rear. The CCTV at the rear belongs to the rail company, and we've requested them as urgent."

Arla snapped her head towards him. "You mean we don't have them yet? That's ridiculous. Let me speak to them after the meeting."

Rob nodded.

Arla faced the assembled staff and continued. "I think he had a getaway car, especially if he was carrying a baby. After what he did, it's virtually impossible to step into a bus or taxi. There's a high chance a cab driver would have reported him. He wouldn't take that risk."

Harry said, "Rebecca mentioned a black Honda following her around. We checked with DVLA—Rhys Mason is the registered keeper of a car matching that description. We're looking for ANPR data on the number plates." Automatic number plate recognition was used extensively from road cameras for vehicle identification.

He continued. "Hopefully we can nail the car down later today."

Arla glanced down at the points written in her notebook. "Any news from the social media accounts? Any new posts trolling Rebecca?"

Roslyn said, "Yes, guv. A couple of hours ago, I picked up some new posts. It's the usual stuff, calling Rebecca's son the spawn of the devil who needs to be put down."

The phone started to ring. It was a hotline from the controller at the switchboard, who was instructed to call only if there was an emergency. Everyone hushed and stared at the phone. Harry broke the spell, striding over to the table and reaching out a long arm to pluck the receiver into his hand. He introduced himself, and as he listened, his lips parted in silence and the skin around his eyes relaxed.

"Send emergency units to both crime scenes. We are dispatching from here, now."

Harry put the phone down, catching Arla's eyes. He spoke to her, but faced the rest of the officers gathered as well. His tone was quiet, but the words fell like explosions in the silent room.

"Grant Stone's car has just been blown up. He was pronounced dead on scene. And—" Harry stopped and passed a hand over his face. "—Rebecca Stone has just been kidnapped from her parents' house."

CHAPTER 45

The heavy odour was sickly sweet, pungent. It made Rebecca gag. She tried to breathe, but a cloth covered her mouth. She took deep breaths through her nostrils, unable to avoid the nausea caused by the horrible cloying smell of the cloth. She recognised the scent from a college science experiment many years ago. Chloroform.

Her head was vibrating, but not from her usual headache. The right side of her face was numb, and she was lying curled up. Her whole body was shaking, and when she tried to move her hands, she realised they were tied behind her back. She couldn't see anything, but heard a dull roar, louder in the right ear.

It took her several minutes to realise she was in the trunk of a moving car. A thin line of daylight entered through a gap, but she was in almost complete darkness, bound and gagged. Even her feet were tied. She stretched her legs and immediately hit the sides. A shard of pain travelled up her legs into her spine, making the nausea worse. She felt helpless, and angry at the useless tears that budded in her eyes.

She groaned with pain as the car hit a pothole, flinging her around the confined space. She curled further into the foetal position, and strained to rub her face against her knees, trying to loosen the rag tied around her mouth.

It was hard work, and when the car lurched again, her head slammed against something hard, making her wince. She decided to lay still and conserve her strength. She tried to piece together what had happened.

When she'd left the barn, she had secured the latch, but it wasn't hard to open. She cursed herself for not fixing a lock on the barn door. She must've become unconscious and then Rhys had carried her to his car. And that was where she was now. She wondered where he was going. It was still daylight, which meant it was afternoon, about four o'clock. Soon, in an hour or two, it would be dark.

She could feel the car slowing as sounds of traffic faded. The car entered an uneven road, jarring her back and head repeatedly. She rolled around, trying to stabilise herself with the tied legs. It was a hopeless task. Luckily, it didn't last long.

Abruptly, the car came to a halt. It was very quiet all of a sudden. She couldn't hear the sound of traffic, which was unusual. Had Rhys gone farther into the countryside?

She heard the driver's door open and shut. Boots crunched on the ground and she heard them coming around to the trunk. A key turned, then sudden light washed over her as the door opened. She blinked in the light, only able to make out the shape of a man leaning over her. She could smell dust and the faint stench of diesel fumes.

The man leaned over, partially blocking out the grey daylight. She still couldn't see properly, but heard the familiar voice. "Are you okay, Becky?"

The solicitous tone made her shiver. Rhys sounded concerned, apologetic even, and it reminded her of the times when he was violent with her, then begged her for forgiveness.

She felt his fingers against her face, pulling the rag free. She breathed in deeply, gulping the welcome, fresh air. He moved to her feet and loosened the ties there. But he didn't free her hands.

"I'm going to make you stand up, Becky. Don't worry, I won't let you fall. Please don't shout. There's no one here. Screaming will only make things worse for you, as I'll put the gag back on."

A strong arm encircled her shoulders, and another pulled her legs out till they dangled outside. Rhys made her lean against the car, his arm around her back. She didn't want to look at him.

They were in a disused yard, old rusty machinery in one corner and a building that looked like a warehouse opposite them. There

337

was a long drive and she couldn't see the end of it. The dirt road was uneven, and she could see the fresh, muddy tyre marks where Rhys had driven up on it. On either side, she could see similar warehouses, an industrial wasteland.

She stood and Rhys kept the arm on her back for a few seconds. She shrugged it off, then looked at him for the first time. He had a white parka on, the hood lined with fur. He was wearing a baseball cap, jeans, and trainers. His eyes ran over her warily, and he stood taut and ready, as if he anticipated her making a run for it.

"There's nowhere to go, as you can see," he said in a calm voice. "If you run, I'm going to find you and then lock you up here." He pointed to the car boot.

He had a three-day stubble on his cheeks, and he was still good-looking. His large brown eyes observed her intently, his thin nose tapering down to full, pink lips.

She looked away quickly, her body shuddering at the conflicted memories that rose up inside her in a tidal wave. It felt bizarre, like she was in a dream from which there was no escape. It was cold, too, and she gripped herself tightly, feeling goose bumps spread down her arms. When she turned to look at him again, his eyes were still locked onto her, calm and deadly.

"Why are you doing this, Rhys?" Her voice broke and she blinked furiously, stopping the prickle of tears. "You took my baby, and now. . . ." Her throat closed, silencing her words.

Rhys raised his eyebrows and shook his head as a smirk appeared on his lips. He grabbed her arm above the elbow in a claw-like grip and marched her towards the warehouse. She stumbled along, knowing it was useless to fight. He was big, and stronger than he used to be. She was tall herself, but would never beat him in a fight.

They went round to the back of the warehouse, and Rhys opened a rusty door and went inside. He flicked a switch on, and to her surprise, white halogen lights flickered to life overhead. The warehouse floor was large enough to park several trucks inside. There were two rooms at the far end, each with a door opening out onto the open floor.

The interior had been cleaned, Rebecca noticed. There were no weeds here, no smell of animal urine like outside. Rhys marched her towards the rooms at the rear and flung open one of the doors. It was an office space, with an old, dust-covered desk, threadbare carpet, and a chair with one leg missing.

He shoved her down in one corner and then squatted in front of her. His lips curled upward as he breathed heavily. A scowl appeared on his face.

"Why, Becky? Why did you leave me? It didn't have to come to this."

She stared at him. He took the cap off his head and ran a hand through his flattened, wavy dark hair. An unwelcome memory seeped into her mind—how she'd rubbed his scalp and how much he enjoyed it. She swallowed hard and snapped her eyes shut. She wished he would just go away, but clearly, he wanted her attention.

Which wasn't a bad thing. She needed to keep him talking, to buy time. She needed to find out where she was. He was obsessed with her, and that was her only weapon at the moment. Her jaws relaxed as she opened her eyes and stared at him like she used to. With an effort, a light smile played on her lips.

"I didn't want to leave you, Rhys. What we had together was good; it could have lasted forever."

His eyes narrowed, as if he didn't want to believe her. His breathing quickened and she saw his hands clench into fists. Good, she was getting under his skin. She drove home her advantage. Leaning forward slightly, she dropped her voice to a husky whisper. "Remember that time we went to Puerto Banús in Spain?"

Rhys rubbed a hand against his stubble. "That was a long time ago," he said in a careful voice.

She didn't want to overdo it. He would see through that easily. She kept her voice even and maintained eye contact.

"Yes, but those were our best days. When we could talk to each other. Then you changed. I didn't want that, Rhys. If you could go back to the way you were. . . ." She lowered the corners of her lips and her eyes fell to the floor. A careful mixture of regret and confusion remained on her face.

"Then what?"

"Then maybe, just maybe, we could try again. Maybe we could go to Spain, and never come back. Or whatever." She shrugged. She smiled again, a little fuller this time. "That would be nice, right?"

It was Rhys's turn to look perplexed, a panoply of emotions playing across his face. He sat down cross-legged. His eyes remained narrowed. "You want to get back with me?"

She shrugged. "We could try, right?" She fought to keep her expression sincere.

He smiled. The snarl reappeared and his eyes glittered. "You fucking bitch. You think I'm that stupid?" He reached forward so swiftly she had no time to move. He grabbed her by the throat and pushed her against the wall, leaning in. She heard his teeth gnashing, his breath hot and heavy. She fought against him but he was too strong. She gagged; the grip on her throat was tight.

"You destroyed everything the day you married that bastard. Now you want to go back to the way it was before?" He thrust her back violently against the wall, just holding her throat. Then he let go abruptly and stood. Rebecca coughed and sputtered, a trail of mucus drooling down her mouth. She slid sideways, then fell forwards, her face resting on the flea-covered, dirty carpet. She didn't have the strength to lift her head.

"You think I'm that stupid?" he thundered. "You destroyed my life; now I'll do the same to you."

Rebecca thought quickly. She needed to come up with a different plan. "Water," she croaked. "Please. . . ." She coughed, making gagging sounds. She turned on the floor, looking up at him. He stood with his fists bunched by his side, an angry snarl on his face. She coughed again, then retched.

"Please, Rhys."

It worked.

Rhys turned and left and she heard him running across the warehouse floor. She straightened immediately and looked around the room. She spotted two shelves above the desk, holding nothing but dust. Her eyes fell on the chair. One leg had come off, and it lay on the floor, with a screw sticking out from the top. Her eyes lit up. Her spine creaked and protested, but she managed to stand. Then she heard Rhys coming back. She lay down quickly, back to her previous position.

He came in and offered her a glass of water. He held it to her lips and she finished it, then leaned back against the wall, gasping. "What are you going to do to me?"

A crafty smile appeared on his lips. "It's a surprise."

CHAPTER 46

The MIR-1 was a hive of activity. Arla was seated at the desk, her eyes on four new TV screens.

Live feeds were not possible at the moment, but Johnson had put in an urgent request at the road and transport command. It was taking frustratingly long to hear back from them.

In the meantime, Arla was using the time to go through the CCTV feeds from around Martha Smith's house and the car park of the doctor's surgery where Grant Stone had been a patient. Grant's housekeeper had told them he was going to the doctor's and Roslyn and Rob were at the site. They had talked to several witnesses who had seen Grant both arrive, then drive off in his golden Porsche.

Uniformed officers rushed in and out of the room, and the radio on the desk squawked incessantly. Harry was leaning over Arla's shoulder and he reached out a long arm to turn off the radio. Then he lifted a finger to point at one of the screens. "There. The man in the blue mechanic overalls. He's kneeling by Grant's Porsche."

"Yes," Arla said excitedly. The figure turned around but they only got a poor view of the face.

The man clearly knew where the cameras were pointing. Arla could make out a black baseball cap and a beard. His hands were covered by gloves. She zoomed in but there was no bare skin visible. She zoomed back, then focused on his boots. They looked similar to the boots Rebecca had found in Rhys's house. She watched the man's gait carefully, putting the video into slow motion.

Then she grabbed her radio. "Duty controller one, this is DCI Baker."

"Controller one receiving, DCI Baker."

"Alert all road surveillance units on Operation Newton to search for a man with a beard and dark glasses. Black beard and dark glasses."

"Roger that, DCI Baker. All units on Operation Newton alerted."

Arla hung up, then grabbed her radio again. She called the three members of her immediate team, telling them what to expect. Harry's eyes were roving around all of the screens. He jabbed his finger at the screen on Arla's right.

"Stop!" he exclaimed. Arla looked at the screen. It showed a Range Rover going down Clapham High Street. She knew the road well, from the usual shops on the side.

"Is that Rebecca's car?"

"Yes it is."

"Go back a frame."

She did as Harry asked. Apart from traffic she couldn't see a great deal, and they scrolled back a couple of more frames before Harry asked her to stop again. "There." Harry's fingers tapped the screen, landing on a black Honda. "That sounds like the car Rebecca had seen following her around."

Arla's eyes widened as she zoomed in on the number plate. Harry snatched up the radio. "I need the ANPR and DVLA details on Bravo Victor 12 Delta Sierra Tango. Black Honda, but different colour also possible." He repeated the number plate, and put the phone down. It rang again immediately and Harry answered, then handed it to Arla.

"DCI Baker," Arla said tersely.

"It's your favourite pathologist, my dear." Dr Banerjee's mellow, warm voice came down the line. "I've been examining the new victim, Martha Smith."

She clutched the receiver tighter to her ear. "Yes, doc?"

"Primary cause of death was exsanguination by bleeding from the uterine artery, as we suspected. There were no other knife marks on the body. From the edges of the wound, I extracted traces of nickel and chromium. The concentration suggests these are residues from a common kitchen knife, easily available in any store. Nothing special about the murder weapon."

"Question is, where has it gone?"

"That's your job, I'm afraid, my dear." Banerjee paused. "Any progress with the case?"

"Plenty." Arla told him what had happened in the last few hours.

"Good Lord." Banerjee sighed. "I'd better let you go, in that case. But I found a couple of other things on baby Reggie I should inform you about." Arla listened, then flipped open her black notebook and scribbled on a page.

One of the uniformed sergeants came in, his cheeks ruby red, forehead shining with sweat. "Guv, there's been a development. A member of the public called. He's seen the e-fit image of the bearded man with Rhys Mason's face. He's a landlord in Tooting, and he rented a room to a man matching it."

Arla smacked her palm down on the table in excitement, and tried to stand. A spasm of discomfort rippled across her belly, and she sat back down heavily. Without missing a beat, Harry took over.

"Send four uniformed units there now. Block off Tooting High Street at both ends. Has MPAS 2 been dispatched?" MPAS stood for Metropolitan Police Air Support Unit, the division that commanded the helicopters used by the London Met.

The sergeant nodded. "Yes, guv. I'll pass the message on to Darren Stevens."

"I'm coming with you," Harry said. "Meet you at the back." He glanced at Arla. "Is that okay?"

She nodded, then pursed her lips and stomped her foot on the carpet in frustration. She felt a corresponding kick in her tummy and rubbed her distended abdomen with a rueful smile. "It's not like I can get very far."

"No, it's best if you stay here. Let me know of any developments."

"Harry," she called out as he rushed off. He swivelled his wide shoulders around at the door, his head almost touching the top of the doorframe. His eyebrows rose in a silent question.

"Be careful," Arla whispered.

CHAPTER 47

Rebecca could hear Rhys's voice as he paced the factory floor, speaking on the phone. She strained to hear, but the words were muffled.

She had heard the key turning the lock when he left. The window in this office wasn't big enough for her to squeeze through, and it faced the inside. The most she could do, even if she broke through it, was end up on the warehouse floor, where Rhys would see her. Not that she could even try, with her hands still tied behind her back. She heard Rhys's voice fading, along with his footsteps. He had left the light on and she rose, getting close to the window. The blinds were drawn and she couldn't see much from the sides. The corrugated sheets of steel that made up the walls of the warehouse were visible in the distance. Some old machinery, rusting and disused, lay dumped in the corner. The back door was open, letting in daylight. She couldn't see nor hear Rhys.

She sat down by the damaged chair, focusing on the rusty screw sticking out the top of the broken leg. Using her feet, Rebecca pushed the leg against the wall.

She squatted in an ungraceful fashion in front of the chair leg. Gingerly, she put her tied hands on the screw and pressed hard, gasping sharply when she shifted too far and the screw hit her skin. She stifled a cry of pain when she felt the warm trickle of blood roll down her hand.

Soon, she was able to begin an up-and-down motion against the screw, ripping at the cloth tying her hands. It was tough going. She knelt on the floor and took a rest. It was still silent outside the room.

She couldn't hear Rhys, but that did not mean he wasn't by the door, listening out for her. She moved to the door and squinted down the keyhole with one eye. As expected, the key obstructed her vision. She looked down the edges of the blind, but she couldn't see him.

Well, she had to take her chances. Already when she pulled, she could feel her hands getting looser.

She squatted over the chair leg and started again. The sharp tip punctured and scarred her skin, but she gnashed her teeth and carried on. Finally, she could wrench one hand free, then both. She rubbed her hands, then pressed the cloth over the bleeding points. Pressure was the best way to stop bleeding, she knew. To her relief, it worked. That meant she hadn't perforated the important radial artery at the wrist. She put the chair back to its original position, and with grim satisfaction, picked up the fallen chair leg. She considered her possibilities.

*****

When the key turned in the lock, Rebecca was sitting in the position where Rhys had left her. His calm and controlled eyes swept around the whole room, then came to rest on her face. Her hands were tied behind her back and her head rested against the wall. She let out a soft moan.

"My hands hurt, Rhys. They're numb. Can you please let them loose? Like you said, I can't escape. There's nowhere for me to go."

Rhys stared at her impassively. He shut the door and stepped inside. He crouched in front of her, his expression a curious mixture of suspicion and a hint of softness.

Rebecca said, "Please, Rhys. I also need to pee. If you don't free my hands, I can't do anything."

He continued to stare at her in an unnerving fashion, then his eyes slid down to her chest and then lower down. A light gleamed in his eyes as his lips parted open. Her eyes closed as he reached out a large hand and cupped her breasts, his hands moving over her chest. She averted her face, kept her eyes closed, and breathed heavily. Rhys withdrew his hand slowly and when she looked at him, his eyes were glassy and unfocused. They were alive with lust, and she knew that look.

"Do you want me, baby?" she purred. "Free my hands. Let me touch you."

His eyes widened a fraction, slipping down to her lips. He leaned forward, stretching his hand out. Rebecca's left hand shot forward, gripping Rhys's outstretched arm. In her right hand she was holding the chair leg like a spear, the rusty screw its pointed tip. She plunged the chair leg with savage force into Rhys's face, aiming for his left eye. She hit the target perfectly.

Her hand jarred from the impact but she gripped the chair leg tightly. There was a horrible squelching sound, a spurt of blood that arced upwards as the screw drove home. Rhys screamed in agony. He slammed back on the floor, and Rebecca jumped on top of him. She pushed the screw in as far as she could, grunting with effort. Sweat blinded her eyes. Rhys howled like a wounded animal and bucked, throwing her off. She rolled off him and ran to the door. He hadn't locked it. She ran down the short set of stairs, hearing him scream behind her.

CHAPTER 48

Rebecca tripped on the stairs and sprawled on the factory floor. She hadn't realised how weak her legs had become. She picked herself up, then ran across the warehouse. She was heading for the door, which, ominously, was shut. As she reached it, with a sinking heart she realised the door was locked. She pulled at it, making it rattle. But it wouldn't open. She heard a sound behind her and turned. Rhys stood at the door of the office. His left hand was clasped over the eye, blood streaming down his hand.

"You bitch!" he bellowed. He clambered down the three stairs and she ran across the floor, to the door at the opposite end. This door was next to a huge rolling gate, which could be moved up and down to let large vehicles in and out of the warehouse. Desperately, she looked for a lever or switch to operate the gate. If there was one, she couldn't see it.

She got to the door before he could. To her dismay, a shiny new padlock hung on this one as well. She screamed in frustration and kicked the door. It didn't budge.

"Like I said, nowhere to go," a mocking voice said behind her.

She whirled around, holding the chair leg up like a weapon. She stabbed it towards him but he dodged the blow easily. They circled around. He moved his hand down from his left eye. It was a ghastly sight, the eye swollen and red, turning black with blood congealed around it and pouring down his left cheek. But he moved easily, with the grace of a boxer, on the balls of his feet. She knew he was in good shape.

"I shut all the doors so we could have some time together," Rhys continued in his mocking voice. She swiped the chair leg at him and missed again. She noticed he was coming closer, completely unafraid.

"Don't come near me," she snarled. Rivulets of sweat rolled down her head, blinding her eyes, but she blinked them away, ignoring the salty sting.

"Yeah? And what will you do?" He smiled.

In one swift motion he reached for her and she cried out, jabbing the chair leg into his arm. It pierced through the full-sleeve shirt he was wearing, the screw embedding itself in his right forearm. He bellowed again in pain and fury.

She tried to wrench the chair leg out, but he had hold of it now. He ripped it from her and flung it away. She launched herself at him, a burst of rage igniting inside her. This bastard had destroyed her child. Her life. He would pay. She wouldn't go down without a fight.

Her hands scratched at his face and then closed around his good eye. She ripped at it, digging her nails in. He screamed and a hand closed around her throat, pushing her back. The grip around her throat tightened and she couldn't breathe. She lifted one knee and smashed it into his groin. The connection was good, and he grunted in pain, leaning forward. The grip on her throat loosened, and she pushed him away.

She turned and fled. Next to the office, she had seen a metal staircase that went up to a grilled walkway that ran along the perimeter of the warehouse, near the roof. It was high up, and she used her long legs to take three steps at a time. She could see Rhys hobbling down the floor, coming up to the staircase. She looked around in desperation. The walkway didn't lead to anywhere. It went around all the way, but was punctuated by several staircases at regular intervals that came down to the warehouse floor.

"You can run, my darling, but you can't hide," Rhys called out in a high-pitched voice, then broke out into laughter.

CHAPTER 49

The MPAS 2 helicopter flew low overhead, the staccato beats of its rotor making the shop windowpanes vibrate.

On the traffic-jammed Tooting High Street, both drivers and pedestrians looked up at the red-and-white-striped aircraft making low circles overhead. Drivers had alighted from their cars, as they couldn't get through. Uniformed officers were trying to placate a number of disgruntled drivers, who gesticulated wildly, angry at being held up.

Tooting High Street was a major artery that led into Balham, Clapham, and the rest of southwest London. Backroads existed, but they, too, got jammed up frequently. Squad cars, blue lights rotating, blocked both ends of the high street, bringing the busy road to a standstill.

Harry's black BMW was let through, but he couldn't get very far. He lifted the car on the kerb, beeping and scattering some pedestrians. This being Tooting, the erstwhile denizens did not take kindly to an unmarked police car disturbing them so rudely.

Fists shook at Harry, followed by fluent curses in Caribbean patois accents. Harry brushed through the throng, not bothering to reply or flash his warrant card. He was a South London boy, born and bred. These people were justifiably angry and always voluble, but ultimately harmless.

He saw Darren waving at him across the road, in front of a butcher shop. He ran across the road, eyes darting up, down, and sideways.

"This is the building, guv. The landlord owns the butcher shop and the whole building. He's here." Darren pointed. Harry saw a small, squat Pakistani man, with a beard and skullcap, standing nervously behind Darren. Harry showed the man his warrant card and gave his name and rank.

"I'm Mr Iqbal," the landlord said. "All of this is for the man who hired the top room?"

Harry nodded. "He's a very dangerous man. He's an expert with explosives, and he worked in the army." He took the e-fit photo of Rhys and showed it to Mr Iqbal again for good measure. "Are you sure this is him?"

Mr Iqbal's eyes widened with fear as he nodded. "Yes, I told your officers already."

"Have you been upstairs?"

"No, the room is locked. I don't know when he left."

Harry nodded. He shifted his attention to Darren. "Did the Armed Forces unit arrive?"

"On their way, guv."

"There's no time to lose. If he's up there, then Rebecca could be as well. We are endangering her life by waiting. Let's go up to have a look."

Darren called up three members of his team, and with Harry at the lead they entered the building through the side door next to the butcher's. A narrow hallway led to a rickety flight of stairs that broadened into a wider landing. Darren's radio squawked.

Harry whispered, "Turn it off. He knows something is up, but best not to give him any warning."

They reached the top floor, and Harry told them to wait at the landing below. He went up the last flight of stairs by himself.

A white wooden door faced him across the landing. He knelt by it and then looked in through the keyhole. He could see drawn curtains and the outline of a table in the dim light. He knelt down and peered through the gap between the door and carpet. Apart from table legs, he couldn't see a great deal. The room seemed empty, or its occupant was being very quiet.

Knocking wouldn't help. He tried the handle. Locked, as expected. He pushed on the door and felt something give, and heard a soft click.

Damn.

He stepped back swiftly, scanning around the door. He found nothing. But something was wrong. He knew he shouldn't have tried to open the door.

Harry's mouth opened and he breathed hard. He raised his voice, directing his words to the officers gathered on the landing below him. "Get out of here, now!"

He detected an odour. It was sharp and acrid, and it assaulted his nostrils. His brows furrowed as he inhaled. How did he know that smell? Then the memory hit him and his eyes widened.

When Arla painted her nails.

A domino of rapid thoughts cascaded down his brain, culminating in the bright flash of the forensic report of the explosive device. TATP. The nail polish chemical used to make the bomb.

Before Harry could move, the explosion ripped across the walls, bursting out of the windows. The walls caved in, showering bricks and debris at Harry, as the impact of the explosion picked him clean off his feet and hurled him down the stairs. He braced for impact by crossing his arms around his head, but he was flipped around, and the back of his skull smashed against the wall. A screaming spasm of agony tore across his brain. He fell on the staircase as debris rained down on him, and the world turned black.

*****

Arla drummed her fingers on the desk. She was used to being in the field, and it was frustrating sitting here. She had last heard from Harry just as he arrived in Tooting. She assumed he was now checking out the apartment, and that she would hear from him again soon. She looked up as both Parmentier and John, the cybercrimes officer, walked in.

Parmentier said, "I heard back from the company that makes the plastic bags the baby was found in."

"Refresh, right?" Arla asked.

"Yes. They make these bags to store meat that is delivered to supermarkets. They have a location for the barcode that was on the bag. It's in southwest London."

"Excellent. Do we have an address?"

"Yes."

"Good. I'm sending an officer down there now to get a list of their distribution clients. Anything else? Did Mary Atkins come up with anything?"

Parmentier snapped his fingers. "Yes, Mary has uncovered something important. She's upstairs and will come down soon." He turned to look at John, who shuffled forward.

"You know that account that's been trolling Rebecca Stone on social media? The Final Countdown?" John asked nervously. "You asked me to track down the IP address, and I told you it's a VPN."

"Yes, I know that," Arla said impatiently. "Have you got anything new?"

"Yes, I do." John took out his phone and scrolled down to a photo of a woman hanging from the ceiling by a rope fixed to her neck. Arla looked at the photo carefully, but the woman's face wasn't clearly visible.

John said, "This photo was posted from that account a couple of days ago. Same IP address."

"So what?"

"Any digital photo, when sent, bears the GPS location of the phone that was used to take the photo. But only if location services is turned on." John pointed at the screen. "When this photo was taken, location services was turned on. Therefore, it gives us a GPS location."

Arla breathed faster, feeling her pulse surge. "Where is it?"

"I looked it up. It's a warehouse inside an old industrial estate on the outskirts of Hounslow. Less than five minutes' drive from Heathrow Airport."

Arla stood up slowly, hearing her heart hammering against her ribs.

"Send two units out there now. That could be where Rhys is hiding, with Rebecca. He's taken out all this cash to get himself a quick flight out of the country with one of his false identities."

She reached for her phone, intending to call Harry and divert him to the site. Instead, the red phone on the desk gave out a shrill ring. Arla picked it up.

"DCI Baker? This is Darren Stevens." Darren's breathing was short and rapid, his words forced.

Fear clutched Arla's guts. She knew Darren was at the site with Harry. "Yes, it's me. What's going on?"

"The room was booby-trapped, guv. There's been another explosion, and the top floor is destroyed. A couple of the pedestrians were injured. Paramedics are on site."

Arla felt a cold sheet of terror descend upon her, freezing the words in her brain. *Why wasn't Harry calling her? Why Darren?*

After a few seconds, she croaked out, "Where's Harry?"

Darren's voice broke. "I'm sorry, guv. He was hurt in the explosion. He's still unconscious, and taken to hospital."

The receiver dropped from Arla's hand as the world fractured and splintered before her eyes. She slumped back on the chair.

CHAPTER 50

Rebecca ran down the metal grill walkway, high above the warehouse floor. She was long-limbed, and had worked hard to get rid of the pregnancy weight. Her strength served her well now. Fear had morphed into rage, an all-consuming, quivering fury that made her want to destroy Rhys. She wished she had a weapon, but she found nothing. The walkway was narrow, only wide enough for two men side by side. It reached the warehouse floor by a number of zigzagging staircases.

Rhys called out to her again. She turned to look, glad she had put some distance between them. He appeared out of breath, holding on to the railing as he stumbled towards her. Blood was still pouring from his left eye, and she hoped she had hit a major artery. The blood loss was making him weaker. Otherwise, she knew he would be sprinting for her.

"Feeling tired, Rhys? You're weak and stupid." She shouted out the words in a taunting voice, baiting him. Rhys had an inflated ego and he would hate her jibe. She was correct. With a snarl, he increased his pace. He was still noticeably slow, and every time he moved his left hand from his eye, blood trickled out. His right arm was soaked in blood too, injured by the screw.

She ran across a staircase. There was no point in going downstairs. He had locked both the exits. At the same time, could she really keep running around the walkway, hoping to tire him out? It might work, but she would become exhausted as well. No, there had to be a better way.

She kept running, doing a semicircle around the perimeter. She was out of breath soon, and exhaustion drove her to her knees. She knelt on the walkway, staring at the floor far down below, visible through the grill. She panted, then glanced quickly to her left as his footsteps caught up with her. A crooked, devilish grin played across his lips as he came forward, sensing his advantage. Rebecca got to her feet and willed her legs to move, noting she was slower than before. However, she hadn't lost blood, and she was still faster than him. She came across the next staircase and looked down. The first zigzag landing was a good three to four metres below her. A thin railing was the only protection against falling to the floor, way down, more than ten meters.

That gave her an idea.

She collapsed on the walkway, gasping. She clutched her back and cried out in pain. The clanging sound of Rhys's boots grew louder as he closed the gap between them.

She was positioned directly opposite the gap of the staircase. When he was within touching distance, she slid her hands along the back wall, hooking her hands on the railing.

Rhys appeared in front of her, leering. He was a ghastly sight, left eye now so swollen and large it was protruding from the socket. Blood still spasmed, turning into reddish-black clots that slithered down his hand, staining his shirt.

"Not that easy, is it, my darling Becky?" The smile became a snarl as his voice rose. "You can try, but you can't win."

She said nothing, only watched him carefully, gasping like she was out of breath.

Rhys bared his teeth. "If I can't have you, no one can."

He launched himself at her, but Rebecca was ready.

She gripped the railing tight, flexed her lower spine and back against the wall, and high-kicked with both legs, levering her entire torso off the floor. She used the strength of her shoulders to lift up her legs, crying out with the effort. It took Rhys by surprise.

Her feet smashed against his chest, knocking him backwards. His arms wheeled in the air as he tried to regain his balance. Rebecca let go of the railing and kicked his legs as hard as she could. Rhys had created a puddle of blood, and his boots were slick on the metal surface. He fell through the gap, sliding down the stairs.

He tried to hold on to the railings but failed. He screamed, the weight of his body losing to gravity. His left hand clawed at the metal railing and held on to a rung. But his body overbalanced, and he fell over the staircase, dangling several metres off the factory floor.

"Becky . . . Becky . . . please, help me."

His face was contorted with pain as he held on to the railing with both hands, his feet wheeling in the air. Rebecca rushed to the staircase. She knelt over the hand that was gripping the railing, sinking her teeth in till they pierced flesh and she could taste blood. She didn't stop, and kept her jaws clamped, increasing the force.

Rhys screamed, a primal, animalistic howl of rage and pain. Rebecca let go and stood. She wiped the blood off her mouth and kicked at his hand as hard as she could. Rhys kept screaming, but his hand came loose.

"No!" Rhys screamed one last time as his fingers gave way. He plummeted to the floor, his body meeting the cement surface with a sickening thud. Rebecca leaned over and winced as she watched the body come to a rest. His legs jerked a couple of times, then he was still.

Her ears pricked up at a sound in the distance. It was the wailing of police sirens.

CHAPTER 51

Speckles of blue and grey floated across a placid black surface. An unyielding miasma of total darkness. The speckles coalesced into larger blobs, like a lava lamp, but they remained black. There was no sound, no glimmer of light, nothing at all. Harry couldn't even hear the sound of his own breathing. He wasn't sure if he was alive or dead, departed to the afterworld. Maybe death was supposed to be like this, a blankness where the senses didn't operate, submerging him in a strange, ethereal world of nothingness.

But how did he know he was in this state?

Or was he imagining the whole thing?

He tried to do something. Move a part of the body he couldn't feel anymore. Contract the eyelid muscles. Twitch a finger. Nope, he couldn't feel or do anything. He began to panic. What the hell was wrong with him? Was he really dead? It confused the hell out of him. How could he be dead, and still be aware of his own mind? Of his own thoughts?

A wave blew across the blue, black, and grey blobs. Like a shoal of fish in the ocean, the blobs changed shape and moved en masse. The wave came again, stronger this time, moving the blobs again but not shifting the darkness. Then he heard it. It wasn't a wave. It was a voice.

A voice he knew. He knew it very well.

It was Arla. At that moment, he felt the blackness jerk and twitch, like a piece of paper being torn. He frowned. The blobs vanished, replaced by peaks and troughs, black hills and valleys. He tried to speak, and was astonished at the sound of his own voice.

"Arla?"

His ears picked up another sound: It was a sob. He felt something warm and wet on a part of his body, and with some effort, realised it was his hand. He tried to open his eyes, but they just wouldn't do their job. It was bloody infuriating.

"Arla?" he whispered again. At least he had his voice. It felt good to be able to use it. This time, he heard her more clearly.

Her voice was tremulous, like she'd been crying. "Harry. Harry, can you hear me?"

His lips were parched dry and his voice cracked. "Yes, I can."

He heard a soft bell above his head and felt a tighter grip on his hand. Footsteps. To his right. Another female voice said, "He's awake. That's good."

He heard a rattle from the foot of the bed but didn't feel any movement. The blackness was receding, he realised. There was a rim of whiteness, pushing the black circle down. His breathing picked up as he felt pain for the first time, tiny cannonballs playing ping-pong against his skull. He grimaced and a soft moan escaped his lips.

"The morphine's wearing off," a female voice said. "We need to dose him up again."

Arla asked, "What did the MRI scan show?"

A male voice answered. "He has a skull fracture. But the brain is unharmed. There's no fluid causing pressure and there's no bleed in the brain. He had a lucky escape."

Harry felt a weird sensation, cool liquid trickling up his arm. It disappeared after a while, absorbed into his bloodstream. The pain was still there, but the whiteness was expanding faster now. He realised then, he was staring up at a white light in the ceiling. His eyes were open. He couldn't move his head and his lips trembled as he sweated with the pain.

Then a shadow appeared from his right, blocking half the light. It was Arla's face, cheeks stained with smudged mascara. She whispered his name. Despite the pain ripping his mind apart, Harry smiled. He smiled because he had seen the woman he loved. He was not afraid to die, and knew it might well be in the line of duty one day. The memory of what happened was coming back to him in a series of rapid flashbacks.

If he had died, his only regret would've been he didn't get a chance to say goodbye to Arla.

And to his baby, whom he would never see.

But now, he had no regrets. He could die in peace. His smile grew wider as Arla's face swam in his eyes, becoming hazy, diffuse. His eyes flickered, closing down again. The pain was receding, and he was floating back into that dark oblivion, where nothing mattered anymore.

*****

"What's happening to him?" Arla asked the nurse. "His eyes are closing." She gripped Harry's large hand in both of her own, pressing them to her chest.

"Don't worry," said the nurse in a soothing voice. "The morphine is just taking effect again. He'll be like this till tomorrow. It all depends on how bad the pain is."

Arla felt tears bud in her eyes again and she squeezed them shut. Her heart was broken into so many pieces, picking them up was futile. The jagged shards would only make her bleed again. Her life had come to a complete halt. At the back of her mind, she was glad that Rebecca Stone was safe and back home. She was a remarkably brave woman, and a survivor. But for Arla, the victory had turned to ashes. She was all cried out. She felt empty inside, her soul a vacuum. For the first time she was faced with the question she didn't want to answer. How could she live without Harry? After Nicole, Harry was the only person she had loved. Would he now be taken from her as well?

The tears came anew. Her body shook with sobs as her head touched Harry's chest, her tears soaking into the bedsheets.

What would she do if Harry died? The father of her child. Her best friend and partner in crime, and what a pun that was. If he'd been awake, he would've smirked at her, made a joke about her horrendous sense of humour, which would get her angry. They knew each other so well, it was like they lived in each other's minds half the time. She couldn't think of a better father for her child. . . . The tears were ugly, big drops, making her nose run and eyes swell.

"There, there now." The Afro-Caribbean nurse pulled Arla towards her ample breast. "He's going to be fine, honey. Don't you worry now."

Another voice cleared its throat behind her, and she heard him say her name when he laid a hand on her shoulder. She looked up at the weary, sunken-cheeked face of Timothy Baker. Behind the square-framed glasses, his blue eyes were dulled. Surprised, she momentarily forgot her predicament.

"Dad? How did you. . . ?"

"I was watching the live news and saw Harry on the stretcher. I was worried you were hurt as well, God forbid." His eyes flickered to her abdomen, warmth igniting in his eyes, dissolving the deeply carved sorrow lines in his forehead and cheeks.

Arla had told him about his impending grandchild, and despite the years of distance that her father had carefully cultivated, he had been overjoyed at the news. It was the first time in decades Arla had heard him excited about anything, and it made her cry. He was no longer the only living relative she had left. There was a new life to look forward to. Maybe he or she would bring her father back into the fold.

Timothy said, "I called the station, and told them who I was. They let me know which hospital. What happened?"

Arla told him the story as Timothy pulled up a chair and sat down. When he put his arm around her shoulders, she sobbed like a little girl.

CHAPTER 52

Commander Wayne Johnson picked up one newspaper from the stack on his desk. Arla and Harry sat opposite him. They were in his spacious fourth-floor office, spindly blocks of grey council apartments surrounding their view.

"Grant Stone explodes!" Johnson read from the paper, then slapped it down on the table with a harrumph of disgust. He picked up the next, biting the words out, face turning purple.

"Police clueless about Grant's death."

He flung the paper to the floor, cursing under his breath. "Unbelievable."

Arla said quietly, "When should we do a press conference? They'll keep asking about Grant till we talk to them."

Johnson ignored Arla and picked up the next paper. *"Terrorist attack in Tooting."*

He sagged back in his red gilt leather armchair, then stood rapidly, pacing the room.

"The biggest mess I've seen in a long time, and I've seen it all," he thundered.

"In order to tie up Grant's death, the explosion in Tooting, and the baby killer, we have to expose Rebecca Stone," Arla said patiently. "And you don't want that."

Johnson swung around to face her. "Jeremy Stone has requested to keep it quiet. So has Mr Cummings. I mean, I can see it from their point of view." He swirled a finger in the air, making a circle. "But you obviously think something else."

Harry coughed and cleared his throat. Arla snapped her attention to him. Harry had been out of hospital for two days. He was back to his normal self, but still had a dressing on his left temple, which he proudly proclaimed made him look like Frankenstein. His scalp had several lacerations, all of which had been stitched. Arla had warned him she would pull them out if he carried on with his crap jokes.

Harry glanced at her and she smiled warmly at him. She drunk him in with her eyes, just happy he was here, right where she could touch him.

Arla asked, "We have to address the media sooner or later, sir. Is it not easier to get it out of the way?"

"Which part? The fact that Grant Stone was a paedophile, or that his daughter-in-law's former lover was one of the children he abused, who then came back to kill him?"

Rhys Mason's notebooks and diaries were found at his old house, and he had also mailed a letter to the station, addressed to Arla. They were nothing but allegations at the moment, but Rhys had provided intimate details of his life with Grant. The journals had made Arla physically sick.

Harry raised both hands and let them fall. "How about all of it? We can't lie, sir. We can't tell the media Rebecca wasn't involved when she's at the heart of it."

Arla nodded. "Harry's right, sir. Besides, I'm going on maternity leave soon. If you want me to sort this out, then we do it now, not later."

Johnson folded his hands behind his back and straightened his spine. His eyes softened as his jaw relaxed.

"Anytime you want to take time off is okay with me, Arla. Both of you have been through enough. You need some downtime."

"Then let's speak to Rebecca now, sir. You know what I want."

Her boss regarded them in silence for a while. "Okay," he sighed. "Do what is necessary."

CHAPTER 53

The black BMW crunched gravel as Harry drove it down the farmhouse drive in Weybridge. Rebecca was staying with her parents and Jeremy was also present.

Harry helped Arla walk on the gravel. He rang the bell and they waited. Christine Walton opened the door, and a brief, tight smile appeared on her lips before vanishing. She was expecting them.

Arla and Harry followed her inside, into the living room. They declined tea and coffee. Christine went out to get Rebecca, and they came back presently, with Jeremy.

Rebecca was wearing jeans and a pullover, hair pulled back in a ponytail. She had no injuries, but her hollow stare and gaunt cheeks told of the suffering she'd endured.

"Have you told the media?" Rebecca asked as soon as she sat down. She had already been to Clapham Police Station and given her statement. Rhys Mason lay in the morgue, and Arla awaited Dr

Banerjee's verdict, but there was no rush. For once, Rhys had nowhere to hide.

Arla said, "Not yet, no. They don't know about Rhys's death, but everything else is already in the papers."

"Please protect my daughter." Christine leaned forward. "She's been to hell and back. You people have witness protection programmes, right?"

"But she's not a witness," Arla said gently. "If anything, she's the victim. And yes, we do have victim protection, but now that Rhys Mason is dead, Rebecca should be fine. The media attention will blow over in a few weeks."

Harry said, "The papers will have some new juicy scandal to feed their readers."

Arla settled back in the sofa and placed her hands gently on her baby bump. "There's just one thing I don't understand."

She looked at Jeremy, who rubbed his hands and moved a foot. He looked pensive, but his movements came to a sudden stop when Arla got his attention.

"Why was the nursery room warm, Jeremy?"

He frowned at Arla. "What do you mean?"

"When baby Reggie was stolen from the room, the curtains were raised. That's what Rebecca found. And they had to have been open for a while, because Rebecca was downstairs. The intruder didn't shut the window, did he? So on a cold day, the windows were open for a while. But why was the room so warm when you walked in?"

Silence.

Jeremy frowned at her, but she broke off eye contact. She stared at Rebecca, whose eyes were wide, fixed on her face.

"Is it possible the window was never actually open, until you opened it, Rebecca? Then you screamed and your husband and Miss Mildred came running?"

Rebecca opened and closed her mouth a few times, then cleared her throat. "Why would I do that?"

"Because you had left baby Reggie in a plastic bag in the Common, when you went for your walk. Didn't you?"

Rebecca's eyes bulged, and a mauve colour engulfed her face. She couldn't speak.

Arla continued. "Dr Banerjee said Reggie was killed by strangulation, twelve hours ago. Not by asphyxiation inside a plastic bag. That makes the time of death the early hours of the morning, around four, five a.m. Only you had baby at the time."

She turned to look at Jeremy. "And you said Rebecca slept in her own room that night, with baby. And the CCTV inside your house proves you correct. Rebecca can be seen taking baby Reggie into her room, and coming out in the morning. She went downstairs where the cameras show her going out for the walk."

Rebecca stood, making a choking, strangling sound. Her hands were fists. "This is rubbish! After all I've been through, how dare you accuse me of this . . . this. . . ."

"Infanticide?" Arla raised an eyebrow.

Rebecca shook her head, then pointed a finger at Arla. She shouted, "But the boot prints! They belonged to Rhys. You saw them!"

"Ah yes, the boot prints. As it happens, our forensic gait analyst confirmed that the boot prints in your house and at the crime scene were the same as the boots you found at Rhys's house."

Rebecca made a huffing sound. "And you need more proof?"

Arla paused as Harry took out the laptop from his backpack. He powered it on, and clicked on a file. Arla put the laptop on the desk and turned it towards the family so all could see.

"On the right, you can see the boot. On the left, you can see the gait predicted by the marks made by the boots. The gait is a zig-zag pattern. Correct?"

Everyone nodded, apart from Rebecca, who breathed heavily, her nostrils flaring. She was glaring at Arla, who ignored her.

"Now, the funny thing is, we have similar boot prints at the warehouse in Hounslow, at Rhys's hideout. Not the same shoes, but Rhys clearly liked using these big builder's boots. However, his gait is completely different. He walks in a ramrod straight line. His gait does not match the gait we found at the crime scene where baby Reggie was killed."

Silence again. Jeremy said, "So what are you saying? Someone else wore Rhys's boots at the crime scene?"

Arla nodded. "That's exactly what our forensic gait analysis software shows. There is no way Rhys walked around in the Common crime scene."

"So, who did?"

Harry pulled the laptop towards him and played a clip of CCTV footage. It was inside Jeremy's house and showed Rebecca walking in the kitchen.

"We took this footage, and analysed Jeremy, Rebecca, and Miss Mildred's gait. Only Rebecca's gait is a perfect match for the one found at the crime scene."

"You're lying," Rebecca whispered.

"Of course, that only proves you were there, not that you killed Reggie," Arla said softly. "The plastic bag baby was found in was from a company called Refresh. And they supply bags to the Weston Parks Farm."

There was a sharp intake of breath from Christine. Arla turned towards her. "That is this farm, Mrs Walton. Your daughter took that bag from here. No fingerprints, of course; she always handled it wearing gloves."

"This is . . . absurd!" Christine exclaimed.

Arla shook her head. "You were delivered a stack of bags on the same order. We have the barcodes to identify the serial numbers. That bag came from this farm, Mrs Walton, unless you didn't get any bags at all."

Christine and Rebecca gaped at Arla. She continued, addressing Rebecca. "You put Reggie's blue cloth, and a pair of Rhys's old boots that you had worn to the crime scene, into a bag and then planted it at Rhys's house. Didn't you?"

"Detective Baker," Rebecca said through gritted teeth, "I think you have lost your mind."

"I don't think so," Arla said calmly. "That blue cloth and the boots are key items of evidence that point the blame to Rhys Mason.

You knew that, of course. Hence you took them with you and then pretended to find them in Rhys's house."

Christine intervened. She stretched an arm out, speaking over her daughter, who was gasping. "Why would she do that, detective? Everything you have said so far just makes no sense. You're accusing my daughter of murdering her own son!"

Arla stared at Christine, then at Rebecca. "When Rebecca went to Rhys's house, Miss Mildred drove her part of the way there. She saw the bag Rebecca was carrying. We have that bag in our possession now."

Harry pulled out a small Ralph Lauren shoulder bag from his backpack and zipped it open, putting it on the table. "You can see the few fragments of mud inside. There are also microscopic fibres of the same fabric as the blue cloth that belonged to Reggie."

"Miss Mildred gave you this bag?" Rebecca asked, incredulously.

"Yes," Harry said softly. "It was not obtained by coercion, and therefore it is valid as evidence."

Rebecca stood again, her face losing colour. "She's lying. She's trying to—"

"Frame you?" Arla said. "No, she isn't."

The sound of a car pulling up on the gravel drive came from outside. Conversation in the room stilled. The doorbell went and no one moved for a few seconds. Then Jeremy stood slowly.

"Any idea who this is?"

Arla said, "One of my detective sergeants. She has a witness with her."

Jeremy went to open the door, and returned shortly with Edna Mildred, accompanied by Lisa Moran. Lisa pulled up a chair for Edna, and the elderly lady sat down. Lisa stood behind her, keeping a watchful eye. Edna's face was drawn and haggard, as usual, but her dark blue eyes were alive, and they swivelled between Rebecca and Christine.

Arla said, "Miss Mildred, why don't you tell everyone who you are."

Edna sat with her back straight and arms folded on her lap. "My name is Cheryl Mason. I am Rhys Mason's mother."

Both Rebecca and Christine gasped, and Jeremy's mouth opened.

The woman they knew as Miss Edna Mildred continued.

"I knew what Grant had done to my son. I threatened to go to the papers, but he threatened me back. He had an army of lawyers, who also had questionable connections in the underworld. They harassed me to the point where I had to change names. Rhys helped me get a different identity and move up to Birmingham. I stayed there for ten years before returning to London."

The truth was sinking in slowly, layering upon the silence in the room. She continued.

"When your job came up," Cheryl Mason addressed Rebecca, "it seemed too good to be true. My son didn't know anything about it, and I didn't want him to be involved. To be honest, after what Grant did to him our relationship has never been the same. Grant paid off my debts, bought me a house, and I lost sight of what he was doing to Rhys. I have to live with that."

The tip of her nose turned red and a teardrop rolled down her cheek. She wiped it off with a tissue and took a moment to compose herself.

"I took your job to see if it would get me closer to Grant. I doubted he would recognise me after all these years. However, I never got to see him. He seemed to have become a recluse, spending all his time in his mansion, or abroad." She shrugged. "I don't even know what I would have done if I did see him. However, I told Rhys where I was working. It was me who left the bathroom window open to let Rhys in. He stole all of Jeremy's memorabilia collection, and left."

Arla lifted a hand and intervened. "Rhys actually left through the nursery window, didn't he? That's why there was the boot print on the flat roof landing, just below the nursery window as well. You left the door of your annex apartment open, and that's how he got in."

Miss Mason nodded. "Yes, he disabled the Wi-Fi so the CCTV wouldn't work while he stole the memorabilia. It was his way of getting back at Jeremy, and Grant Stone. The nursery window was larger, and I opened it for him to escape, then shut it, as it was shut before. I helped him to escape via the rear, then brushed away his footprints, so no marks were left in the snow."

"Most importantly," Arla said, "when you let Rhys into the house, Rebecca was still out walking with her son."

"Yes." Ms Mason nodded. "It was the best time. I knew Jeremy would stay in his room, busy with work. But if Rebecca and the baby were around, I couldn't let Rhys in. He would be caught."

Abruptly, Rebecca stood. Her face was bleached bone white, and she was shaking like a leaf in a storm. She raised a trembling finger towards Ms Mason. "I trusted you. And you. . . ."

Ms Mason showed no outward emotion. She didn't move a muscle, apart from her lips. Her words were like arrows, slicing through the air towards Rebecca.

"I betrayed you because I wanted to hurt you, like Grant hurt my son. I could sense something strange was happening. I didn't know what you had in the bag you took to Rhys's house, but I did have my suspicions." She shook her head. "I know I'm not a saint, and my son was a twisted and damaged individual, but for you I have no words." She held Rebecca's eyes.

"You're evil," Miss Mason whispered.

CHAPTER 54

Rebecca threw her head back and laughed. It was a high-pitched, cackling sound. She turned and shifted her attention to Arla.

"You trust this scheming, lying nobody over me?" She pointed a finger to Ms Mason. "I am a well-known public figure and she's already admitted that she changed her identity. For heaven's sake, she just told you she let Rhys Mason into my house."

"And she will be charged for being an accomplice to burglary," Arla said firmly. "But Rhys Mason did not kill your baby, Rebecca. *You did.*"

Rebecca remained standing and put both hands on her waist. "Really? Tell me, Detective Baker, if I did such a ghastly thing, then why would I leave the body in a public place for someone to find?"

Arla shrugged. "Only you can explain what happens in your mind, Rebecca. But if I had to guess, maybe you wished to implicate Rhys Mason. If you could cast enough suspicion on him, then he would be behind bars for the rest of his life."

Arla kept her eyes on Rebecca and reached inside her coat pocket. She pulled out a small, green, rectangular piece of folded paper. It was a doctor's prescription. She said softly, "Or it could be some other reason." She held up the prescription, so Rebecca could see it clearly. Christine sat stock-still. Jeremy leaned in, frowning as he stared at the prescription.

"This is a prescription in your name, Rebecca, by your doctor. The tablet is called olanzapine. It is commonly prescribed for psychosis." Arla settled back on the sofa again. "We spoke to your doctor, and also the psychiatrist he referred you to. You have a condition called puerperal psychosis. It's rare, but it can be a severe form of psychosis, where a woman starts to feel her baby is her mortal enemy."

There was pin-drop silence in the room again, punctuated by heavy breathing. Rebecca was slumped backwards, her mouth open, eyes downcast. Only Christine leaned forward, hands clasped over her knees, glaring at Arla.

She continued. "It was your psychosis that made you kill your son. Then, you tried to frame Rhys for it. With his history of stalking you, both physically and online, he was the perfect suspect. But it doesn't end there. You murdered Martha Smith as well, didn't you, Rebecca? And then stole her baby."

Jeremy gasped. "What?"

There was no comment from either Rebecca or her mother. Arla continued. "The morning Martha was murdered, you said you went to see the doctor. It's true that you did. You registered your name at reception, picked up your prescription, and then left. That gave you enough time to take the bus to Martha's house. There, you killed her with a kitchen knife."

Christine was shaking her head. Her cheeks were sunken, and she breathed heavily. "This is ridiculous, detective. These allegations have no basis whatsoever. I would like you to leave." Christine rose. "Right now."

Harry said, "Please sit down, Mrs Walton. We are not leaving without searching these premises, and the outbuildings."

Rebecca stirred, her eyes sliding over to Harry. He continued. "The CCTV cameras didn't pick up anyone entering Martha Smith's house. The intruder came in through the back—that was you, Rebecca. You put the baby in a bag, suitable for the purpose, I presume. Then you left through the back as well. We didn't find your car on CCTV. But when we searched for your mother's car, we found it on a road leading to Martha Smith's house."

Harry glanced at Arla, who nodded imperceptibly, giving him the go-ahead. He continued, addressing Christine. "You deliberately parked on a road that didn't have cameras. Your daughter joined you, after a short walk, and both of you, with the baby, came back to this house. That return journey, we do have on CCTV."

Arla said, "And we have the footage on the laptop now, if you wish to see."

Neither Rebecca nor Christine moved. The silence stretched on.

Harry spread his hands. "Therefore, we would like to conduct a search now, if you don't mind."

Jeremy stood. "Is this true?" he asked his wife, then his mother-in-law. His lips were trembling and sweat rolled down his forehead. He raised his voice. "Is this actually true?"

The front door opened, and footsteps marched down the hallway. Mr Walton appeared, wearing cords and a heavy farmer's anorak, with a flat peaked cap on his head. He looked bewildered as he pointed to the door. "There's a police van outside, and they want to come in." He stopped, his eyes taking in everyone in the room, coming to a rest at Ms Mason. He came farther in, then frowned at his wife. "What's going on, Christine?"

Arla answered for him. "Your wife and daughter are being charged with murder and also the abduction of an unborn infant. It is our belief, if the baby is alive, he or she is hidden somewhere in this house. Is there an outbuilding that the women use?"

Mr Walton's jaw almost hit the floor as he leaned forward, holding on to the edge of the sofa for support. "What are you talking about?"

Arla said, "Could you please answer the question. Is there a building on the premises that Rebecca frequents?"

Mr Walton nodded slowly. "Yes," he said as if in a daze. "The barn. I built her a room there, and recently she had it cleaned out."

"Does it have electricity, running water, and heating?"

"Yes. Why do you ask?"

Rebecca stood abruptly and pushed her father to one side. She charged out of the room, only to be tackled at the door by a uniformed officer. She slammed into him, pushing him back to the wall. She was as tall as him and the man was taken by surprise. Two more officers piled in, and it took three of them to restrain Rebecca in the hallway.

Arla glanced at Christine. The older woman sat with her spine ramrod straight, wide fixed eyes staring into nothingness. Her shoulders were pinched, neck muscles taut as she shivered once.

Arla leaned towards her. Rebecca was screaming outside, shouting curses and thrashing around, even after she had been handcuffed. "You knew your daughter was in a desperate state of mind," Arla said softly. "But you still helped her. Why?"

Christine didn't answer for several seconds. Arla repeated her question.

Christine slowly turned her face towards Arla. Her voice was a dry whisper. "I thought she would get better if she had another baby."

Arla shook her head. "And you didn't know she would have to murder another woman to get that baby?"

Christine said nothing, averting her eyes. Arla asked, "Did Rebecca follow me to the antenatal clinic? Is that how she found Martha Smith?"

Christine was silent, head bowed for several seconds. Without lifting her head, she nodded.

Arla asked, "Did she choose Martha because her husband was gone for several days in a row with his work? Martha was alone, and therefore an easier target than some of the other women, who had family around them."

Christine lifted her head. She wouldn't look at Arla, but nodded again in silence, eyes fixed on the floor.

Arla stood. "Christine Walton, I am arresting you on charge of being an accomplice to murder and abduction of an infant."

Harry stepped forward and handcuffed Christine, then handed her over to a uniformed officer. Mother and daughter were taken out to the police van. Ms Mason also left with them.

Lisa Moran appeared, holding a portable baby cot in her hand, the type that fits into a car seat. She was smiling. She lifted the cot on the table and pushed back the hood. A baby lay sleeping peacefully inside, little fingers curled around its face in perfect repose.

Arla's heart lifted in a shining halo of sunlight. All the police officers in the room crowded round the cot, wide smiles on their faces.

The only exceptions were Mr Walton and Jeremy, who sat on the sofa, a distance apart from each other, too shocked to speak.

CHAPTER 55

Arla had never felt pain like this. She had known it was coming, but never imagined it would be this bad. She'd had an epidural, but still the waves of white-hot agony lashed against her lower belly.

She could see the midwife, positioned between her legs, fingers reaching inside her. "Push, push, almost there. Go on, push!"

Arla closed her eyes and summoned her inner strength. She cried out as she pushed down with all her might, focusing on the weight between her legs.

"That's it, again! Again!"

Her head fell back on the cushion, and she panted. Sweat caked her entire body, and she was exhausted. She heard Harry's voice. "You can do this, darling. I know you can." He gripped her hand and squeezed it. "Take a deep breath and try again."

A low wail escaped Arla's lips as the pain hit her again. There was only one way to get rid of the pain, and that was to push harder.

She just wished she had more strength to do it. She grunted again as she bore down on her lower abdomen as hard as she could. It felt like she was pushing her intestines out along with the baby.

"The head is almost here," the midwife said in a perfectly normal, almost bored voice. "Do that once again, go on."

Arla increased her grip on Harry's hand, almost pulling him down to the bed. She screamed out as she heaved downward. This time she felt something dislodge and move, and all of a sudden the weight seemed to pass out from her, flowing out. Tears erupted from her eyes as she saw the scrawny, shrivelled pink figure appear on the bed.

The midwife picked the baby up by the legs and smacked its bottom. The door opened and a doctor rushed in. He took the baby from the midwife and put it in an incubator. A suction machine was placed around baby's mouth, clearing out the airways. Then the lusty cries began, and the doctor's shoulders relaxed. The baby was wrapped up in a towel again and handed to Arla.

"It's a baby girl," the midwife said. Arla clasped the little shape to her bosom tightly, all exhaustion and tiredness forgotten in the blink of an eye.

She couldn't stop staring into the tiny, wizened face, the little button-like nose and tiny brown eyes so perfect, it took her breath away. Tears dimmed her vision and she kept wiping at them.

Harry's face was right next to hers and he reached out a finger to touch baby's little fist. He sniffed and wiped the tears from his face.

"I guess we know her name already, don't we?" Harry asked, his voice choked with emotion.

"Yes," Arla said. A shroud of joy and sorrow floated down from above, covering her like a comforting blanket. She would never get back what she had lost, but maybe life had a way of opening a new door when another remained forever shut.

Her heart broke as she kissed her daughter's forehead, but it also filled her with the dance of rainbow colours. The forlorn music carried her to a bitter-sweet, blue distance where she saw her sister's face again, glowing in the sunshine of eternal memories. Lost, but never forgotten.

"Nicole," Arla said, her tear-soaked voice bubbling through a sea of happiness and regret. "Her name will be Nicole."

THE END

Printed in Great Britain
by Amazon